WHEN DISTILLED FROM RAGE

AILEEN & CALLAN MURDER MYSTERIES
BOOK SIX

SHANA FROST

Website: https://shanafrost.com

WHEN DISTILLED FROM RAGE

First Edition.

Ebook ISBN: 978-93-5627-001-5

Paperback ISBN: 978-93-5635-891-1

Large Print ISBN: 978-1-7384994-0-3

Written By: Shanaya Wagh as Shana Frost

Copyedited by Rosie Walker

Proofread by Charlotte Kane

Cover design by GermanCreative

BOOKS BY THE AUTHOR

You can find an entire (latest) catalogue on the
website: Shanafrost.com/books
Here's what you can read next…

Aileen and Callan Murder Mysteries
When Murder Comes Home
When Eyes Don't Lie
When Birds Fall Silent
When Red Mist Rises
When Old Fires Ignite
When Distilled From Rage

Banerjee and Muller Mystery Series
Smokes of Death Beer

For Janae
Your critique and ideas made this story whole

SCOTTISH GLOSSARY

Bairn- Child/Toddler
Bampot- Crazy
Banlaoch- Female Warrior
Eejit- Idiot
Loch- A Scottish Lake
Wee- Little

This book is written in English (UK)

PROLOGUE

July 26th, 2005

'You think we can find him?' Daniel McIntyre had a youthful gleam in his eyes, but his broad shoulders made him look much older than eighteen.

Callan Cameron set the newspaper on the rock and raised an eyebrow at Daniel. 'Neither of us is a detective.'

They sat in the woods by the Senior Citizen Care Centre, a few minutes' walk from the school. They'd graduated that summer, but their friend Blaine Macgregor still took a piano class there.

Heather swayed around them, adding tranquillity to the afternoon. The newspaper shone under the sunlight. The headline read:

Aaron Ridge missing.
Reward of £5,000 for information about his whereabouts.

Callan's mother had called the missing man 'a drunk'. So had the shopkeeper who'd sold Callan a new canvas board that morning. And no one, not even the man's friends, hoped to ever find him.

Blaine, short and bony, dropped his backpack next to Callan's and plopped onto the grass beside Daniel. He'd grown a moustache, which clashed with the freckles on his boyish face. Blaine wiggled his fingers. 'Ms Willoughby would rather my fingers fall off than play a single note off key. She's worse than a drillmaster!'

'Yet you wouldn't give it up,' Daniel said.

'I love it.' Blaine peered at the newspaper. 'Do you eejits want to solve this?'

'Five thousand pounds is a tidy sum of money, and they just want information about Mr Ridge.' Daniel pointed at Callan. 'Plus, your father's a detective. You must have some detection skills.'

'Buzz off, bampot! Your father can build houses and look at you, you can't even hold a screwdriver.'

Blaine cracked up. 'Callan's right, you know.'

Daniel smacked Callan on the head. 'Bastards! Who fixed the damn ladder when you snapped it sneaking into Pat's room?'

Callan sobered up. 'That was a fluke. But if my father finds out we're snooping into his colleague's case, he'll have my hide and you know it.' Callan checked his watch. The dial had a splatter of red paint he'd forgotten to clean. 'It's four forty-five. Do you want me to drop ye off, Blaine?'

Blaine snorted. 'You're such a show off.'

'Aye.' Daniel joined in. 'Mr Cameron should never have got you that car.'

'He didn't get me a car!' Callan harrumphed. His father had been delighted to hand Callan the keys to his ten-year-old truck. Callan could never sneak out at night; its engine rattled so loud, the noise would give him away. 'He bought himself a new one.'

Blaine's lips turned down. 'Paw won't let me drive.'

Callan jostled Blaine's arm with his shoulder. 'Hey, you've always got me. I'll drive you to your first sold out show.'

Blaine laughed and jumped up. 'A sold out show. That's the dream.'

Daniel stood up. Callan followed suit and kicked a stray pebble. The thing had been pressing against his right ankle. He plucked his backpack. 'Until that sold out show, I'll get you two eejits home.'

'Aren't you meeting Pat tonight?' Daniel asked.

Callan shrugged. He'd had a row with his girlfriend that afternoon and she'd stalked off to her best friend's. Callan kept his tone light. 'I have to get our esteemed piano prodigy home.'

Blaine smirked, lifting a side of his mouth. 'I know I can always count on you, Callan.'

'That you can, Blaine. That you can.'

CHAPTER ONE

Present Day

Gravel crunched under the sedan's tyres and a white mist whispered, tickling the silhouettes of trees in the darkening sky. It was summer, but impending rain had cut off the rays of sunlight.

Aileen crept through the night like a spy. That's what Mr McCloughan wanted: to be discreet.

The dark clothes and black scarf camouflaged her in the shadows, but her heart thundered louder than the clouds rumbling in the sky.

A stray tear of rain smacked against the windshield. The trees trembled in the breeze.

Storm had eclipsed the spring.

She jostled as the car hit another patch of uneven road. The further she travelled from the centre of town, the rougher the roads were. They reminded a traveller of their location: the north-western wilds of Scotland.

Gravel crumbled, and a stone bolted. Her sedan shook like a plane in turbulence. *Damn it.* It was time to trade this city car for a truck. Even if she'd look like a mouse driving it, given her short stature.

Dark brown strands of hair escaped her ponytail and Aileen tucked them behind her ears. When would she find the time to hack them off?

'Gosh!'

The pelting rain slowed her progress, a white curtain as angry as the wind. At least it offered a veil to hide behind. No way could anyone spy her out now.

Her eyes strained to see the sign that would lead her to Loch Fuar's most prized distillery and export: McCloughan's.

McCloughan's was the first tumbler of whisky Aileen's gran, Siobhan, had toasted her with. And typical of her gran, she'd tried to trick Aileen into drinking before she turned eighteen. Aileen learned to be firm with Gran early on, especially regarding whisky.

Her forehead relaxed at the thought of the ninety-year-old Siobhan. Nothing slowed that woman down.

And this weather won't slow Aileen either.

She hit another ditch and hoped her car wouldn't crash into a rock and leave her stranded out here, especially given the spotty mobile connection. Again, the farther away from the centre of town you went…

Through the downpour, she spotted a dark sign with gold lettering. Under it shimmered an image of a waterfall cascading into a tumbler.

She'd found them.

Despite the deserted road, Aileen indicated left and braced for the ride on an unpaved track. Mc-Cloughan's were known for their 'Highland experience'; tyre tracks etched in wet mud were difficult to drive along but showcased the rugged landscape.

She gritted her teeth, used all her might to steer, and trained her eyes on the road. Her headlights caught fronds shivering in the wind on either side.

Crash.

'Ouch!'

She'd hit a deep ditch. The engine let out a groan. If her petrol tank burst…

She pulled into an empty car park. Using her sedan for this trip was not incognito, but it would have been foolish to walk here or hitch a ride.

When her boyfriend found out her plans for tonight, they'd had another one of their rows, leading to physical blows. Or rather, she *tried* punching, and he deflected with a kiss. Then the night had turned sweet.

Aileen huffed out the remnants of irritation at

being in love with a police detective, aka a walking bodyguard-cum-safety alarm system.

She knew how to take care of herself, thank you very much. But he always worried she'd land herself in trouble, often listing out instances when she'd been in jeopardy.

Last night, she assured Callan she was in no danger from the McCloughan Distillery's patriarch, Mr Pluto McCloughan – the man walked with a stick.

His retirement was a loss to Loch Fuar. The heir, Jack McCloughan, had fallen far from the tree, so said the rumours according to trusted gossip-monger-in-chief, Isla McIntyre.

Aileen stepped out of her car and straight into a puddle. 'Hell!'

The night was turning from irritating to worse. She glared at her boots. Who'd clean the crusty mud from them later? She didn't have time for this. But why was she here, then?

She breathed through her nerves. A girl needed downtime, even if it included a bit of sleuthing. *Especially* if it included sleuthing.

She shut the car door behind her and a chill flashed through the air.

Time for the fun to begin.

Aileen waited for her eyes to adjust so she could peek through the trees and see. There: the outline of a stone building, just one storey tall and topped with a typical peaked roof. Next to it stood another building with a chimney, exposed bricks, and a frieze carved above the door.

Pluto McCloughan's house. That's what Ethan, the pub owner, had told her.

Aileen splashed her way towards it, careful to not switch on the torch. She always carried it, a hangover after solving a few murder cases on her own.

The wind tugged at her raincoat's cap and spiked goosebumps on her skin.

If her feet slipped and her arse landed in the mud... she shook her head. Wet clothes, muddy shoes and soggy underwear were a recipe for disaster.

Her face dripped, and eyes stung from the moisturiser that had dissolved in the rainwater. Aileen put one foot in front of the other.

The house grew larger as she neared. A golden glow emanated from the ground floor rooms. Pluto McCloughan was waiting for her.

She veered around a puddle and stepped under the awning. At last.

Aileen took a minute, surveying the silent building next door, the distillery. The patter of rain prevented her from hearing the waterfall, the natural resource distilleries in the Highlands used to fashion their whisky.

She flicked a glance at the car park behind her, shrouded in blackness. The pitch-grey sky swallowed the views McCloughan's brochure waxed poetic about. Where were the endless mountains, the stone bridges and tartan-striped peatlands?

So much for long summer days…

Aileen faced a door which sported roughened, exposed wood to match the outer brick structure. She banged the barrel-shaped door knocker.

Within a second, the door swung open to reveal a face topped with tufts of white hair, and a beard and eyebrows to match. All he needed was a Santa suit.

'Ms Mackinnon!' A smile split his pink lips to reveal yellow teeth. His cheeks glistened in the lamp light. 'Come on in, lassie. The rain's a pisser.' His Scottish burr rang through each word, and his booming voice echoed through the house, despite his earlier command for her to be discreet.

He settled a large hand on her arm and yanked her in. 'Ah, some whisky would do ye good.'

Aileen smiled. 'That would help, yes.' Her boots and raincoat dripped soggy mud around her. She tried not to step on the hallway rug.

McCloughan caught her gaze and snorted. 'Ricky!' he roared.

Footsteps stomped against the stone floors and a tuft of dirty-blond hair appeared.

McCloughan nodded at the skinny man. 'Grab the lassie's coat and shoes. Get them dry and warm.'

Aileen thanked McCloughan and Ricky.

The patriarch waved off her gratitude. 'Manners me maw hammered into us lads. A good smack on our bottom is all we needed. Sometimes I wish I'd done the same with ma Jack. Bloody sod.'

Aileen padded behind McCloughan, relieved at not being weighed down by a coat and gumboots.

Photo frames littered every surface and covered the walls. The man sure had a lot of friends and happy memories.

'Let's sit by the fire in the drawing room.'

She followed him through a doorway to their right; the one with the warmest glow. Embers of fire crackled in the massive fireplace. The mantel held more photographs. Several lamps on side tables shone, highlighting old art on the walls and ostentatious furniture. All seats faced the same way: towards a huge throne-like chair in the centre of the room.

Aileen gasped as she noticed a circle of revolvers attached to the wall behind the throne. Was this a drawing room or a Great Hall in a palace fixed with artillery?

McCloughan chuckled at Aileen's expression. 'Aye, ma forefathers sure loved hunting in these forests and peatlands. Now they're heirlooms gathering dust.' He gestured to the room. 'And my dear Linda sure loved decorating. This entire house was a canvas she painted on. I didnae have the heart to change a thing when she passed.' His eyes twinkled with love and longing for his late wife.

Aileen bowed her head. 'I'm sorry.'

'Ah, don't be. A whisky will cheer things up.' The man clomped over to a table in the far corner where whisky decanters sparkled. He splashed generous amounts of golden amber into two crystal tumblers. Enough to loosen Aileen's tongue.

Everything about this man oozed abundance. He lived well and lived big.

'Oh, take a seat, lassie. Don't be so stiff.'

'I'm sorry I'm late.'

'Later the better.' He grinned, handing her a tumbler. 'It's been ages since I entertained a woman this late in the night. My skills may be a wee bit rusty, but respect my maw drilled into us, too. With a spatula.' He raised his own tumbler. 'Drink up.'

Aileen intertwined her hands around the glass, took a sip and grimaced. Unadulterated whisky trickled down her throat, blazing warmth in its wake. Her muscles sparked with life and the heady aroma of malt sent her tongue tingling. 'Wow, Mr McCloughan. This is—'

'Pure dead brilliant? Ha! That's the expression I'm going for when someone tastes our ambrosia. But… But that's not the case anymore.'

Aileen frowned. Ethan had refused to tell her much except that Mr McCloughan wanted the distillery accounts audited by a trained forensic accountant. 'What do you mean, Mr McCloughan?'

'Oh, please. Call me Pluto, lassie. It's only right considering I'm letting ye into the fold when I tell ye this.' He studied the liquid against the light. 'Ever since the first whisky was made in these Highlands, the McCloughans have been quenching thirst. We persevered when the taxes were too high in the 18th century. From then until the doctor demanded I take a back seat, this nectar was as pure as a drop of gold. And no'? No' it's just scented water with a bitter taste.'

Spittle flew and his eyes widened in rage. 'Bah! Is it the water that's turned? Machinery gone sour? No! No, it isnea. It's that wretched son of mine. The damned pest's fooling about. This whisky ye drink, lassie, is from ma personal collection. Sitting in barrels I bottled as a wee lad. And no'? No' ye should taste what we sell. It looks all right, but to a trained connoisseur, it tastes like shite! There's something wrong with it. Something foul…'

He shook his head. 'I won't have it, lassie. I won't have that imbecile run our name through the mud. Find out where he's cutting corners. How much he's secreting into his own pockets. I'll pay ye handsomely. Anything to save this place.'

Aileen swallowed. 'Oh, but I… I—'

'Seventy years of my life I gave to this place. And to see it reduced to this? Do this before I breathe my last. Lord kens I havenae got long, not with all the pills the doctor's making me swallow each day. Say ye'll do this for me, lassie.'

A long checklist of tasks ran through her head – an inn full of guests, the new catering business she planned to start as a buffer for the downtimes, her responsibilities as a friend, girlfriend… Her eyes landed on the man who looked like Santa Claus in so many ways.

The *no* sat on the tip of her tongue.

Her dormant curiosity reared its head.

Callan would kill her.

No. Say 'no', Aileen. Just a simple word, one syllable—

'Yes. Yes. I'll do that for you, Mr McCloughan. I'll go through the books. Do you have a record with you?'

Oh, damn.

'WHAT THE HELL?' CALLAN BLINKED AT THE SHEET of paper. 'What does this mean?'

Detective Chief Inspector Rory Macdonald sighed. 'Don't make me explain it to you.'

Callan slammed the piece of junk on the table. The desk rattled with the impact. 'How dare they?'

'You know there have been talks. And it's not environmentally friendly.'

'It's not environmentally friendly to provide a murdered eighteen-year-old the dignity he deserves?'

Rage burned Callan's lungs, and his nostrils flared. He held on to his senses. Barely. Blaine Macgregor, his best friend, had gone missing fifteen years ago. When Callan solved his missing persons cold case, he'd discovered their mutual friend had murdered Blaine. But he'd never found Blaine's body. All they knew was the Erwins had buried him somewhere in the peatlands that sprawled on one edge of Loch Fuar.

Callan saw shadows flickering in Rory's eyes. His boss didn't like this order either.

'It's bloody politics, isn't it?' Callan growled. Everything always boiled down to politics.

Rory hated diplomacy. The language of politicians. 'I'm sorry. The environmental group protested, and the council responded with this. You know what it's like when elections are right around the corner. And it doesn't say you can't find Blaine Macgregor, it says—'

'The police are ordered to evacuate their current excavation on the peatlands unless they can prove with evidence that an object of importance to their case or the remains of a missing person are buried there.' Callan hated his photographic memory sometimes. 'That's bollocks.'

Rory pushed back his chair with a squeak against the floor. He stalked to the window. 'It's shite and I know it, damn it! But that's an order, acknowledged and backed by the higher ups. There's nothing I can do. Environmentalists proved, with stats, what happens when you dig the bog. Plus, this council has an Environmental Protection Committee. They won't back down. And since we've been unable to find anything concrete in the last six months…'

Callan didn't need reminding of that epic failure. Mist and frozen ground halted their progress in the winter. And in spring they found nothing but a couple of old coins.

Where the heck did the Erwins bury Blaine?

Gerald had confessed to killing Blaine in a fit of rage and said his father buried the body for him. When Callan met Gerald Erwin at the prison, the eejit smirked and denied knowing where the body was hidden.

Callan's next stop was Dr George Erwin, Gerald's father. The man refused to open his front door, let alone talk. And then he'd claimed in court – and continued to tell whoever would listen – that he condoned his son's actions and would never hide a murderer or a body, contrary to what he confessed in the beginning. But criminals and their stiff-collared, Rolex-wearing lawyers meant diplomacy.

'I can ask Dr George Erwin again.'

Rory huffed, tainting the windowpane. 'He'll report you for harassment. He pointed us to a location, didn't he?'

'And Blaine isn't there! Now Erwin says he had nothing to do with the murder. That's a lie but we can't prove it. And now we're not allowed to search. He can use this to get his son out of prison. A murderer can walk scot-free because we don't have a body.'

He hadn't worked hard enough or asked the right questions to rescue Blaine fifteen years ago.

And now Callan couldn't find Blaine's body to give him a proper burial.

Rory shook his head. 'We have enough evidence, Callan. You just want to find Blaine for your peace of mind. Admit that.'

Callan didn't wrench his mouth open. He didn't want to admit the guilt that ate him every single day.

'You should do what you set out to – give Blaine a memorial and close that chapter of your life.'

Callan's girlfriend's words echoed back to him. She wanted him to let go of the past and the what ifs. But he'd still held hope. And now it was gone, banished by one sheet of paper dripping with politics and diplomacy.

Callan had truly failed his best friend.

CHAPTER TWO

Aileen pulled the first ledger closer. Her wristwatch told her it was a few more hours until dawn.

Pluto's minion, Ricky had set her up in a loft with no power outlet, not even for a bulb. She worked by torchlight.

The torch flickered. Oh no. Did she have batteries?

Aileen flipped the page and—

Boom. Boom.

Something pierced through the silence.

Gunshots.

Her legs crumpled, crashing her to the ground. Her arms covered her head.

Were they close?

Her body vibrated, thoughts looping into each other to flash images she didn't want to come true.

'You're safe. You're safe,' she whispered to herself.

But was she safe? What if the shooter got closer? What if—

Her heart throbbed towards a heart attack.

Fear kicked her into action. She hunched over and crossed to the loft's window, squinting to pick out any silhouettes. Nothing.

Silence filled her ears. Dust particles slowed as they floated under the moonlight.

Who was out there?

Aileen turned, pressing her back to the wall. Had she dreamt it? No way.

Focus.

She glanced at the desk which commanded the loft, its surface topped with dust-coated leather ledgers, and receipts hanging out of drawers.

Up here, with the full moon's spotlight pouring in from two massive windows, she might be safe. Or illuminated like a ballerina on the stage.

And Pluto was down there with Ricky. She had to wake them up.

Aileen scrambled out of the door and down the corridor. The staircase walls closed in on her.

She stumbled, just one false move from breaking her neck. Her feet landed on the second floor and she managed to steady herself. 'Shots fired! Get up! There's a shooter! Call the police!'

Crap. She'd forgotten to call the police.

Her fingers shivered as she hit 999. Callan would be pissed.

The moment someone answered, she gabbled down the phone, breath rattling in her throat as she continued down the stairs.

Somehow the operator understood and asked her to stay on the line. Units were on their way.

This far out? She'd be lucky if they even found the McCloughan property.

Her feet hit the first landing. 'Pluto, Ricky! Wake up!'

She heard no sound except her feet thundering over the floorboards. Had they gone out to investigate?

She descended the last flight to get to the living room. 'Pluto?'

Moonlight pooled on the carpet like grey puddles of water. The unshuttered windows revealed the stillness of the night outside.

Where was the shooter? Who got shot?

Aileen ran into the throne room and to the circle of revolvers on the wall.

She stammered to a halt. Even if she climbed, she couldn't reach them. All that armed glory for naught. She couldn't shoot either, could she?

Thoughts fogged her mind, evaporating her survival instinct. She had to keep herself safe. Especially now that she'd run down here like an eejit.

She scanned the landscape outside, hoping to glimpse the shooter before they broke in.

Why were they here? Who'd be out there in the night?

She dived underneath the long sofa by the fireplace, pulled her legs in, and wrapped her arms around them. A stupid move, in retrospect. Her arms would quickly go numb in this position. What would she do with a limp limb?

Her breath panted as if she was wearing a microphone, so loud she was convinced that the shooter would make her out like a—

Her nose twitched. *Ignore the carpet's bristles.* They stank, reeked of wet cloth not dried for days.

She held her breath but couldn't, couldn't—

Crash. The front door cracked against the wall.

Her heart banged against her ribs in fear.

Footsteps barged inside, loud as a horse's hooves.

Aileen bit down on her lip, hoping to stop the trembling. Useless.

The barrel of a revolver dangled in her field of vision.

She yelped.

A giant hand grabbed her arm and tugged. 'Ye wee bastard!'

Shit. Aileen jabbed at the man's torso, then kicked him.

He didn't move.

Her whole body quaked, as if an earthquake shook the world.

'Who are you?'

She gulped oxygen into her lungs, which burned with the effort. 'No…' Her voice grated against her vocal cords, a ghost speaking. 'No—'

'Who—' A gust of breath blazed across her neck. 'Are you?'

'Don't hurt me! Please.' *Don't cry, don't cry, don't cry…*

'Jack, you're scaring the poor girl.'

She froze. Jack?

'What's she doing in my father's house? Call the bloody police!'

Jack tightened his grip on her arm until she shut her eyes and squirmed with pain.

'You'll do no such thing! Let her go!' Heavy footsteps pounded into the room. Pluto. 'Let her go. Now.'

Jack McCloughan's grip on her loosened, and her feet hit the floor. He stuck close, the intensity of his rage scalding her back. 'Who is she, father?' Spittle landed on her shoulder like missiles meant to detonate.

'None of your business.'

'Someone fired shots in our backyard and it's none of my business that a stranger is in your house?'

'Exactly.'

'Father—'

Aileen cleared her throat. 'I'm Aileen Mackinnon.'

The air pulsed for a beat. 'What?'

'Ai-Aileen Mac—'

'A Mac… How dare you? How dare you allow a Mackinnon on our land?'

'It's my house and I'll do as I please.'

'Are you joking?'

'Jack, Pluto, please.' A woman hustled over, holding her hands up. Her dressing gown camouflaged with the upholstery of the chairs in the room.

When Jack opened his mouth, she shook her head, her cornrows bobbing around her small face. 'The poor girl's afraid. We are humans and can afford courtesy towards people who need our help. Besides, the police are here. I think she called them?'

Aileen nodded, her ears registering the wail of sirens. The cacophony echoed louder until tyres splattered mud and headlights splayed across the windows.

The woman answered their knock and ushered them in. 'We're grateful you could come.'

'Aileen Mackinnon?'

Aileen raised her arm for a handshake and realised it shivered like a twig in a storm. She tucked it against her side. 'That's me.' She said.

'Are you alright, ma'am?'

'I believe she's in shock,' the woman said.

The police officer pulled out his phone. 'I'll get the paramedics.'

'I… I don't need…' But neither of them paid her any heed.

Jack introduced everyone to the officers.

'She needs a whisky,' said Pluto.

'Ma'am, why don't you sit down?'

Aileen bit her lip. *Get a grip*, she said to herself. *Tell them*.

'Shots. I heard two of them right before I called. They were gunshots, I'm sure. I think I saw the flash of a spark as well. Somewhere in the peat-lands. I thought it was near, yet far… from here. And I decided to run down to warn Pluto and Ricky.'

'Ricky?'

Aileen bobbed her head. 'Aye, Ricky. But no one answered me.'

As she focused, careful to include all the details, her trembling stopped. Yet the paramedics insisted on checking her and draped a blanket over her shoulders.

She wasn't a mouse, dammit.

And she certainly didn't want to be wearing a blanket when she had to face the man who'd stalk in here soon. He won't blow a gasket, he'll blow her up.

Her worries came to fruition when a dark grey SUV barrelled in through the main gates towards the car park, spewing mud and water. Only one man she knew drove like the hounds of hell were nipping at his back wheels at 3 a.m. Equipped with a new car and sturdy wheels for roads like these, her man was incorrigible.

Detective Inspector Callan Cameron slammed the truck's door so hard it rattled. His gaze scorched a path towards her despite the distance and the window separating them.

Oops. If she were dramatic, Aileen would say his footsteps thundered towards them and the grey in his eyes swirled like storm clouds in the dark sky. But she wasn't dramatic…

'Detective—'

One glare at the police constable shut him off. And then the fire singed her.

'McCloughan.' He nodded, his short-cropped hair giving him a militaristic look. His chiselled jaw muscles twitched, not helping her cause. She loved her man to bits but—

'I'd like to have a word with Ms Mackinnon in private. Excuse us.'

He stepped in front of her and held out his hand.

She set hers in his on autopilot. Her hand shook again.

'Hell,' he said, and pulled her up.

The next thing Aileen knew she was out of the McCloughan's house, with bricks digging into her back and a growling man pressed to her front.

'What the hell?'

CALLAN YEARNED TO RIP INTO SOMETHING. IN THE thirty minutes it took him to drive here, his heart had lodged itself in his throat. How many times had she made him worry so? He had to lock her up and chain her to her inn. Not humanitarian thoughts. 'I told you not to do this.'

Aileen lifted her chin, informing him she was up for an argument. 'How could I have known something like this would happen?' She was shaking like a leaf but she'd argue. Stubborn eejit.

'You drive down here, alone, in the middle of the damn night. What did you think would have happened?'

'I called the police—'

'And weren't you lucky your phone had service? Or I'd be investigating your murder right now. Ever thought of that, Aileen?'

'I'm fine. See?' She tugged at his right hand and placed it on her chest. 'Feel that? I'm alive.'

'Oh, I don't need to feel your heartbeat to know that. You ratting out stupidity is enough.'

Aileen narrowed her eyes. 'I'm going to chalk that up to stress.' Her soft lips pressed against his. 'Don't you dare insult me next time. In case you forgot, you're not the boss of me.' Then she ducked under his arm and strutted inside.

How many times would she put herself in trouble and get away like this? It didn't matter. He'd save her every time. Not that she needed saving…

Callan ran a hand through his hair. This night

shift was getting to him. Not only had he seen not the sunlit world in a while, the shift was so silent that even Lieutenant General Warren didn't call to complain about his neighbour's cat.

'Detective?' The police constable, Officer Kirkpatrick, stepped forward out of the shadows.

Callan grunted.

She pulled out her notepad. 'Mr McCloughan, the younger one, says he heard at least three gunshots coming from the peatlands. His wife confirmed that. The elder Mr McCloughan said he heard nothing, only the commotion in his living room. And then Mr Ricky, he… well, he didn't say much.'

'Did Aileen Mackinnon hear three gunshots?'

'No, she heard two. That's what she told the operator. Should we check it out?'

He'd have to speak to every person inside. 'Get your partner to put them in separate rooms. I don't want them communicating with each other. And tell him to get statements. We'll go into the peatlands.'

Now that they had a case to solve with witnesses claiming to have heard gunshots at the peatlands, they could go investigate. But the bog was where devils hid, even in summer. Dark mist called it home, like the smoke from a witch's cauldron.

He almost called off the search until dawn, but if there was something to find, they needed to locate it before the grey clouds shrouding the moon burst into rain.

'Come on.' His voice sounded distant to his own ears. But he put one foot in front of the other, heading for the dark and deadly mass of hell. 'Better get this done with.'

They passed the big house, leaving the distillery on its other side. Behind it was a smaller cottage, with just one floor above and a lamp glowing behind a netted curtain.

Jack and Sarah McCloughan's house.

Behind it, Callan's torch highlighted a hedge, bobbing with some summer flowers he couldn't name. In the night, they didn't appear as jolly as they were meant to.

'Here.' They walked through a small gap in the hedge, and Callan's wellies sunk into the peat.

Damn rain. The police constable's wellies made a sucking sound. Something about it grated on Callan's ears and an image flashed in his mind of a Second World War gas mask.

Sweat trickled down his back. Callan loosened the zip of his well-padded jacket. The smart dashboard in his car told him the temperature was in single digits. Why then was he sweating?

Mist glided over the peat, surrounding them like a cage.

Callan looked back to make sure he wasn't alone. He wasn't scared, but he was reassured by the silhouette behind him, draped in neon yellow.

His muscles turned to lead. He drew in a breath that burned his nostrils. *Get a grip, Cameron.*

'Sir?'

He stopped. 'Aye?'

'Should we go in separate directions?'

And risk one of them landing in a ditch and hurting themselves with no mobile service? 'No, let's take a zigzag route and cover max territory.'

Stone markers demarcated the part of the bog that fell into McCloughan land. They stuck to the low fence, then swished to the right and continued straight.

One advantage of smartphone technology was the compass, which proved handy now that he'd learned to use it. Especially tonight when the clouds surrounded them and obscured their vision from all sides.

They walked to the other low fence and back again in a diagonal line. The mist puffed around them.

Callan checked over his shoulder to make sure his police constable hadn't tripped or wandered off.

'How large is their land?' Officer Kirkpatrick said.

He didn't know. 'Don't dally.' Callan trudged ahead, focused on the ground and his compass, hoping his phone wouldn't die.

The night would lighten into dawn soon, one advantage of summer. And the shadows of trees, too giant to be real, would fade away. What sort of creep loomed over humans like that?

Another rivulet of sweat trickled down his back,

and he could feel a giant soggy spot under his armpits. It was the late night exercise. It *had* to be the exercise.

Callan breathed through his teeth, suppressing the pictures of masked giants, screams, and—

'Sir?'

He almost missed the squeak and gag. Almost walked away.

His torch caught the one spot where the mist wasn't threatening to overpower his world. A boot.

He skirted his torch around before making his way to it.

His wellies were a blob of mud and his hands frozen bloated digits.

Cold sweat zinged a shiver through him.

Denim-clad legs emerged from the dark, attached to a torso covered with a blue overcoat and—

'Ah, hell!'

There was a bloodstain where the man's heart should be. And his face…

Callan breathed through the belly-souring sight.

The man's skin had sunken into his bones, his lips tainted blue. The eyes stared into space. White hair flickered in the breeze, the only movement.

'Call SOCO.' They'd need a slew of scene of crime officers. Not only because the crime scene was a wide area, but also because the dead man was once important in Loch Fuar.

Callan felt his gut drop at the implication of what his mind registered.

Dr George Erwin. Dr George Erwin was dead, shot to death. And he'd taken with him the secret location of Blaine's grave.

In that moment, the little optimism he had of ever finding Blaine splintered. Now his best friend was truly lost forever. Callan's eyes prickled. Hard damn luck.

But the doctor had the worst of it.

CHAPTER THREE

The sun had banished every grey cloud from the sky and a breeze swayed the heather brushes, but Callan's thoughts were sour. He wanted to howl, rip something apart. But nothing short of a miracle could make things right again. He'd never find his best friend. Erwin took that secret to his grave.

They'd erected a tent to protect evidence from the rain, and its white sheets fluttered in the wind.

Callan swiped a hand over his face. Heat doused him in beads of sweat. The mist had faded, bringing the shrouded scene to life: shrubs spotted with dew drops, wet earth effusing its scent and a silence weighed down with death.

Dr Brown rushed in with pinched lips, the bags under her eyes more prominent than ever, her hair a violent tornado of grey.

He stepped back to let her do her job, and followed the markers towards the layby. There was no point in pondering the what ifs. Aileen was right. It was time to move on. Easier said than done.

Two vans appeared beyond the white and blue striped police tape, and several cars dotted the road – more traffic than this area had ever seen. Many cars appeared coated in liquid chocolate, just not as sweet.

One car sat in the layby, the emblem on its bonnet informed Callan it didn't belong to any of the hordes of officers prowling the area. An honest police officer's salary didn't stretch enough to afford a high-end luxury SUV.

Callan crossed his arms and waited for Mr Halston, who was overseeing the processing of the scene. Halston addressed a collection of officers wearing white scrubs, directing them to sweep the car. Instructions complete, he turned to Callan. 'Can you believe it? The guy must've been a zillionaire!'

'Or his killer. Or a witness.'

Halston shook his head. 'Found papers inside. Dr George Erwin. Never knew being an NHS doctor paid so handsomely.'

Callan narrowed his eyes. 'It's our business to find out. What else did you find?'

'Still sweeping. But,' he gestured for Callan to follow him onto the road. More yellow markers spread around a litany of tyre marks. 'We parked out a bit before we cleared this area for the other cars. These tyre tracks were here before we arrived. Don't belong to that car.'

'A getaway car?'

Halston shrugged. 'But there was another car here, and it sat beside Erwin's in this layby.'

'Why haven't they paved his bloody road?'

'The McCloughan charm.'

Not so charming when you had a murder to solve, was it? He shook his head. 'Can you identify the car?'

'It's a long shot, but we can get you some details. Detective, given the large area of the crime scene, we're going to need time to process all of it.'

Callan grunted, wondering how much more time they'd take than their normal pace. The SOCO teams were always swamped. He wasn't any good at diplomacy, but barking out orders? Apart from Aileen, everyone else listened to him. 'I'd like to know if you find any other DNA on it, besides Erwin, I mean. And his wife.' Oh crap. He'd have to visit Erwin's wife and look her in the face and say her husband was dead. He could imagine how well that would go.

Callan thanked Halston and went off to harass Dr Brown.

Their crime scene spanned the entire McCloughan property. They had found Erwin's car a good ten minutes away from the body. What was that man doing hiking around in the peatlands at night?

Callan pulled out his notepad and began sketching. His photographic memory would recall what he needed, but sometimes putting things on paper helped him work out the missing parts of the story.

Erwin's high-end SUV – because a sports car would crash on these roads before you even pulled it out of the shop – was facing the peatlands. So he was here to meet someone. He hadn't reversed it to make a quick getaway.

Besides, the man had walked out here.

Callan gazed at the markers which trailed from the road to the peatlands, and then over to where he'd found Erwin's body.

Two sets of footsteps, both wide and large. Both with an equal gait. Erwin was here with someone his own height.

One shoe had a zigzag pattern to it and the other was wavy. The zigzag one belonged to Erwin, so Callan had been told. The man, if Callan was any good at gauging heights, was about five feet and ten inches. Average.

The forensic team should be able to deduce the shoe brand, hopefully as elite as the car and not something common. But he didn't believe in luck.

Callan got back to his assessment. Erwin met his killer here. But…

He crouched next to one set of prints – zigzag

over wavy. But the wavy print stamped over the zigzag in some spots.

The killer, if he assumed the wavy prints belonged to the killer, hadn't considered hiding footprints. And if the wavy pattern had stamped over the previous pattern, that meant Erwin and his killer hadn't walked side by side. Someone had followed Erwin.

Callan traced the footsteps and found both patterns criss-crossing each other, solidifying his theory. But nothing was a given until proven.

Callan scribbled down on his notepad: *Any previous crime committed in this area?*

The peatlands were a vast patch of land, some of it privately owned. But the weather was a great deterrent for locals, even in summer. The mist dominated a landscape spotted with ditches. You could fall inside and break a limb, or your neck.

But someone had shoved bullets into their doctor.

Callan nodded at Dr Brown, whose white scrubs were now stained with peat. 'Have anything?'

'You'll have to wait for my report but...' She huffed. 'Two entry wounds caused by bullets. I'll have to run tests to give you more than that.'

'Two wounds? So two bullets? You sure?' Didn't Jack and his wife claim they heard three?

'Two entry wounds don't mean two bullets, Detective. You aren't that naïve. And I can count. As far as I can tell, there are two wounds. Maybe I'll change that in my report. The soggy mud, despite the tent they've set up, makes it difficult for me to study much in situ.'

'Does his autopsy take priority?'

'I do the best I can, Detective.'

She was the best. He knew that. He thanked her and let her go. Like him, she had burned the midnight oil and then some.

He glared when a yellow-vested officer rushed towards him. 'Er, sir. Jack McCloughan is, er, throwing a fit.'

Callan massaged his forehead. He had asked the McCloughans to shut up shop for the time being, as per protocol. And Jack was having none of it. If there was one person of interest who'd be the most difficult to handle, it was him.

'Get PC Robert Davis to handle him.' He wanted to know what Halston had found in Erwin's car. Especially if he'd found the man's phone. If they knew what he'd been doing here, they could have a lead.

He pivoted on his heels to head back to the layby and winced. His right knee throbbed but he still had a couple hours of work to do and – he glanced at his feet and wiggled his prosthetic foot – his Wellies could take a little more drudgery before the mud swallowed them whole.

Aileen relaxed in the chair, blinking away sleep. After the rush had worn off, all she craved was bed. And they weren't letting her go.

No, she sat her butt in an armchair in the library and, for the first time in her life, didn't want books around her.

The McCloughan's library had floor to ceiling bookshelves cramped with a variety of books – peeling spines and fresh colourful ones.

She rested her head against the backrest and considered drifting off to sleep. How long had it been?

Dawn flirted with the windowpanes, peeking through the drawn blinds. The air was lighter in here since she cracked open a window, bringing in the scent of soil after a storm.

An occasional voice, steps or snippets of conversation drifted in. If not for them, she could've been at the spa.

Her eyelids almost shut and the images of that night flitted in. The ledgers, the dust, the darkness, the gunshots. The cash account someone had scribbled in with ink.

The gunshots.

She sat up straight and stuck her hand into her satchel. Her fingers wrapped around the yellow notepad she lugged around and flipped to the page where she'd been taking notes.

Why did Pluto maintain handwritten records?

His age had to factor, but he wasn't the circus

master anymore, was he? No, that was the snarling lion, Jack McCloughan.

So why did Pluto have a handwritten account of the business?

When he'd said he wanted her to audit the records, she'd hoped for a file from his son. Or some stock registers detailing the poor whisky he distilled. Yet all she had were sneeze-inducing ledgers.

Who owned those ledgers? Why did Pluto suspect his son?

Something didn't add up.

Or it's your sleepy head cooking up a mystery when there isn't one.

Aileen rolled her eyes at herself and realised she was back to the negative self-talk. She needed sleep.

A knock at the door swiped off the haze. Aileen smiled at the head that popped in.

Police Constable Robert Davis. The man wore his entire uniform, right down to the chequered hat and thick boots. 'Morning.'

'It's morning already?'

He released a nervous laugh. 'You don't look so well.'

A coffee would fix that, along with an explanation of why they'd locked her in here.

The carpet cushioned Robert's footsteps as he crossed to the window and peered out. 'It's a terrific property. They do engagement parties in their restaurant out back, too.'

'What's going on, Robert?'

He sighed and plopped himself on the seat by the windows overlooking the distillery. 'George Erwin was found murdered.'

Her gasp echoed through the room. 'Oh no! Callan—'

'Is still out there, investigating. But…'

Her boyfriend wouldn't be happy. Crushed, more like it. Now that Erwin was dead, he'd taken the secret of Blaine's grave to his own.

She hoped Erwin had written the location down somewhere, and the police would find it when they searched his things. But deep in her heart she knew there was little hope of that happening.

Robert shook his head and pulled out a notepad. 'Could you tell me what happened? Then I'll let you head out.'

She told him about the two shots, her running down from the attic, calling the police and then Jack and Pluto's argument. It seemed surreal, especially because it all happened in a blink surrounded by the night.

'That's all you remember?'

'Yes. Everyone followed Jack into the room. Well, everyone except Ricky.'

Robert scribbled something in his notepad and thanked her. 'We'll get in touch if there are any further questions.'

'Is Callan done?'

'I expect not. It's a large crime scene. Do you need a lift?'

Aileen shook her head and stood, glad to be heading back. She'd missed breakfast for her guests, but her best friend Isla had agreed to stock up some fresh bread and scones with jam. Not the ideal breakfast. That'll teach Aileen to take on assignments she had no business getting into. *Eejit.*

She followed Robert to the first landing and down the stairs to the living room. The staircase crowded in on them, as narrow as in medieval buildings. Her shoulder caught on a nail, tearing her shirt sleeve.

'You can't shut us down!'

The bark popped up the hair on the back of her neck.

'That's illegal!'

Her steps faltered as she recognised that voice. Jack McCloughan. How could Pluto's son have such a short fuse compared to his father? Apples and trees. Sometimes gravity didn't work right.

Her foot connected with the last flight of steps and—

'Bullies, the lot of you. As if I'd kill a man! It's business. We have employees to pay and customers to sell to.'

A low murmur hit her ears – the other police officer explaining procedures to Jack. When one of her guests had had a dagger lodged in their gut, she had to shut her business down, too. Especially when they all became murder suspects.

Jack's gaze met hers over Robert's shoulder and he stiffened. 'Ah, that's how it is, isn't it?' He waved, drawing the attention of another yellow-vested officer. 'Mackinnon – the rotten devils! Mayhem everywhere they go. And now here comes murder. *Murder!*' His boots stalked towards her.

She backed away, and her foot caught the stone step behind her, nearly toppling her backwards. She held on to the wall. 'Mr… Mr—'

His stubby finger stabbed at her. 'You can never trust a Mackinnon!'

Her cheeks burned, hands trembled. Why did this man hate her so much?

Robert stopped in front of Aileen. 'Please, Mr McCloughan—'

A muscle on Jack's brow twitched. 'Don't you get in the way!'

Robert didn't move. 'You must know, sir, we've asked you to remain closed for today because it's protocol. It's nothing got to do with anyone.'

'A bunch of bollocks! My father messed it up, as he often does. Dear god! Someone dead in our backyard? Why would you think we did it? It'll taint our business forever! Ask *this* woman!' He stabbed a finger at her. 'A man dies on the first night she's here. It's either a bad omen or… or she did it!'

'I didn't!' The words exploded out of her before she could think. She had been accused of murder before. But not like she was the evil eye. She wasn't a timid mouse, either. Not anymore. 'You don't know me, sir! And I suggest you stop pointing fingers.'

'Or what will you do? Aim the revolver at me?'

'Mr McCloughan—'

Aileen cut Robert off. 'If we are into throwing accusations — you do realise, don't you, that you were the one carrying a revolver when you barged into the house? What's to say it wasn't you?'

She stepped down one stair. Jack McCloughan towered over her by another few inches.

Her gran, Siobhan, wasn't tall either, and men burlier than Pluto bowed at her feet.

'Are you threatening me?'

Aileen lifted her chin. 'No, I'm informing you, Mr McCloughan. I've unearthed a few mysteries of my own. And if it was you, be sure that DI Callan Cameron will find evidence to prove so—'

'Fraternising with the police, are you?' The twinkle in the man's eyes was menacing. 'I remember another suck up like that. Guess it runs in the genes, eh? Eean Mackinnon's daughter, aren't you? That man sweet-talked his way into getting whatever he wanted. And then spat it out as if it were junk! Nothing but an arse, that man! And you are just like him.'

'I... I—' Words stuck in her throat. This man knew her father?

'Get out of our property! And don't come back again.' With that, he turned and stalked away.

It wasn't until the door slammed behind him and all of the police officers slumped their shoulders that Aileen's mind came to terms with what he'd said. Jack McCloughan knew her father and didn't like him much. For once she couldn't blame the man. Her father was a tough pill.

She cleared her head and made her way towards the front door. She needed sleep. The rest – Pluto, Jack, the audit, the foul stock of whisky – she'd think about later.

Farewell, hellish night.

CHAPTER FOUR

Callan left the SOCO team to work its magic: gather samples and segregate them to study in their lab. He had to talk to the people in the house. The police constables had gone through hell babysitting four adults who hadn't had any sleep.

And now Callan sat opposite Jack McCloughan, whose nostrils flared like a bull's before a fight.

'You can't shut us down!'

'We're not—'

'There's nothing wrong with our distillery!'

'Sir, we are processing evidence—'

'In the bloody distillery?' He followed that with more cussing. 'Did the Mackinnon woman tell you to do this?'

Callan frowned. 'Why would she tell me to shut down your distillery?'

'Because she's sour blood.'

Callan looked up from his notepad. 'Care to elaborate?'

'You can't shut us down.' Jack was a broken record.

'I want to know what you heard tonight.'

'Two gunshots.'

'You said three?'

'Two, three… What does it matter? Someone's dead and our business is under threat. Have you considered that someone could be after us?'

Callan scribbled down 'delusional' in his notes. 'I haven't considered anything yet, sir. But I'd like to ask you some questions about what happened last night.'

Like a child denied his treat, the man folded his arms and stared out the window.

'Mr McCloughan?'

'I was working. There was an issue in our stocks. It had to be late, I think around 2:30 a.m., because my first instinct was to check the clock on my desk after I heard the shots.'

'Where is your office?'

'I have an assigned desk in the distillery's office. But my wife and I have dinner together every evening. So I was working from the spare bedroom in our house.'

Their house had a woman's touch to it, with pastel blues, pinks and a lot of white sleek design. The net curtains were the only rustic aspect about this place. The dark blue throw pillows added character to the living room, as his sister would say. Several memorabilia lined the walls.

'My wife used to be an interior designer until we moved here to run the family business.'

Callan made a note. 'Did you know Dr George Erwin?'

'I was raised here so I do. But I hadn't heard from him recently.'

The man's balding head told Callan that Jack McCloughan could be almost the same age as George Erwin.

'Does he have any reason to be on your property?'

'Unless he fancied a dram of whisky in the middle of the night, I don't think so.'

Callan needed more than one-line answers. 'What did you do after you heard the shots?'

'I called out for my wife. We pulled on our coats and then heard the commotion in my father's house. Then there was a stark silence right before I entered the house with my revolver. I thought it was a burglary and the gunshots were intended as a distraction. And, well, I found that woman. But my father wasn't there.'

Callan raised a brow. 'He wasn't there? Despite the gunshots and the commotion?'

'My father's an old man.'

Jack looked away, telling Callan he didn't believe the excuse. 'What about your father's aide?'

'Ricky? I don't know what he was up to. He's often missing.'

Callan frowned at the odd description.

Jack uncrossed his arms. 'I'm mighty sorry about that old chap, but I've got some damage control to do since you won't let us allow employees in either. So if that's all…'

Callan thanked the man and left.

Once outside, Callan strode over to the bigger house.

The moment he stepped inside, a paramedic walked over. 'Old Mr McCloughan wasn't feeling up to it. We got Dr Eric Macdonald in and the doctor's given him some pills to help him rest.'

'What about Ricky?'

'The thin-as-a-stick lad? He went to drop off the doctor.'

Callan snarled. 'Didn't I say not to let anyone out?'

'Hey!' Robert waved as he jogged towards them. 'I took Ricky's statement and Aileen's as well.'

'And Mrs McCloughan?'

He shrugged. 'I figured you'd like to talk to her.'

Callan did. He gestured to the house. 'Do they have any overnight or live-in staff?'

'None. They have a local gardener whose son helps around the house. But they don't stay on the property.'

Callan nodded. 'Where is Mrs McCloughan?'

'I moved her to the library about an hour ago.

First floor. Although I think she must've dosed off; it's quiet in there.'

Callan stalked towards the stairs. As he climbed, he noted the stair carpet battered with mud crumbs. His shoulders brushed against the narrow walls.

On the landing, a stone floor spread out to reveal three doorways, one on each wall.

Callan saw the books through the open doorway to his right and stepped inside.

Mrs Sarah McCloughan sat on the seat by the window, her feet dangling. Not sleeping then. She was reading.

A floorboard creaked under his feet and Mrs McCloughan jerked upright, her eyes cloudy. She adjusted her nightgown. 'Sorry, I was so engrossed in this book. The author is… Sorry, you're interested in last night. What time is it?' Mrs McCloughan peered out of the window. 'Clearly late morning. I was in the living room reading when Jack started his fit. Then your colleague said I could lock myself in here.'

'Nine a.m., ma'am. Would you like some tea or coffee?'

With a wave of her hand, she faced him. 'Your colleague offered, and I've had some toast.'

Callan selected a wooden chair by the table, its legs thin as a deer's. It creaked when he sat. 'Could you tell me what happened last night?'

'I was half asleep. I'm a reader and… well, I love to read late into the night. Jack and I, we thrive in the dark.' She laughed, the light glinting off her cheeks and hitting her eyes. 'But I had had an arduous day and couldn't keep my eyes open. And then I heard the shots. Two of them.'

Callan paused in his note taking. 'Two shots. Are you sure?'

'Aye, because I jumped when the first sounded and clutched my blanket when I heard the second. Then Jack shouted for me and within five minutes we were out the door.'

'You didn't think the shooter would come after you?'

Her smile faded. 'We heard the Mackinnon girl screaming. Jack acted annoyed, but he was scared, really. He thought it was a burglar. He brought his revolver along. And then as soon as I closed the house door, we heard another shot. This one was farther out, almost faint. You wouldn't have heard it unless you were listening for it. And the girl's screams almost drowned it out. We heard it because we were outside.'

Mrs McCloughan clenched the fabric of her nightgown. 'Jack barrelled through Pluto's door. Though I must say, Pluto took an awful lot of time getting to the drawing room. The doctor insisted he take the bedroom opposite the library. He can't climb up two floors like he used to. So we had the bed, and his furniture moved one floor down.'

'He's an old man. I'm sure he needed time to descend the flight of stairs.'

Sarah shook her head. 'He is a cat in the dark. Perhaps he was in deep sleep because of the medicines.'

'What about Ricky?'

'That poor boy. I wouldn't be surprised if he hid under the bed with terror. He hates loud noises. It triggers him.'

Callan noted it down. 'Does he suffer from PTSD?'

'No, Detective. I think he's just a wee bit of a scaredy-cat, our Ricky is. Heart as pure as a bairn and just as easily startled.'

The spouses had different takes on the same lad. A point to further research. Callan made a note of that and followed with questions about Erwin. The woman didn't know him; she wasn't from Loch Fuar. She'd met Jack at work when she was living in Ireland.

Callan thanked her for her patience and answers before leaving the McCloughan's for a more disturbing meeting.

It was time to tell Erwin's wife.

AILEEN GNAWED ON HER NAIL, STARING AT THE blank page in front of her. Starting a culinary business was harder than she'd thought. Even with Isla McIntyre guiding her.

Isla had tasked her with listing items she could sell.

After returning from the McCloughan's, Aileen tossed, turned and after twenty minutes gave up on sleep. The best way to get Jack's words out of her mind was to focus on work. Work that wasn't related to the case. If she wanted Dachaigh to survive, she had to get her restaurant business off the ground.

But she was faltering at the first step. How did one come up with a menu? What could she cook well and sell?

The problem wasn't her ability to cook, it was the quality. She fed her guests and the people she loved. But apart from an occasional courtesy comment from her friends and guests, she'd never received compliments.

Well, her boyfriend told her just how much he appreciated her food after he'd scarfed down everything she cooked for him. But the man ate anything, as he was always hungry. His comments didn't count as qualification enough to—

A knock on the door startled her.

Was she expecting guests? Perhaps it was Callan, here for round two of arguing. The night shift made him grumpier than his usual irritable self.

She rolled her eyes and paused. Since when did Callan knock? And why would he knock on the front door? Last minute guests, it had to be.

Aileen smiled as she grabbed the door handle and pulled. 'Welc—'

Words died in her throat, and a squawk pierced the air.

Faces she'd never thought she'd see here…

The woman stood willowy and tall. Her fitted white sweater and trousers matched her bag, in stark contrast with her brunette bob. She sported some blond highlights that were not there the last time Aileen saw her.

The man beside her, also tall, had his salt and pepper hair combed as if a hairdresser had worked on it that morning. He wore a dark grey sweater and black trousers with semi-formal shoes, something Aileen was sure was the rage in high-end Italian stores.

'Mum? Dad?'

Ann Mackinnon stepped through the door and halted in front of Aileen. A scent of sweet flowers smothered Aileen's nostrils.

'You need to step aside to let guests in. And have you gained weight again?'

Aileen swore she saw the edges of the woman's nose turn up. Grey eyes scanned Aileen from head to toe and found her lacking. Then the woman flipped her head to take in the desk and meandered into the reception area.

Try as she might, Aileen couldn't crack a smile. She pressed herself to the door and gestured for her father to enter.

Eean Mackinnon climbed up to the porch, revealing two large suitcases at the foot of the stairs. 'I see this place is still the same.'

Aileen blinked, trying to come to terms with the situation. 'Um, I… er…'

'Don't gawk, Aileen, it doesn't suit you. Get the bags in.'

She didn't even think before following her mother's instructions, it was so ingrained into her conditioning.

She placed the bags down and found her hand shaking as she shut the door. Wasn't it ironic that her reaction to gunshots was the same as seeing her parents?

'Wh— what are you two doing here?'

Another knock on the door.

Aileen opened it and she partially wished she'd bolted it for life. Why?

Siobhan Mackinnon scowled at her son from the other side.

Every time her gran visited, Dachaigh lit up like a shop during Christmas. Only now, her gran and her father were here together. And with Aileen there too, this was catastrophic.

Siobhan stabbed her walking stick on the stair and pushed up as if her hips were fifty years old, not ninety. She held up the stick and lifted her chin, her dress floating in the breeze.

'Gran!' Aileen raised an eyebrow. 'Did you cut your hair?'

Siobhan patted the fluffy white cloud and shot a grin at her grandwean. 'We have a new young doctor at the nursing home. I'm ninety, not dead.' She stalked inside, the walking-stick a prop to wield power instead of a device to help her walk.

Her cerulean eyes burned with the embers of love as she gazed at Aileen. Siobhan leaned in, her faint floral perfume stoking the calmness hiding in the recesses of Aileen's nerves. 'I wanted to warn you, but I only had an hour to pull it off.'

Aileen frowned, taking in Siobhan's mauve knee-length dress. 'What did you do?'

'Saved you.' Siobhan sniffed. 'No gratitude in today's children. None.'

Aileen's gaze travelled to where her parents had disappeared into the drawing room beyond the reception area. She pressed her lips and muttered so only Siobhan would hear. 'We'll talk after I get them settled in.'

Her gran bustled towards where Aileen's parents were. 'Help Nurse Nancy get the bags.'

'Yup.'

At the sound of a car's lock clicking in place, Aileen looked over to her right and smiled as Nancy hauled in two more bags from the car. She attempted a wave. 'It's quite the party. Makes up for missing Christmas, I suppose.'

Aileen couldn't remember the last time their family had assembled for Christmas or any other tradition. She couldn't remember the last time her family had gathered, full stop.

She shrugged. 'What do you know about this?'

'That I packed our bags and we were out the door within fifteen minutes when most mornings I have to argue with Siobhan that it's time to wake up.'

A conspiracy. That's what Aileen sensed.

'You head in first. I'll get these.' Aileen stepped out and muttered a curse. Her father's high-end rented SUV idled by the kerb. He couldn't leave it there.

Damn it all. She'd take ten gunshots over this.

She lugged the suitcases behind the reception desk, sure her parents had loaded theirs with boulders to show her how incapable she was.

Her jagged nerves transformed into a scowl.

Aileen pushed the bags against the wall and wrung her fingers. She didn't want to think about how she'd get them upstairs to the rooms.

Now or never…

In the living room, her mother sat on the sofa with her legs crossed and back stiff, taking in her surroundings. Her father was on the phone, standing by the long window overlooking Loch Fuar.

'I guess you haven't had breakfast,' Aileen said to no one in particular.

Siobhan followed her into the kitchen, eyes twinkling for gossip. 'So, I gather you're alone.'

'The inn's almost full. I'm not sure where I'll accommodate all of you.'

'You're not a fool, lassie. That's not what I asked. Last I heard, Callan was on the night shift. That can't be good.'

From the moment Gran first saw Callan and Aileen together – when they'd gone to the nursing home to question her about a clue – Siobhan took it upon herself to nag them into being together.

Aileen shook her head. 'Answer a more pertinent question. What are they doing here?'

Siobhan sat in the nook beside the back door and stared out at the Highlands. 'There's such beauty in summer. I always loved sitting here watching the sunlight give birth to nature.'

Aileen brought out a fresh can of beans.

'My boys never liked it much. I don't understand why. And my eldest believes his daughter shouldn't like it either.'

The can crashed to the counter. 'He wants me to go back to the city?'

Siobhan huffed. 'Back to your old life.'

'Why, Gran?'

'Your parents' new cook is a good friend of Maurine's nurse. So Maurine told me they were off on a little holiday. My son and his wife on a non-business trip? Ha! Whoever heard of such a calamity? Then she heard they were taking a train and a ferry, so they had to pack light. It doesn't take

Einstein to piece it together. So I called and asked them to pick me up.'

'I'm sure Father was happy.'

'I don't pay attention to my son's happiness just like he doesn't to his daughter's.'

Aileen rubbed her forehead. She'd landed in a worse mess than she'd anticipated. 'Do you know why they want me to go back?'

'I know a lot, but I can't read minds. If only I could.'

'It would be a disaster because you don't under-stand *privacy*.' Aileen piled toast on a plate. 'Come on, let's eat.'

Her father wandered in first, face set in a scowl. Her mother followed, eyeing the food. 'Don't you serve smoothies? This will clog your arteries.'

Aileen blinked.

Siobhan smacked her stick against the floor. 'Dachaigh is known for its wholesome food, Ann. Not bird pickings.'

'Siobhan—'

'Why don't you all have a seat and I'll bring the coffee?' Aileen chipped in. She didn't want her mother and gran to get started.

Nancy took the cue to sit down and spoon some eggs into her plate. 'This looks scrumptious, Aileen.'

It took her family five minutes to get seated and begin bickering about the size of the plates, the colour of the coffee, the lack of a tablecloth, the sun…

Aileen felt the stirrings of a headache.

Siobhan gestured at her. 'You look like a corpse. Didn't you get any sleep?'

'I was busy.'

The twinkle in her gran's eyes foretold trouble. Siobhan would find out what Aileen had been up to. Perhaps she already knew.

'Out on adventures? Working with the police?'

Her father snorted. 'Adventures? Working with the police? This is Loch Fuar, Mother. The worst crime it's seen is when Little Dorothy stole her friend's pencil in 1960.'

'I understand how someone such as you would say that.' Siobhan placed her cutlery down. 'What are you working on right now, Aileen?'

'Ah… I…' The people at the table caused her to zip up about the McCloughans. If Jack hated her family, chances were the feeling was mutual. And she didn't need a lit matchstick near a bomb. 'Just restless. Isla is helping me with some business planning.'

'I'm not talking about Isla, darling. I want the details of your case…' Gran said.

'Oh, please, Mother. If you consider driving into the main square an adventure, then it is. Nothing ever happens at Loch Fuar.' her father said.

Aileen bit her lip. If only he knew.

CHAPTER FIVE

The doctor's house stood in resplendence, just like his son's: beige brick walls, a frieze at the entrance decorated with sea waves and a crest in the centre, a brass handle and a nameplate emblazoned with 'Dr George Erwin'.

No mention of the wife. As far as Callan remembered, Melanie Erwin had hidden under a hat and a handkerchief when she'd attended her son's trial.

After punching out a quick text to Robert to get a list of firearms certificate holders in the area, Callan had driven from McCloughan's country estate to this high-end community in Loch Fuar.

The door opened before Callan could knock. Melanie's cropped hair fell to her shoulders in sheets and matched her dark eyes.

She blinked at Callan once, twice, and awareness dawned across her face. 'What's happened?'

Callan cleared his throat. 'Mrs Erwin, can we go inside?'

'Tell me!'

This was the hardest bit, no matter the victim. Callan took a breath. 'I'm sorry to inform you. Your husband was found dead this morning—'

A sob wrecked her, seeming to pull the strength from her limbs. Callan rushed in to hold her arms and keep her from hurting herself.

He hated this. Melanie had been through a lot. She hadn't known about her son's crime; her husband had covered it up and hid it from her for fifteen years. When the truth came out, she'd attended every single court session. And now she had to deal with her husband's murder.

The house was darker than Jack McCloughan's modern setting, with more timber. Antiques, plush carpets and fancy light fixtures with the view of the lawn behind suggested opulence and old money.

All that hadn't saved the Erwins from disaster.

Melanie sank into a leather armchair and pulled her legs into herself like a child trying to hide.

'Could I get you some water?'

She shook her head.

'Can I call someone for you?'

'Aye, ask… ask your team if they've made a mistake, will you?' Her doe eyes pleaded with him, huge pools of sadness in her face. She whimpered. 'Not George. Not my George.'

Callan sighed. 'Mrs Erwin——'

'You're sure, aren't you?'

'Aye, ma'am, we are.'

Another sob, this one seemed to come from her soul. Her head sunk between her knees. 'Oh, George… George… George.'

A heavy ache pinched the spot between Callan's eyebrows. He rubbed it, hoping to dissipate the stress, but it only built up. What could he say to this woman? Sorry never seemed enough.

Death was permanent; it never brought the person back.

'Could, er… could I get some tea for you?'

Melanie dropped her legs to the floor and clutched the chair's arms. Her fingers were like twigs: lean and long. The knuckles poked out like the cheekbones on her face.

Her delicate shoulders shivered. Melanie Erwin had been the image of vitality a few short years ago. But now, stress had eaten her from within. Pity for her seeped into Callan's bones and his heart ached.

'Mrs Erwin?'

She blinked and reached over to a small button built into a side table. 'Let me ring for the maid.'

A silence descended on them, Melanie wrung her fingers until footsteps approached over the carpeted floor.

A petite woman in a black and white maid's uniform rushed inside.

'Crista, please get us some coffee and cookies.' Melanie dashed a tear away. 'And a snifter of brandy for me. I… I need it.'

Crista raised an eyebrow, but nodded and scurried out of the room.

'She's a sweet girl.'

Callan had to talk to Melanie about her husband's case and leave. He didn't have time for a coffee. But it was past ten and he hadn't had a drink in nine hours, and his eyelids were growing heavier.

And Melanie needed someone. She hadn't asked him about her husband and experience told him she still hadn't processed the news.

She arranged herself elegantly on the chair – legs tilted with feet flat on the floor with her body angled towards him. She tucked her auburn hair behind her ears and gripped her fingers together.

Footsteps clicked towards them again, along with the clink of coffee cups.

Crista arranged two porcelain cups with golden rims and matching saucers on the coffee table. A brandy snifter in a gleaming crystal glass joined the set.

'Thank you, Crista. Oh, the cookies!'

Callan waved his hands. 'That's alright, Mrs Erwin.'

'See to the ironing, will you? The detective and I need to talk.'

Crista beat a hasty retreat, a little red in the face. Callan waited until he heard a door close elsewhere in the house. 'Mrs Erwin—'

She poured his cup and handed it over.

He salivated at the scent of freshly ground beans, and paused to take in the aroma until he caught himself and straightened up in shame. This woman's husband had just died and here he was…

'Mr Erwin was found at the McCloughan's property early this morning, Mrs Erwin.'

Melanie poured a snifter and downed the amber-coloured liquid in one go. She winced before slamming the crystal onto the wooden table. 'I prefer brandy over whisky. Doesn't make me much of a Scot, does it?'

'Everyone has their preferences.'

She lounged back in the chair, her previous decorum forgotten. She stared at the timber frames on the ceiling, a hazy look on her face.

The clock ticked away. Callan had finished his coffee before she spoke again. 'George is dead. It wasn't an accident?'

'No, ma'am. Gunshots were reported at half past two this morning. When we answered the call and searched the scene, we found your husband.'

'Shot to death?'

'Aye.'

'Who killed him?'

'That's what we're investigating.'

She startled upright, hands once again clutching

the arms of her chair. 'Someone shot him to death? In the distillery?'

Callan wanted to spare her the details, but she had asked for them, and would hear it in the news soon.

He leaned on his elbows, made it a point to look her straight in the eye and tell her they had found her husband on the peatland.

She covered her face, the tears now dried up.

'Where were you last night between two and four a.m.?'

'Where any ordinary human is that late – in my bed. What was he doing on their land? He never went to them for anything! Erwin preferred Speyside whisky throughout our marriage, Detective. I-I know my husband.'

'Do you know what your husband was doing at the bog?'

A sob burst from her, and she covered her mouth. 'No, but to rendezvous that far out of town? That's not like George at all. I have… have nightmares some nights, about the poor boy, what Gerald did. I… I'm sorry about the lad. So sorry!'

'Mrs Erwin, it was not your fault. Why don't we talk about last night?'

She massaged her forehead, letting her shoulders droop. 'Last night was bad, so I took a pill and went to bed. It's a strong dose, so I didn't wake until Crista came in this morning at eight. George wasn't around, and it had me worried. And then you…'

Now she cried unabashed tears of agony. 'Oh, my George!'

Callan scratched his leg through his trousers, unsure what to say. 'Mrs—'

'He never was a morning person. And I just felt it. The bed was so cold this morning, as if he hadn't slept in it at all. And I thought… Oh, I thought, "he's done it again, spent the night in his chair again. And now he'll moan of a sore neck the entire day!" So…'

Her bloodshot eyes crumbled with pain. 'So I went to his office, and it was empty. I searched the house and saw his car was gone. And I knew… Oh, I knew…'

'Mrs Erwin, let me call someone for you. Please.'

She gasped, pressed her palms to her heart. 'I don't know. I… Call Eloise, please. She'll be here. We have no family.'

'Eloise?'

'Eloise Wagner, my neighbour.'

Callan frowned. Wagner? As in their local councillor's wife? The same councillor who'd prevented them from digging for Blaine in the peatlands?

Rage towards the man burbled in his gut. He shoved it aside. Now wasn't the time for that.

He found an Eloise Wagner in Mrs Erwin's phonebook – aye, the lady still used one – and dialled.

Eloise Wagner was quick. She didn't dally. He

heard the car door slam outside and opened the door to a brunette, her hair flowing like she was starring in a shampoo commercial.

She wore a deep green fitted dress and gold jewellery, more suited for the country club or mall than to meet her recently widowed friend.

Callan shrugged.

Eloise made a beeline for Melanie, engulfing her in a hug. 'Oh, darling, I'm so sorry. So, so sorry.'

She peered over Melanie's head. 'Are you sure?'

'Oh, they are, El! They are!' More sobs.

Callan gripped the front door handle and nodded. 'I'll take my leave.'

A nod was all he got as a dismissal from Eloise as Melanie Erwin fell apart in her friend's arms.

Just as well, because he was about bone dead himself. What a body couldn't do, telling the next of kin did. Balled you over with the flood of sadness, no matter how shitty the murder victim was when they were alive.

Aileen slammed the car door and tilted her head back. The pale blue sky shifted above her. So beautiful.

And this life was under threat again.

She shook her head, enjoying the breeze playing with her hair and caressing her face. Each inhale carried a bucketful of oxygen – pure, clear air.

Out here, away from the main town of Loch Fuar, the Highlands played a more beautiful symphony. How could it get more gorgeous than this? But it did. When she rested her head next to Callan's and gazed out of the window at Dachaigh, life got blissful.

Aileen huffed. One battle at a time. Now, she had to focus on Pluto McCloughan.

She'd only sorted through some of the receipts. The ledgers and the receipts were all in a mess, and messy accounts rendered the numbers incoherent. Today she'd be doing one of her favourite tasks – filing.

Aileen rubbed her palms together, both in anticipation and to generate some warmth. It was summer, but an icy breeze swept across the Loch Fuar. The puddles were gone; mud crumbled under her boots.

At four, her gran had ushered her out the door to go do some sleuthing. Not because she wanted Aileen to have fun but because she 'didn't want to stare at two long lawyer faces with no whisky in ma hand'. Until midnight, Siobhan and her nurse were playing innkeeper.

Aileen studied Pluto's house in daylight – two storeys, and topped with loft windows peeking out of the roof. Curtains hid the view inside. She frowned. Who'd draw curtains in summer? The screen next to the front door shimmered.

Aileen's steps faltered. Someone was watching her.

Not someone friendly, because they didn't bother opening the door for her. Did Pluto not want her services anymore? Would he ask her to leave? He was too much of a gentleman to turn a woman away. And she'd worked on her negotiation skills.

She wanted to see this audit through. Not only was it a great escape from her parents, but something about it tickled her curious bones.

Something was brewing here apart from whisky. And Jack's initial reaction to her name showed that this family had ties with hers. She remembered it despite the shock, and the way he spat out her father's name.

She needed to know what the feud was about.

Step one: knock on the door.

No one answered. Aileen tapped a foot, waited.

She reached for the barrel knocker and struck it against the door three times. Again, she waited.

A solid minute later, the door squeaked to reveal Pluto, bags under his eyes and a frown on his forehead. The moment his eyes met hers, the frown metamorphosed into a smile, but this time it didn't reach his eyes. 'Aileen! I thought we'd lost you for good.'

She walked in and grabbed his hand. 'I hope you're doing well?'

'Not as well as I'd hoped, lassie. A murder on our land! Oh, come in first.' He led her to the living room, which smelled of air freshener and soap. There were no mud stains on the carpet, nor a chair out of place. 'The stress isn't so good for me, my doctor says. Any other day, I would've scoffed at that, but I feel it now. Whisky?'

Aileen shook her head. 'Callan's working the case, and he's the best.'

Pluto averted his gaze and cleared his throat. 'Aye, I've heard of him and how he found justice for his friend. It's a shame about the excavation coming to a halt. That's just… just… Well, it all boils down to politics, I suppose.'

'Callan is tenacious.'

'At my age, I think some things are better left alone. All I wanted was to find out who's messing with my business. And now someone's dead.'

She knew that feeling more than anyone else — how trouble found the person more than the other way around. But justice, even served cold, made this world a better place. Aileen rubbed her thighs and said, 'I was making some real headway last night and was hoping to continue now.'

'Are you sure you want to?'

'Yes, but I'd like to begin early. And if you don't mind, I'd like to work in the library instead of the loft.' She patted her satchel. 'My laptop needs charging.'

His bushy eyebrows furrowed to form a snowy line. 'The loft? What were you doing in the loft?' Realisation set in. 'That wee bastard! Don't you worry, lassie. I'll set you up in my favourite spot in the library and you can work your magic.'

He led her to a spot which faced towards the distillery. Not the peatlands, Pluto insisted, because the bobbies were still crawling about that place.

Pluto shook his clenched fist, displaying anger for the first time. 'Some eejit murdered Dr Erwin and now we're shut for business until they process all the evidence. Damn it all to hell! We've had to turn away so many visitors and there're spirits that need to get to retailers. A huge loss.' He grumbled as he waddled away, telling her he'd be next door in his office.

Aileen set up her laptop and added extra sweetness to her smile when Ricky walked in with a stack of ledgers and receipts. The man had hefted entire drawers stuffed with receipts instead of transferring them into bags, or better yet, filing them.

He smiled back, but it wasn't genuine: a challenge gleamed in his eyes as clear as the Koh-i-Noor diamond. He didn't believe she'd get through this work. Well, he didn't know who he was messing with.

She hadn't ever audited handwritten ledgers, yet she'd sorted through intangible messes and unsorted big data. This was amateur's play.

Aileen took off her jacket, arranged the desk the way she wanted, and pulled the blinds low so the sun wouldn't burn her tired eyes.

The clock ticked as the sun crawled closer to the

west. Her back ached, but she didn't stop. She piled away the receipts in separate stacks by date. Then she separated out the ledgers that corresponded with that timeline. This process was mundane yet engrossing enough to clear her mind. Aileen repeated this until she had five piles corresponding to five years. Five years since Jack took over, she gathered.

She used her colourful clips to pin each pile into months.

When she sat back and worked out the cricks in her neck, Aileen had sixty different files and as many ledgers. And it was 7 p.m. She had to leave.

Her stomach protested, but the beautiful summer sky was still alive with sunlight.

She'd be at Dachaigh in forty-five minutes. And if this weather persisted, the drive would be pleasant.

Perhaps she'd call Callan to hang out. After all, his night shift was over.

She was wrapping up when she heard it, at first so indistinct that she almost missed it. She strained her ears. Two voices were spitting hate at each other.

A frown crinkled her forehead as she made her way towards the right-hand side wall. Was there a hidden passage behind these books?

Aileen hadn't a clue about the house's layout but—

A deep rumble tickled her ears, followed by a muted one, and then the rumble again.

She slipped out of the room and paused. In the library, a carpet had hushed her footsteps. Out here on the first-floor landing, every step and breath echoed off the exposed stone floor. Aileen doubted the two people on the other side wanted her to eavesdrop.

Why was she eavesdropping?

She was here to dig out the truth. The true reason Pluto wanted her to audit the accounts.

Considering the state of the accounts, it was clear to Aileen that Pluto needed a traditional accountant, not a forensic one. And in this mess, there was no way Pluto could point the blame on Jack. He had no authentic accounts to study, let alone enough evidence for fraud.

'I told you, you idiot!' Pluto roared. 'Do not, I said, do not tell him!'

Ah, the voices were in the adjacent room to the library. Pluto's office.

Ricky's tone was so timid she failed to reconcile him to the man who'd led her to the loft. 'He asked—'

'And you blabber? Where is my phone?'

'Sir?'

'Get it to me!'

All went silent, and then muffled footsteps approached the door. Ricky was about to step out.

In her hurry to move, her foot caught and she tripped. 'Oh!'

Shit.

The door opened to reveal Pluto, mouth agape, ready to spit out more venom.

'I'm sorry! I was only coming here to let you know I was done for the day, not… not…' Eavesdropping? *Eejit.*

His face smoothed. A smile graced his lips, but again it did not reach his eyes. 'Don't worry, lassie. Ricky's always muddling into something when he's asked not to. Did you find anything?'

'I… I,' Aileen wrung her fingers. 'I only just got started. It'll take some time.'

'Sure.' Pluto winked. 'Until then, I'll be glad for the female company.'

'Er, of course.' It was on the tip of her tongue to ask questions about the state of the accounts and why he really suspected his son when there was no stock register or samples of the whisky they sold.

Despite Pluto's smile, the anger radiated off him in tides. Whatever Ricky had done, it had pissed off Pluto.

She smiled, wising up. 'I'll see you tomorrow.' And hurtled out of there.

CHAPTER SIX

Callan taped a picture of Melanie Erwin to his murder board. He had the Mc-Cloughans up there beside a writeup about their characteristics, too.

He didn't know if Julian Wagner was involved but you never knew with politicians. If they could toy with the fate of a murdered eighteen-year-old, they were capable of anything.

The latest piece of paper he'd printed was the list of firearms certificate holders. In the Highlands, the list ran long, especially with residents staying further out of town.

Once he taped everything on the board, Callan jotted down notes about the crime scene: the body, the two or three gunshots the witnesses had heard, and the exact distance from McCloughan's house to where they'd found the body.

The property stretched over a hundred acres, but Erwin was found less than a kilometre away from the house. In the darkness the distance felt longer and Callan had taken a zigzag route. But the shooting took place close enough for the residents to hear a shot and far enough for the police to not suspect one of the McCloughans.

Callan drew a question mark between Erwin and the McCloughans. How were they connected? Erwin wasn't Pluto's current doctor and perhaps the family had consulted him for minor infections…

Pluto's wife… Linda? Aye, he remembered hearing about Linda McCloughan and her passing a few years ago. He made a mental note to look into that.

The phone interrupted Callan's musings. 'Hell,' he muttered.

'Detective.' The caller didn't bother with a hello. 'I have Dr George Erwin's call logs with me and I thought you should check them out. I've sent you an email.'

'What about his calendar? Do we know why he was at the bog?'

The technician huffed. 'Erwin didn't have a passcode on his phone. That's pretty old school, considering, but he *was* old. And it sure saves time for us.'

Callan pressed his computer's power button and waited for it to wake up. 'What's his cyber security got to do with anything?'

'Because as he was a doctor, he wasn't stupid. And he didn't use his phone for anything else but for its primary reason – to call people.'

The computer hummed to life, and the browser popped open with an error message. Callan tapped the refresh button. When the page didn't load, he barraged successive clicks on the mouse. Stupid internet. 'What does that mean?'

The technician groaned. 'Detective, what do you use your phone for?'

Callan chewed on that question. What did he use his phone for apart from fighting the urge to hurl it towards a wall? 'I call or text.'

A long pause. 'Er, most people use it for emails, social media, photos, and storing their entire life's data on it. Erwin's phone is clean. Clean in a way that I believe he literally didn't use it for anything but calling people.'

'Do we have reason to believe he had another phone?'

'Maybe. I can't say. Although he has a few contacts saved, like his wife and a few colleagues, I'm guessing.'

Callan's email finally pinged, and he hit the attachment button to download the call logs from the technician. 'He had nothing else on his phone apart from call logs?'

'Yeah, and no social media either. That's weird, because most people use at least one platform.'

Callan didn't. Using his phone and the dashboard on his new car was painful enough. 'Has your team found anything else? Did he have a smart watch? A geo tracking app?'

'Nope. If I find something, I'll send it to you.' The technician hadn't grumbled about his workload once and had called Callan instead of Callan nagging at him. Since the voice on the line was new, Callan reckoned the lad was still wet behind the ears.

He disconnected the call and hit 'print'. The printer creaked to life, its sound muffled under the stacks of filing he'd never got around to doing. Perhaps when Robert got back he'd set the bastard to work. Until then, Callan needed to find a lead in this case.

If his photographic memory served, George Erwin's phone was a latest model. A tech had found it in the bushes, its screen cracked and unresponsive. But the technician had somehow got it to work.

Callan hunkered at his desk with the printout, eyes scanning over the long list of calls. It would be a long shift.

Thirty minutes later, Callan had five numbers of interest. Erwin called a slew of people yesterday, and each call had lasted for varying minutes. But… these five numbers were ones the man dialled regularly: Callan could trace repeat calls to each of these numbers over at least a week.

It wasn't the wife – Callan had eliminated her.

And George Erwin had no other children apart from Gerald, who the Erwins no longer spoke to.

These five numbers of interest weren't saved on Erwin's phone. Almost as if he didn't want anyone to know about their existence.

Did that mean Erwin wasn't in fear for his life at the bog?

A seasoned criminal would have deleted the call history, adding at least another layer of defence between the data and the police.

Callan had learned in a cyber security class — which cost him a few brain cells — that data couldn't really be deleted. That knowledge helped him. Every time Rory hounded him about the papered mess in his office, Callan informed him physical data was safer.

He frowned at the phone numbers he'd jotted down in his notepad.

Technology wasn't completely useless. Aileen had told him of an app which tracked the owner of a particular number. But sometimes security could hinder the search.

The first two numbers belonged to people in London, the app said. But to check once himself, he dialled the first number and got a dead tone. Someone had already ditched it.

He tried the second one, and it rang. His heart thumped in anticipation. He tapped his desk.

'Hello, Mystics and More Self-Care store!' a voice chirped.

What made people so energetic in the bloody evening? 'Hi, I got a call from this number. May I know who I'm speaking to?'

A scuttle sounded down the line, something crashed into someone and a female voice said, 'Oww!' And then, 'Hello?'

'Hi, this is Dave. I got a call from this number?' Callan didn't want to tip off any criminals by giving his real name.

A pause. 'I'm sorry, Dave. I think you've misdialled. This is Sharon and I haven't made a call to a Dave all day.'

'Sorry, I must've made a mistake. Thank you for your time.'

For good measure, Callan searched for the Mystic and More Self-Care store and found one in a small town in Wales. The owner, Sharon Reeves, was in her late fifties and very active on social media.

Someone had used their number to call Erwin. That didn't mean Sharon knew anything. It was more likely that the real caller had used their number as a spoof.

Spoofing was easy enough via apps. Even he could do it. Callers rerouted the location of the caller, like a mask, to appear like they were calling from somewhere else.

Callan hit the email icon on the computer and grumbled until the computer spit open the app. Then he composed an email to IT asking for information on these numbers.

George Erwin was perhaps dealing with some shady criminals or someone smart enough to cover their tracks. But not enough to wipe his phone log clean.

Callan moved on to the other three numbers.

The internet didn't refresh, causing him to cuss at it. He didn't have time for this tomfoolery. Callan grabbed the landline and dialled the middle number on his list. Good old grunt work paid off better than sitting behind a hellish screen.

When the first ring came down the line, he almost fist-pumped the air.

'You've reached Mr McCloughan's office.'

Ice froze Callan's veins. McCloughan? Ha. So they were in touch with each other. He now had a connection. 'Could I speak with Mr Mc-Cloughan?'

The feminine voice didn't respond, and he could hear the soft tones of a conversation not meant for his ears.

'Sorry, Mr McCloughan is not in the office. We had to shut the distillery for the day.'

'What about Pluto McCloughan?'

Another muffled conversation. 'Sorry, none of the McCloughans can come to the phone right now. We've been swamped with calls from the media and we are not giving a statement.'

Ah, so it was the official McCloughan's Distillery phone number. 'This is Detective Inspector

Callan Cameron, ma'am. I want to know who you are.'

Another pause. 'I'm their marketing manager and now their media spokesperson.'

'Is this your private line?'

'Er, not really. We have a common landline number. It rings at all the connection points.'

'Okay, where are you working from?'

'Jack's house.'

When Callan had ordered no one to enter their premises. Callan rolled his eyes. That man was a stubborn arse. 'Thank ye,' he said, and disconnected the call.

Callan deduced that someone in the distillery was in touch with Erwin and were smart to do it on a semi-public landline. He needed to check each phone and its outlet himself.

He noted that on his to-do list and moved on to the next number.

This time someone answered after the first ring. 'Hello, Mr Wagner's office.'

His blood froze. Bloody Wagner. His hunch was right again. Politicians and their noses were in everyone's business, especially their wife's best friend's husband.

'This is Detective Inspector Callan Cameron. I wanted to know if Wagner's in the office.'

'He is, but unfortunately he's busy at the moment in a meeting.'

'Alright, thank ye.' Callan scratched his chin,

thinking about the notice Wagner had signed for the Environmental Protection Committee.

And that stay on the excavation could protect Erwin's son, evidence or not. Politicians and criminal lawyers: a pair of slippery eels.

Blaine had joked once about Callan becoming a lawyer when they'd been thinking of careers knowing Callan didn't have a sweet tongue. He told it like it was.

Mr Macgregor had insisted his son become a doctor, while Blaine wanted to play the piano. And his dream hadn't been unfounded. He would've flourished. Denied opportunities…

Callan set his jaw. When he met Wagner, he wouldn't sugar-coat a word for that bastard.

Happy with that lead, Callan turned to the final number on his list.

He dialled the number, a normal mobile phone this time, and waited. The tune rang out and went blank.

Callan redialled. No response.

Hell. He needed that internet app again. This time when the thing spluttered to life, Callan didn't thank the machine, he cussed it out. 'Work, you, hellish torture—'

The app loaded onto the screen. Callan gritted his teeth and typed in the phone number.

A circular 'loading' icon flashed on the screen. Callan tapped his finger on the desk, then tapped his feet and was almost ready to hurl the computer to the floor when the page loaded.

A name.

For a week, George Erwin had spoken to this person, for the better part of half an hour each time.

And last night Erwin had called again, but it went unanswered.

Callan frowned at the man's name. Eean.

But his surname itched Callan's skin. *Mackinnon.*

Who was Eean Mackinnon?

It was time to pay Dachaigh a visit.

THE DOOR CLICKED SHUT, BLOCKING THE COOL wind and paling sky. A sense of trepidation squeezed Aileen's heart. A murmur drifted from the library, but it wasn't the voices she wanted to hear.

'Aileen?'

She shut her eyes and willed for things to go back to the way they were.

'Where have you been?'

She straightened her spine at her mother's question, and infused steel in her tone when she said, 'I was out.'

'Don't you have work to do around the inn?' Ann Mackinnon flicked her straight-as-a-ruler hair behind her ear. She would not smile for her daughter. Aileen believed her mother's lips were incapable of lifting up, but they sure tilted down.

'I don't see why I have to keep you updated with my whereabouts, Mother.'

Ann crossed her arms, her fingernails glinting a pale pink shade. Her white trousersuit didn't have a single crease nor a speck of lint; it fitted her like a model on a runway. Unlike Aileen, her mother took great care of her looks. 'Your father and I took great pains to come here so we could speak to you. It is important. Especially when you're being difficult. Why weren't you answering your phone?'

'I thought we discussed the matter already.'

'You cannot possibly want to spend your entire life here! For god's sake, this is a holiday destination for people who like that sort of adventure. Not a place for a forensic accountant.'

Aileen bottled up the irritation at her parents. They still considered her move to Loch Fuar as temporary. 'Phone connection is spotty here.' Her phone had rung and Aileen had ignored it.

'Your father and I would like to speak to you about this. Now.'

'Mother, I told him this morning, and I repeat: I'm not coming back to the city.'

Ann's hair shook like a pleated curtain, few wrinkles on her face thanks to her many facial appointments. 'We'll see about that.' She turned, sauntering towards the library.

A few curses worse than 'bloody hell' slipped past her lips before Aileen followed her mother.

She should've known her parents were lawyers for a reason. They didn't fight; they asked questions, put forth statements like in a debate, and forced your hand. They'd have a plan of action, like they always did when arguing cases.

Aileen never succeeded in her arguments against them. Even as a teenager.

When she reached the library's threshold, her feet faltered. 'Father, I hear you want to talk to me.'

Eean looked up from his book and frowned. 'We felt it was right to speak without your grandmother present. She has a sway on you. And at her age, she isn't thinking logically.'

Her mother sat on a high-backed chair. 'Let's discuss this like adults.'

Aileen massaged her forehead before walking into the room and leaned against a bookshelf.

Her father's brown eyes fixed on her. His gaze was colder than she remembered. 'Is this what you do? Run a loss-making inn and frolic around all day?'

Ann stood up from her chair. 'Look, sweetheart, we know the last year was tough for you. But it's not too late to fix your life. You can come live with us for a while.'

Aileen narrowed her eyes. Her mother bulldozed over her every time she expressed her dreams, and now she was doing it again. 'I don't need to fix my life, nor do I need your help to fix my life. It's wonderful as it is.'

'Taking handouts from strangers is a wonderful life?' Eean scoffed. He stabbed a finger at her. 'You had a fiancé who was willing to help you till you made partner and a decent name for yourself as an accountant. You had a house that you could've sold to purchase a bigger one with him and been happy, financially secure. This, this life here, is not for you. This is a loss-making business, a liability.'

'I'm sorry, Father, but like I've told you before, the picture you just painted is not for me. It's not fair of you to judge when you never wanted this life for yourself—'

'There was a reason for that! I don't want my daughter to waste her life in a good-for-nothing hole in the middle of nowhere!'

'I have friends here!' The lilt in her tone told Aileen her anxiety was spiralling towards the summit. Words fought to slip out and anger spewed into her core like lava. But experience enabled her to restrain the rage. Her parents didn't appreciate her passionate arguments. They would wait till she was done, and debate with her the consequences of her passion. Then, under their disappointed gazes, she'd give in to whatever they wanted her to do.

She needed to stay calm.

But that intention went out of the window when Ann gripped her arms. 'Aileen, you cannot be happy in a place like *this*. We let you explore your wild side, but we cannot let this quarter-life crisis continue any longer.'

Eean joined in. 'It's only right you see sense now than regret later. We spoke to Liam. He is willing to take you back after everything you did and how you ran away. Take the offer. I'll speak with your former boss and get you a new position.'

Liam is willing to take you back after everything you did.

Perhaps that sentence summed up everything her parents thought about their only child.

Hurt gnawed at her heart and any hope of acceptance from her parents burned to ashes. Aileen had worked so hard to gain their approval all her life. From making sure she studied late into the night and earned outstanding grades, to going to the salon so her mother didn't comment on her hair's dullness or her chipped nails.

She hadn't acted under their influence for so long. Still, even now her brain kicked into gear, ready to comply with their demands.

Conditioning.

Her parents weren't wrong, a part of her justified. She had taken a handout from a relative she didn't know existed until he died. And her inn would still struggle if she couldn't successfully set up a restaurant.

Her parents meant well. They had always wanted her to succeed, see her become a lawyer like them, and join their firm.

She hadn't wanted that, and she'd crushed their high hopes. 'I… I think I'll…'

'Aileen, think about it before you give us an answer.' Her mother squeezed her shoulder and for the first time, Aileen saw something other than frost in her eyes. Worry. 'Think about what the city can offer – a job, nice restaurants, shopping centres, museums, bookshops. And friends. What do you have here but heather?'

She blinked at her mother, struck again at her summation of Loch Fuar.

What didn't she have here? she wanted to ask. What about Isla? Callan? Her parents hadn't met her friends. Aileen wished they didn't, especially her boyfriend.

'Mother, I—'

Her father cut her off. 'We'll leave tomorrow. Pack your bags. I have a contract to draft for a client. And two meetings with international clients scheduled after we return.'

'Tomorrow? I'm *not* leaving tomorrow!'

He waved off her protest. 'Don't be ridiculous, Aileen. Time doesn't wait for anyone, especially in the city.'

'Eean!' Ann faced her husband. 'We can give Aileen a couple of days.'

'There is nothing to decide. It's decided. We're leaving tomorrow.'

'Father—'

'You have no prospects here. Do you wish to wither away alone in these wilds? Don't be stupid.'

No one called her stupid, not even when she ticked off Callan. He didn't dare insult her. He raged, threatened. But he was all bark and no bite. With him and in Loch Fuar, she felt like herself, as an adult whose opinions mattered. And everyone respected her for who she was.

Her mind zapped back to another conversation in this room with another lawyer who had belittled her and her business. The reminder pumped steel into her veins. She straightened her back and lifted her chin. 'I'm quite capable of making my own decisions. At this moment, I'm not inclined to leave. All I can say is I'll think about it.'

'Think?' Her father shook his head. 'We don't have time for your childish behaviour. Pack your bags.'

'Didn't you hear *anything* I said?'

'No, Aileen, not when you're acting like a tempestuous child. Pack your bags.'

'No!'

'Aileen! Don't raise your voice at your father. In fact, don't raise your voice, that's not civilised.'

'Mother—'

'Listen to us.' Her father stalked towards her. 'I'll speak to Liam. Let me call him right away.' Eean pulled his phone out, dismissing Aileen's turbulent thoughts and words.

'I don't—'

Crash. A shatter pierced her ear, and glass rained.

She never got to complete her sentence, nor did Eean get to hit the call button. It might've been fate but—

Aileen covered her head, braced for more 'Get down!'

The sound of a car's engine revving blasted through the library's splintered window.

Headlights pierced Aileen's retinas and just as soon disappeared, leaving her blinded.

'What—'

Her parents stayed braced, ducked with hands covering their heads. She would laugh if it wasn't for the grenade in the middle of the room.

Light glittered on the shards of glass, as if the stars in the night sky had plunged into her library. A gust of cold air blew in.

Aileen slid towards the wreckage, and her heart rate kicked up a notch.

It wasn't a grenade. But it was still a threat.

It was a stone wrapped in paper. She squinted to see what was on it and gasped at the picture of a skeleton. Below it was printed: *You shouldn't have come.*

CHAPTER SEVEN

Callan's truck bumped over the stone bridge and zoomed its way to the whitewashed structure that loomed ahead. Dachaigh was so out of the way, this road never saw any traffic except for guests' cars.

He turned right into the inn's car park and the tingling in his chest dissipated. What in the world was Robert doing here? The man had been called to someone else's house earlier, hadn't he?

Callan was out of the car and rushing towards the inn before his car door slammed shut. Dachaigh was almost like his home, since he spent most of his downtime here. But not this afternoon. His office chair had had to suffice.

The warmth enveloped him, and he longed to sag his tired body into the barstools in the kitchen. This part of the house sat in darkness,

92

but he followed the golden halo in the drawing room and paused, eyebrows furrowed. 'Siobhan?'

She startled awake and jerked a hand to her chest. 'My heart isn't what it used to be, lad! Don't scare me!'

'Aren't Horror Nights supposed to be about startling yourself?' Siobhan enjoyed that show accompanied with a finger or two of whisky.

She waved him towards the library. 'They're in there.'

'They?'

Siobhan gripped Callan's palm and squeezed. 'She needs you.'

Callan spotted Robert as he trudged towards the reception area, notebook in hand and his hair sticking out like he'd tried to pull it. He said something to someone behind him.

What was going on? Who were *they*?

Callan nodded at Siobhan and took a deep breath as he stalked towards the voices. They were almost shouting, drowning out his footsteps.

'I don't see why you had to involve the police. It's nothing of consequence.' A male voice said.

'Someone threatened you,' shouted another female voice.

'It was a prank, Ann.'

Where was Aileen? Had someone threatened one of her guests?

She didn't need this after the shooting.

Callan walked through to the reception desk and—

'Callan!'

Aileen stared at him, eyes wide. She stood next to an unfamiliar man.

Callan assessed the two unfamiliar faces. City folk, affluent. The man looked a bit like Siobhan and the woman had the same hair colour as Aileen except for the blond highlights.

Robert cleared his throat and addressed Callan. 'Er, someone threw a stone through the library window. There was a note tied to it which said, "you shouldn't have come" and had a skeleton printed on it.' He held up the evidence bag.

'When was this?'

'At eight.' The woman with the straight bob spoke, and it struck Callan how similar her stance was to Aileen's, along with the shape of her face. She tilted her head up. 'We were all in the library, and Aileen had just returned. Hence, I remember.'

Returned from where? At eight?

He sent a cool look his girlfriend's way that conveyed he'll be talking to her about her evening escapades in private later. Callan didn't need three guesses to know where she'd been. Aileen must have returned to the McCloughan's, thick-headed woman that she was.

'Did you check for footprints outside?'

Robert stuffed the rock into his bag and nodded. 'Tyre marks on the mud road. No footprints. If that's all, I'll head back.'

Callan bobbed his head once. 'Night.'

'Who are you?' The woman – Ann – said.

'Detective Inspector Callan Cameron.'

'I'm not sure this misadventure warrants a detective inspector's attention.'

Callan faced the man and wondered where he'd got the upward tilt of his nose from. This had to be Aileen's father. And the woman to his left must be her mother. He didn't know of them – neither Aileen nor Siobhan ever spoke of their other family members. All Callan knew was that she had an uncle who specialised in criminal law.

Aileen cleared her throat, looking anywhere but at the people around her. 'This is my father, Eean. My mother, Ann. They're here for a visit.'

'I'm sure the Detective Inspector would rather investigate the library than make conversation with us, Aileen.' Her mother crossed her arms and gestured to the doorway behind her. 'That's the library.'

He knew where the library was, but before he spoke to her parents, he wanted to speak to his girlfriend.

She needs you.

These were her parents, but their stiff postures and Aileen's flighty behaviour told him all was not well.

Callan pointed to the library. 'Aileen, could you show me how it happened?'

She made a sound, between a squeak and a yes, and then without a word turned and fled towards the library.

They entered the room without disturbing the shards of glass and waited for her parents to head into the drawing room.

'This is a mess.'

'They threw it hard enough to shatter a large chunk of glass.'

Callan put his arm around her shoulder and pulled her in. 'What's going on?'

'Hell if I know!' She looked up, and he sucked in a breath at the tears swimming in her eyes. 'My parents turn up in Loch Fuar for the first time in more than two decades. Siobhan invites herself over. All this without a single phone call informing me they'll be here. I haven't seen them for… I don't know how long! And they want me to return to the city with them. Tomorrow.'

Ah shite. Callan pulled his girlfriend closer, caressing her back with his other arm. 'To do what in the city?'

'So they can slot me back into the life I left behind.'

He frowned, unable to understand her meaning. 'Is that what you want to do?'

'If I wanted that, I'd have taken Ken's money, sold this place and headed there first thing. Instead,

I searched for your unconscious arse in the rain overnight!'

He wasn't sure what to say. And he wasn't enough of an eejit to crack a joke about their previous case.

A part of his brain knew she was too intelligent for Loch Fuar with her specialised degree and training. But she'd shirked her city lifestyle and never spoke of wanting to return.

'Did you tell them that?'

She swallowed hard and burrowed into his chest.

'Aileen, darling, I can't help you unless I know what's going on.'

'I know. I know. It's just so complicated and I haven't had the time to wrap my head around it.'

He continued his caresses and kissed the top of her head. 'Did they tell you why they are here all of a sudden?'

A head-shake.

'Do they need you in the city for something health-related?'

She gaped. 'What? I'm such a selfish idiot! I never asked.'

He squeezed her closer. 'It's alright. You can talk to them. What else did they say?'

Aileen stiffened. 'That they had a job lined up for me, my old job with… with… Liam Darlington.'

It took him a beat to realise. 'Crap. An ex?'

Aileen's arms wrapped around Callan, and she

pressed her nose to his chest. He almost didn't hear her when she said, 'We were going to get married.'

His hands froze and his heart stuttered – cracked? His mind numbed itself.

Aileen's fingers dug in his back. She looked into his eyes with tears rolling down her cheek, damping his shirt. He didn't give two hoots.

'An ex-fiancé?'

'I…' Aileen took a deep breath and let it out. 'Aye, but it's a wee bit more complicated than that.'

'I'm sure calling off an engagement to someone is complicated. Why didn't you marry him?' He heard the bite in his own voice and hated it, but the venom in his blood didn't hold back. She'd never told him. Never mentioned any ex, let alone a fiancé.

'I didn't marry him because… because…' Her breath caressed his jaw. He had to strain to hear what she said. 'If you'd asked me back then, I would've said being married to someone, wearing their ring had nothing to do with romance. Now I know there's an entire galaxy between being in love and wearing a man's ring.'

Callan was afraid to ask, but he had to. 'You didn't love him?'

She sniffed back tears and nodded. 'We didn't live together, and I realise now he barely saw me. So the lack of love was mutual. He didn't worry about me, didn't care what I was doing. Only when my actions didn't fit in with his reputation, he belittled me.'

'Is he the reason you left the city?'

Aileen shook her head. 'I know now he was my parents' pet. Just wanted to suck up to one of the best lawyers in the business.' She swallowed and wrapped her fingers around his forearms until his arms almost numbed. 'I never…' Tears leaked from her eyes like water from a tap. 'I never want to return to that life again. Please don't let me go.'

The remaining shards of Callan's heart broke at the utter anguish in her eyes. She'd never asked for his help before. He pulled her closer still, held her tight. 'I've got you, love. I've got you.'

And he let her weep.

SHE'D DROPPED A BOMB ON CALLAN, AND HERE HE was. Another differentiation between loving someone and wearing their ring.

One day she'd have enough courage to tell him everything. Right now, the lack of sleep, the gunshots, and the stress of her parents all threatened to drag her under. She leaned on him.

He was the only man she'd ever loved with all her being.

'Can we head to your place?'

His lips touched her forehead. 'I have to speak to Eean Mackinnon. I believe that's your father?'

'Why?'

He sighed. 'His name's come up in Erwin's investigation.'

'No way!'

'It's what it is.' Taking her hand, Callan led her to the drawing room. Her heart thumped, afraid of what her parents would make of them. But part of her beamed – she'd finally get to show him off.

Someone had turned on all the lights in the drawing room and her gran was not happy about it. 'Switch them off, Eean.'

'You should go to bed. I have work to do.'

The moment Siobhan spotted Aileen and Callan, she grinned and sat up straight. 'I wouldn't miss this for the world.'

'What do you mean?' Her father squinted at Aileen, then his gaze flicked to her hand in Callan's and then to her man. 'I see. You knew about this?'

Siobhan spread her hands. 'Is there anything I don't know?'

Aileen squeezed Callan's hand.

He squeezed back and let go, trying to reassure her. 'Sir, I'd like to speak with you regarding a police matter.'

'I don't want you investigating whoever threw that stone in there. It was a prank.'

'It's not about that, Mr Mackinnon.'

Her father waved his hands. 'I'm not here to interfere with the police. I am here to make my daughter see sense. Now I know why she won't leave this godforsaken place. Because of you! Thus, I'm not inclined to speak to you.'

'Eean.' Ann's voice was sharp, a warning.

He shut up.

Ann sat on the other sofa, legs crossed and back straight. 'You never told us you have a beau, Aileen.'

'Ann, that hardly matters,' said Eean.

Ann glared at him and Eean sat back again. She scrutinised Callan, met Aileen's gaze, and nodded. 'What questions do you have for my husband?'

'I'd like to have a word in private with Mr Mackinnon, please.'

Callan rarely said please. In Aileen's opinion, he used that magic word not to be cordial, but to rein in his temper. She felt the anger still radiating from Callan after what she'd tried to explain about her former relationship. If he'd lost it from what little he knew, he'd blow up when he heard the entire story.

Not now.

'Father, please talk to him. It's important.'

'Nothing's as important as a daughter of mine wasting her time running an inn.'

'Oye!' Siobhan sat up now. Her smile disappeared. She was not someone to take nonsense, especially from her own son. 'What are you calling a waste of time? Don't forget, son, I fed and clothed you and your brother with the income provided by this inn. You might wear fancy suits and drive high-end cars, but don't disrespect your roots.'

She stabbed a finger at him. 'If you had half a mind and some eyesight, you'd notice how happy your daughter has been this last couple of years. But you see nothing except pound signs and your esteem in others' eyes.'

That truth bomb rendered Eean mute.

Siobhan flipped her hand. 'You can't see she's happy, that she has friends here. She's met a man, a *real* man. And he wouldn't have got close if I hadn't vetted him first.'

Aileen squeaked.

'Aye, I watch out for my grandwean. I know when she's fighting for her life in the hospital and who's looking after her. I know when she's struggling to keep this inn working and who's helping her. You,' she pointed at Eean, 'don't know a damn thing. So if you don't stop harrying her, so help me god, I'll shove your arse out the door. Pack your bags or stay here to enjoy the peace and don't disturb ma grandwean. Ungrateful arses.' Siobhan flicked a glance at Callan. 'What questions did ye have for him?'

'This is a police matter—'

'I just stood by your girlfriend. Don't give me the official crap.'

Callan squared his shoulders and waited a long while before he spoke. 'This morning Dr George Erwin was found shot to death on the McCloughan grounds. When we looked into his call logs, we realised he'd been speaking to you at length this last week. I want to know what you were talking about.'

Silence.

'I don't know what you mean.'

Callan pulled out his notepad and recited a number. 'Is this your phone number?'

'Yes, it is.'

'We have evidence that Erwin called your number several times in the last week. In fact, he called you last night but the call went unanswered.'

Why was her father involved with a man whose son had almost killed her? Were they friends? Unease roiled in her gut.

Eean raised a brow without moving another muscle in his body. 'I don't owe any explanation to you, Detective.'

'Father, please help him out. A man is dead.'

Had he played a part in a man's murder? Goosebumps littered her arms.

'I wasn't even in town last night. But this boyfriend of yours insists on questioning me like I'm the guilty party.'

Callan snapped his notepad shut. 'What did he talk to you about?'

No answer.

'Do you know why he was at the McCloughans'?'

Her father had an excellent poker face that hid all his thoughts. A face that quaked witnesses when they sat in the box. And it made her sweat more than any scowl ever could.

'What is your connection to the Mc-Cloughans?'

Siobhan made a sound. 'He hates the Mc-Cloughans.'

'Why?'

'I don't know. Tell him, Eean.'

Her father didn't crack his lips apart. Just stared at his fingers in his lap.

This was a waste of Callan's time. Her father would not answer him. Her parents didn't arrive until late morning. Chances were, they had nothing to do with George Erwin's death. Right?

What business did her father have with that man? To call him on the night of his murder?

It was too early for the medical examiner to confirm the details of the death, but she hadn't seen the body herself – thank god – and there were only a handful ways you could shoot yourself in an open area.

'Thank you, sir.' Callan reached the same conclusion as her. He faced the rest of the group. 'G'night.'

Aileen followed him outside, not wanting to answer her parents' questions or pepper them with her own. She focused on Callan. 'Is it true? That Erwin called him?'

He leaned against his car. The sun had set, splashing the abyss above in dark shades. She basked in the light breeze, a bit too cold for summer.

'It's beautiful out.'

'There's a restaurant by the Loch. It's new.'

Aileen smiled. 'I'd love to go as soon as we get this mess cleaned up.'

Callan dipped his head and kissed her, soothing out her anxiety. With a loud growl, he let her go. 'I'm not giving your gran a free show.'

'She's watching?'

'Aye.'

'Incorrigible.'

'She loves ye.'

Aileen nodded. 'I love you.'

'Love ye, too. And we'll dine at that restaurant. Soon. I promise ye.'

Aileen smiled because she believed his promises.

EEAN MACKINNON NARROWED HIS EYES. 'THAT WAS Callan Cameron's case?'

'Yes, sir.'

'That's all you have?'

'Yes, sir.'

This wouldn't do. He needed more information. If he wanted any sort of sway in this situation, he needed knowledge. Knowledge had brought him here – to all this fame and fortune. 'The Chief Constable owes me. Get the entire damn file on

Cameron. Now!' He smacked the phone on the table and glared at his computer screen.

Detective Inspector Callan Cameron was a force to contend with. The man joined the police force at nineteen as a patrol officer. Had completed the drudge-work successfully, and efficiently.

Then he caught the Lewis case. And his work in that case – almost flawless for a rookie – attracted the attention of some of the higher-ups.

He knew of veterans who screwed up with such cases. But an officer still wet behind the ears in the Edinburgh police force did all the right things and used his mind. So why hadn't he enrolled himself after his final exams? Had he taken a gap year after graduation? What had he done during his gap year? And why did his supervising officer call him a loner? Blanks Eean intended to fill with a thorough report.

Know your enemies well; keep them close. That's how he played.

And what he knew of Callan Cameron wasn't enough to please him. Not yet.

The phone rang.

'Speak.'

His assistant swallowed. 'The chief asks if he could get to it in a couple of hours? It's sensitive data and—'

'Next time he wants me to wake my arse up ASAP for a slip up his officers caused, tell him I'll sleep on it. I don't care if he's dining with the Queen!'

'Er—'

'I want the entire file on DI Callan Cameron. And I want it now!'

Police officers. No matter their rank, they could not be trusted to do their job.

He cut the call and waited for his email to ping.

CHAPTER EIGHT

Callan's eyes prickled from staring at the screen. Never in all his years did he think he'd get addicted to technology. But here he was, eyes popping with red veins.

What did he get for all his trouble? Files on two model citizens.

Eejit.

The moment Dachaigh faded in his car's mirrors, he'd called Robert to ask him what he'd found about the stone. And Robert must have grown into a competent enough officer because, for the first time, he knew what Callan was asking him.

He gauged Eean as a sought-after lawyer, and his wife the crème de la crème in family law. As for the stone, someone had used a pebble as the missile and a 70gsm A4 size paper for the missive. They'd driven to the inn, hurled the stone through the window and scurried away before anyone could react. And Dachaigh had no cameras near the library.

Aileen needed more CCTV. She wouldn't like his suggestion, but you needed protection when you lived that far out.

Although, currently, she needed protection from the people inside the inn.

Callan pushed the files away, upsetting some papers on his desk. He didn't care. He'd spent the night in his office chair, something he no longer made a habit of doing – and it was an easy habit to break when you had a warm bed and someone to share it with – and he now faced a case somehow involving Aileen's father. A bloody mess.

Callan faced the murder board looming over him. He'd added Eean Mackinnon to the list. IT still hadn't found the spoofed numbers. But now he would pin Dr Brown's report.

He pushed off the chair, groaned at his leaden muscles, and uncapped the marker.

Dr George Erwin had died between 1 a.m. and 3 a.m. after two bullets pierced his left leg and heart. The shot to the heart killed him, whether instantly or not, Callan wasn't sure. But the man bled out.

To shoot someone in the dark, the killer must have good eyesight and lots of target practice. And they probably had a gun license, or nicked it from someone who did.

The team hadn't found the murder weapon, just a bullet lodged in George Erwin's leg. It had come from an antique firearm.

He had to first match the shoe to its Cinderella. Callan grimaced. Bad analogy. But he needed a list of people who owned antique firearms in these parts and if anyone had reported them stolen. He'd set Robert to more work.

He was tapping at his computer when the phone rang. 'Crap— Hello?'

'Ms Melanie Erwin reported a break-in at her house.'

Hell. 'I'll get there.'

The Erwins' driveway was littered with vehicles: the SOCO team and a police cruiser. A couple of yellow-vested bobbies hustled around, their radios crackling.

Callan marched in through the porch and into the living room.

Melanie Erwin sat on the same armchair, chewing on her forefinger and staring at the carpet. Someone had drawn the curtains and her friend, Mrs Eloise Wagner, read a book on the sofa.

Neither woman glanced at him, but a constable waved him through towards a doorway at the back. A dark timber beam formed an arch so low it brushed the top of Callan's head. The brass-hinged door was of the same shade and as thick as the door to a bank's vault.

'This was his office. We were here to collect his

electronics,' Mr Halston, the head SOCO, said. 'Mrs Erwin showed us through here.'

Callan stood at the threshold and eyed the room, arms crossed. It was big enough to accommodate a desk as big as a billiard table in the centre. Through long windows he could see a professionally tended back garden.

'How did they get in?'

Mr Halston pointed to a timber door next to the windows. 'That leads to the back garden. And it had a muddy handprint on it.'

'The handprint isn't Erwin's?'

'We've taken samples. But we're not sure how they got in.' He pointed to the back door. 'This door locks automatically when shut. Needs a key to open from the outside. And no one's tampered with the lock.'

Callan frowned and turned his attention to the room. The desk could've been his own – paper and stationery strewn all over. A printer rested on a bureau by the left wall. Timber panels continued the wooden theme and a photo of Erwin holding his degree hung on the wall. On the other side was the bookcase. The wall beside the entrance held framed certificates and more photographs.

Erwin had used a large leather chair, and there was one visitor's chair, also made from timber.

The officer gestured for Callan to enter. 'This study alone must have felled an entire forest.'

'How did Mrs Erwin know there'd been a burglary?'

'As I was saying, she showed us in and screamed. She said there's a cabinet missing. George didn't like anyone touching it.'

Callan saw the depressions on the carpet where once had stood a cabinet against the wall littered with certificates and pictures.

He crouched next to the indents. 'It can't have been a huge cabinet if someone stole it. And based on the width of the legs…'

'There are sleeker designs available on the market. Melanie says it was like a filing cabinet – sturdy.'

'Aye, if Erwin wanted to keep the style consistent like he has in the living room and in here, I doubt he'd have a modern, sleek cabinet. Do we know what files he kept in it?'

Mr Halston shook his head. 'The wife said no one stepped in here: no cleaning, dusting or arranging anything. She only came in when they shared afternoon tea while he worked.'

'Wasn't Erwin retired?'

Halston shrugged.

'What about the safe? Is there one in here?'

'It's under that huge-arse table. Thick steel with a keypad, the only piece of latest tech.'

Callan nodded. 'Did you get the rest of the electronics?'

'We're processing them. But the man was fond

of paper, based on the mess on that desk. It'll take us a while to process it all.'

'Alright. I'll have a chat with Mrs Erwin until then.' He trudged back to the living room, taking in the white walls and the timber. Stained glass windows would've made this place a church.

Callan halted when he didn't find either woman in the living room.

'Eloise left.'

The back of his neck tingled. This woman could sneak up on you. Callan took a deep breath and faced Melanie Erwin.

Her cheekbones protruded, straining her pale skin. She'd shoved her hair up in a militaristic bun and applied a pinch of make-up − something on her skin and lips. Callan only noticed because it made her wrinkles appear flaky.

Her dark eyes scanned him like an X-ray machine. 'I saw you in court. Heard what you said about my son. You're a good detective. It cut deep to know what a beast I birthed. I never knew. And George supported him. Is this his payment for that sin?' A tear streaked down her face, cleaning up the makeup as it went. 'What is my fault in all this that I must be punished so?'

She crossed to the armchair and crumpled into it, sniffing and trembling. Her bony shoulders stuck out under her cream shirt. When she bent her head, Callan could see that she was balding. Her wrap-around skirt fell around stick-thin legs. Was she sick? Or was she starving herself?

Callan took a seat on the sofa. 'I'm sorry, Mrs Erwin.'

She blew into her handkerchief before straightening. 'Do you have more questions for me?'

'I wanted to know how your husband seemed these past few weeks.'

'He hated retirement. Couldn't sit still. So he did what he'd been doing for the last ten years. Woke up each morning, worked out or went for a walk, before locking himself in his study for the rest of the day. What he did in there was a mystery to me. All we shared was tea at around four in the afternoon before a supper at seven. That's the only time we saw each other. After Gerald's trial, we barely spoke.'

Her lips shivered until she bit down on them. 'I couldn't stand it.' Her words rushed out in a sob. 'I couldn't stand what he did to that young boy. How could he? My son killed an innocent boy all because of his rage. Stupid, stupid, stupid!'

Callan let her cry it out, unsure what words would give her relief.

She straightened her shoulders again and nodded. 'Sorry. I'll try my best to answer all your questions.'

'What did the cabinet in the study look like?'

'It was a filing cabinet made of teak wood, very simple. George never liked me touching his official things, especially that cabinet. He didn't allow the maid in there either and locked his study whenever he was out.'

Paranoid, much? What was the man doing in his study all throughout the day?

'Have you left the house since you last went into the office?'

Melanie nodded. 'I couldn't sleep here. Not when there are so many memories… Eloise was kind enough to invite me to her house for a couple of days. She drove me down here this morning; the police said they had a warrant to go through George's things. He'd hate it. All these people going through his things, but… he can't speak now. He's gone.'

Those all-seeing eyes landed on Callan, direct and unblinking. 'I've thought about it. When I woke up that morning, I knew. Did I tell you? I knew he hadn't come to bed. He was more pensive than usual when we ate our supper. It was to do with work. I didn't ask more, and he didn't elaborate.' She wrung her fingers. 'When you arrived, I almost expected it.'

'Was anything else taken from the house?'

'Only that cabinet. I had my jewellery lying on the vanity in our room and no one touched it.'

And a safe in plain sight remained unopened. Someone wanted that cabinet.

'If you have any clue about what could be in that cabinet—'

She shook her head.

'Or if you remember, please let me know.'

'I don't know… I never went through his things. I trusted him. Trusted my son, too, and see where it's led me!'

The front door opened, and Eloise Wagner rushed in. The book in her hand crashed to the floor. 'Oh, Mel. Oh, Mel…' She gave Callan a stink eye and wrapped her arms around a sobbing Melanie Erwin.

Melanie was shaken worse than he'd thought. What fault was it of hers?

'How long are you planning to hide out here?'

Aileen groaned, massaging her forehead. 'Siobhan told father off last night. No sooner she goes to bed than he starts again.'

Isla McIntyre, baker, business owner, gossip extraordinaire, wife, mum and Aileen's best friend, plopped into the chair behind her desk.

They sat in Isla's office, a small space beside the kitchen in her bakery. A large – and, unfortunately for Aileen, empty – playpen dominated the room. On shelves sat miniature food that added a sugary dream-like feel to the cream walls.

Aileen leaned back in her chair, caressing the hot coffee Isla had thrust into her hands with a not-so-sweet compliment. 'You look worse than a starving rat.'

'Let me get this straight. They came here on a weekend-long excursion to get you to pack up your *life* and leave – in a day?'

'They don't think much of me. And I rarely argue with them. Because this happens.' She stubbed her forefinger on the desk. 'They act like I can't think for myself, that I'm stupid and petty. And they know I'll trot along like a trained horse at a parade.'

'You're twenty-nine. You don't need their approval, nor did you ask them for any help.'

'That doesn't matter to them. It's their reputation that's the issue. I could be the best innkeeper in all of tourist-trap Loch Ness, always operating at full capacity and winning every Scottish Thistle award going, and they'd still try to drag me away.'

Isla narrowed her green eyes into slits, like a cat about to pounce. Her already flushed face turned an even deeper shade of beetroot. She leaned in, her words hissing like a viper's. 'Absolute heartless bastards! What are you going to do about it?'

'They tried to get me to leave again. Siobhan said a few words and then I left mother and son arguing to come here. Callan says he has my back. But… I want to know what my father's connection is with Erwin and his death.'

A hint of a smile whispered across Isla's face.

But the coolness of it made Aileen shiver. 'Do tell,' said Isla.

Aileen explained it all: the audit, Erwin's shooting, her father's phone calls and the bad blood between him and the McCloughans.

'Why hasn't Callan asked your father to stay back until he can close this case?'

'He can't do that unless my father's a suspect. Since they placed him in his office in the city, thanks to CCTV, he clearly wasn't here. And now I'm not sure who can help me sort these connections.'

Isla tapped a finger on the arms of her chair, nodding her head. 'Ever considered the library?'

'Library? As in old newspapers?'

'Newspapers especially in a small town should have all the juicy gossip. What if there's some dirty secret connecting your father to Jack or perhaps even George Erwin in one of the old papers? It's worth a try.'

Macy Walter smiled at Isla. The single mother of two looked harried, but the smile smoothened out the lines on her face. She ran a hand through her auburn hair. 'I'm sorry about my state. My younger one's at home with fever, but I couldn't take another day off. So my mother's watching him. There's a flu spreading in school. How can I help?'

'We're looking for older newspapers.'

Libraries were Aileen's happy place, but scouring dusty old newspapers? She hoped they had a quicker way of getting through them.

Macy frowned. 'Er, I'm assuming that's for some sleuthing? I've heard of your adventures, Aileen. Unfortunately, you're going to have to do some sleuthing to get what you want. Because, er…'

Their library's system was outdated. They had a digital record of papers that weren't in their archives. Everything else, almost a hundred years of records, had to be hand-searched.

But they didn't know which year they were looking for; it was about to be a long day.

Macy led them down a corridor lined with bookshelves on both sides. They reached the back, a sort of place where electricity was as scarce as the browsers.

She pointed to black leather-bound books gathering dust on the shelves. 'That's it.'

'Er… Those are bound newspapers?'

Macy nodded. 'Aye, and, um, they should have the year printed on them.' Then she pointed to the rows of bookshelves disappearing into the distance. 'Those are the rest of them. And the ones that are still older are in the basement and… um, I'll need to call my colleague to get them for you.'

Aileen shook her head. 'I don't think we'll need those.' She hoped not.

Isla squinted at the books Macy had pointed to. 'What timelines are all these?'

'The recent past, so the 1950s to the 21st century, I think? I'm sorry, no one's accessed these in a long time.'

'That's alright, Macy. Thank you.'

'As you can see, you are the only ones here. So go wild.' Macy sauntered down the aisle towards her desk, leaving Aileen and Isla to exchange a look of horror.

'When I said we should check newspapers, it seemed much simpler in my head.'

'With a fixed date, it would've been, Isla.'

Isla tapped her finger on her chin, eyeing the rows of books. If they'd been any other books, Aileen would've been salivating at the prospect of going through them. Now, she shuddered.

'Okay, I have a theory.' Isla interrupted her musings. 'We have narrowed down the suspect list to four people.'

'Four suspects?'

'Well, three suspects and one murder victim. Dr George Erwin is dead, so we'll leave his case to Callan. But Pluto approached you. Thus he's one of our persons of interest. Then his son, Jack, who barked at you is another. And your father, well… he never stopped barking at you.'

When Isla put it that way… Aileen snickered.

'Let's begin with the most familiar of the three — your father.'

'He left Loch Fuar in 1974 and returned here

when I was five. That's the last he's been here before now.'

'Not because he hates Siobhan?'

Aileen rolled her eyes. 'They meet up every now and again, either at his place or at the nursing home. They bicker the entire weekend and do it all over again next time. I'm not sure if they love it or hate it. My father hates this place. For its lack of opportunity.'

Isla held up a finger. 'Or because someone scorned him. Let's start with 1974.'

A year seemed simple enough to locate, didn't it?

Aileen took out a random leather-bound book and shook her head. '2003.' She pulled the one next to it. '2003.'

She tried one on the shelf below it. And still got the same year.

Isla plucked one from the shelves beside it and got a '2002'.

They exchanged a look. 'Next time, Isla, let's bring some snacks.'

Isla giggled, and they continued along the aisle. They dragged out a book from each of the shelves as they progressed. Row after row, like an endless tunnel stretched out ahead of them until—

'1975?'

'No, let's try 1974.'

Another five minutes of pulling books out of

their dust-coated homes, Isla and Aileen grinned. 'Victory never tasted so dusty.'

Aileen rolled her eyes. 'I should've thought of coming here before.'

'To hide? Without me?' Isla scoffed. 'You need help, or you'd be in a mental facility.'

Isla hefted five books, and Aileen pulled her weight, dragging six others. Guess the exercises her boyfriend forced her to do were working.

The sound of books slamming on the wooden table echoed through the library like shots of a cannon.

Isla dropped into a seat. 'Well, that's my strength training for a month.'

Aileen opened the black book encrusted with '1974' in gold and then 'Vol 1' in a smaller font. 'Let's get cracking.'

But after ruffling through six doorstopper books, a paper cut, and too-many-to-count sneezes, all that was cracking were their necks.

'It's a mistake, Isla. A stupid mistake.'

Isla groaned and rested her head against the chair's backrest. She winched. 'These are hellish chairs! I can't feel my arse anymore!

Aileen would rather spend time with her parents than do this. But she needed more information. How could she find it? Her eyes widened. 'Isla, why don't we look into Pluto first? He gave me receipts to sort through for the last five years. Let's look at the 2017 newspapers.'

They put the huge leather-bound dusty books back, brushed off their shirts and lugged themselves up the aisle to where they found the slightly less dusty 2017 newspapers.

'I swear I'm getting Daniel to give me a massage. And then some.' Isla wiggled her eyebrows. 'You should try it too with Callan. A massage and then—'

'Isla, focus.'

'Married to a man like this, it's surprising I can even think straight.'

Aileen remembered Callan's promise to take her on a date at the new restaurant when things settled, and she smiled. 'Aye, it's a miracle.'

They got back to work. October 3rd, 2017.

'Isla,' Aileen leaned in close. 'Look, Linda McCloughan's obituary.'

'Pluto speaks of her so often. He loved his wife and that shows. He's written such sweet things about her here, and he's still heartbroken over her.'

'I suppose they were married more years than they were single.'

'And then some.' Aileen's heart cracked for the man left to figure out the rest of his old age alone after a lifetime of loving someone so dearly. 'He mentions Jack and his wife here. And here,' she pointed to a news article. 'There's an article on Linda.'

Isla and Aileen read the article together, sighing and humming about the woman's work. She'd volunteered to serve in the navy. That's where she'd met her man. Then she'd worked as a nurse at a naval base before moving to Loch Fuar when Pluto took over the distillery. She'd taken up a nursing job in the local hospital and always had a smile for her patients.

Almost the entire town had gathered for her funeral, showing their respect for the woman and support for her family.

The article had a photo. Jack and Pluto stood with Sarah in the centre. Pluto had his head bowed, and Sarah was speaking to him. Jack, beside his wife, looked like someone had petrified him into a husk – the image of a sorrow-filled son.

So what made Pluto think Jack would drag their brand through the mud? What turned their relationship so bitter?

For a town that prided itself on the efficiency of its gossip hotline, the paper revealed nothing of the McCloughans' personal woes.

Aileen turned the page when—

'Hold on?' Isla flipped the page over to the obituary. 'The line about her smile… Look what Pluto's said about his wife here.'

'Linda's smile for her patients never faded. She dealt with their loss as she would any family member. A sensitive yet utterly caring soul, my dear Linda was never concerned about herself.'

'She was a nurse until the year before she died, wasn't she? In the local hospital?'

Aileen gasped. 'Oh, yes! Linda was a nurse at the same time George Erwin saw patients at the hospital. We have a connection!'

'Aye! A scorned colleague or an angry patient out for the nurse and the doctor who hurt them, or a family member of a patient. There is an endless list of motives!'

'But he's been retired a year now. And she died five years ago.'

Isla rolled her eyes. 'Ever heard of revenge best served cold?'

But they didn't know if George Erwin and Linda McCloughan actually worked together. They needed someone with enough knowledge, or access to the medical grapevine…

Aileen clicked her fingers. 'Oh, I know! We need to talk to Eric. Eric Macdonald!'

CHAPTER NINE

Callan shoved his hands in his pockets and stared at the ground beneath his feet.

He'd let Eloise Wagner take over the care of her friend and joined Mr Halston to find clues the thief left behind.

Outside the back door, despite someone having locked it from the inside, they found the way the thief had left. And entered, perhaps. George Erwin, for all his smarts, had tucked a key in the flowerbed.

Now they stood in the botanical paradise of Erwin's back garden, which he clearly paid someone to tend. The gardener had done a great job, save for the two drag marks which plucked out fronds of grass and exposed black soil.

Callan pointed to the depressions in the mud. 'It looks as if someone dragged the cabinet here. These marks match those on the carpet inside.'

Mr Halston followed the pattern through the soil to the Erwins' driveway. The concrete road split into two when it reached the house – one led to their front porch and the other to the side of the house under a porte-cochere of sorts.

The car in the driveway near the porch belonged to Melanie.

'If the marks are to be believed, someone simply drove a car here, opened the door and towed the cabinet out.'

'It would appear so.' Halston tugged his mask down to scrub his face. 'And the rain wiped out much of the evidence.'

Callan tapped his foot on the tarmac while he thought. Eventually he said, 'Let's see what they've found in Erwin's office.'

Another SOCO leaned over the drag marks, measuring out the depressions in the lawn. 'A footprint.'

Callan nodded and strode inside the office, which was crawling with scrub wearing officers and contained a mountain of papers.

Was this his future? Callan hoped not.

He stepped over the heaps of paper behind Erwin's chair and crouched under the desk. Erwin had placed the safe on his right, where it took most of the leg space. It was a thick metallic monstrosity with a keypad, which leaned against the desk's leg so Erwin could reach in while sitting in his chair. Callan knocked against it.

'Sounds stocked. Does anyone know the password?'

A SOCO flashed an LED light over the keypad already wiped for prints.

Callan pressed the buttons highlighted with fingerprints. It beeped and then the safe opened. 'Ah, hell.'

He had expected a few pounds, some jewellery, documents maybe. But he never dreamt of finding a twelve-by-twelve-inch box filled to the brim with cash. Hard cash, and not tenners either.

'Shite!' Callan couldn't help himself, just couldn't. He understood the need to print everything out, shirk technology. But to keep hard cash at home in a safe, with the key to this room in the flowerbed outside? This was as stupid as the people who kept a safe right next to their back door.

A whistle from behind him had Callan backing away. 'That's easily my annual salary times two, at least.'

Where had Erwin earned all this from? The man retired after serving in the National Health Service, for god's sake. Not a profession that made you a millionaire.

And the wife said she had no clue what he did in here.

Callan straightened. 'Find out if there are any logbooks, ledgers, or any sort of record to tell us where this money came from.'

Stacks and stacks of cash never came from legitimate sources. Erwin was probably into something illegal and that was where he could've angered the wrong people. Like the spoofed phone numbers Callan's colleagues still hadn't located.

And this safe was jam-packed. He turned to the right and froze. The large picture of Erwin at his graduation.

'Hell! We need to check behind that picture. It's large enough to hide another safe.'

He hefted the gilded frame, left it weighing down on his muscles. It took the help of two more to get it down without cracking the large glass covering.

This safe was similar to the other one, maybe six inches taller but just as wide. Its grey metal glinted in the light from the large windows.

Natural light was a premium in Scotland and gave Erwin a backdrop of the garden. And from the feel of the house, the man was as ostentatious as one could be. But Callan wondered how private the study really was.

Callan retreated from the wall safe and let the SOCOs work their magic. He stalked over to the window, careful to not crunch any papers.

The glass wasn't tinted to hide the view from onlookers. There were no privacy screens or netting, and no curtains to hinder the view − not even the sort that hide half of the window.

The windows exposed too much for a man who hoarded cash. Sure, a safe protected the cash from sticky fingers but from people whose blood pounded only to steal? A lock was nothing but a hiccup, no matter how advanced the security.

And someone stole a cabinet. Why not all this cash?

An amateur? Or were they looking for something specific? Something more precious than cash?

A gasp went up behind Callan.

He swivelled, and his jaw fell open. He'd struck gold. If he were an actual treasure hunter, he'd have literally uncovered the bounty. More cash. Heaps of it, crammed into the safe. Erwin had no more space, not even a tiny sliver to stock one additional pile of notes.

'What the heck was this man into?' an officer said.

'Nothing legit.' Callan wove his way back to the safe. 'Found any fingerprints?'

'I reckon it should be the owners, but we'll check.'

'The logbooks?'

'Still searching.'

If Callan ran an illegitimate business, where would he stack the evidence of his dealings? On a computer? Erwin didn't trust technology. In a cabinet? Most likely.

If they were secret, coded ledgers? Callan cut off his imaginative brain.

'The man wasn't expecting to die.' He scratched his chin. 'Why would he then leave his office and his work in such a disarray? He'd hide all this money. Route it somewhere else.'

Erwin cared about what people thought of him. He wouldn't leave his dirty laundry out to dry if he had an inkling he was about to die.

So why didn't he have space in his safe for more cash? Despite the mess in the rest of his office, he kept these two safes clean. Well oiled.

'Check if there's a logbook in the safe. Or find another safe where he could've stored the cash.'

Callan squinted, taking in the room.

Papers on the desk, papers by the wall, papers on the floor, papers on the visitor chair, papers on the bookcase and papers resting on the tongue of the printer…

A paper on the printer…

With gloved fingers, he reached out and plucked the paper with its black ink on white.

A skeleton glared back from the centre of the page. And below it was printed, 'you shouldn't have come.'

Ah heck.

Could George Erwin have threatened Aileen's father the other day? Thrown the stone?

No way. Erwin was already dead by then.

Callan's eyes strayed over to the cabinet. Did the thief use Erwin's printer to throw them off their scent? In that case, how did they know what the threat had said?

'Log this into evidence as well and try to match

the paper and ink with the one stuck to the stone someone hurled at Dachaigh's library.'

How the heck was Aileen's father involved in this? So many questions he needed to answer before the Mackinnons left for the city. Hopefully without his girlfriend in tow.

He was in a damned pickle.

AILEEN TWIDDLED HER THUMBS. 'ARE YOU SURE?'

'He's here like clockwork, every afternoon. Maybe a surgery ran over.'

Aileen tugged the apron off the stand and put it on. 'No point in me sitting on my arse. Put me to work!'

She had done it plenty of times, and even now they fell into their old dance. Customers bustled in, gave their order. Some sat around, some left, but there was no sign of Dr Macdonald. What if he didn't come in today? There was always tomorrow. Or by visiting the hospital—

There he was. Aileen grinned.

The man's hair stood up as if he'd ran a hand through it. A smile graced his pink lips, lighting up his light blue eyes. If it weren't for his Scottish brogue, the man could be Nordic. With that and his broad shoulders, Aileen was sure people faked injuries to just see him.

'Aileen Mackinnon! What happened to the inn?'

Isla bustled over, wiping her hands on a kitchen cloth. 'Just the man we were looking for! Do you have a few minutes to spare?'

He blew a raspberry and looked at his wrist-watch. 'I have a date with several beautiful ladies. So make this quick.'

'What would your ladies like today?'

He rattled off a large order, and bought two of almost everything Isla had in stock. The man took a box full of treats for the Senior Citizen Care centre every week and volunteered there three times a week.

'And a jam scone? Right. That's on us. Have a seat and we'll be right there.'

Aileen rang him up while Isla held a hand over her mouth, speaking so only Aileen could hear. 'If I weren't married, girl, I'd go for that.'

Isla was as loyal as they came, but whimsical fun. Aileen patted her back. 'There's only one man in this world who can keep up with you. Come on, and behave!'

The bakery wasn't too busy, so Isla pulled up a chair at the table by the window. Eric dug into his scone, his tea beside his plate in a to-go cup. 'I survive on coffee, so I've told myself to substitute it with tea now and then eventually water. Step by step, isn't it?'

Aileen rolled her eyes. 'Tell that to Callan.'

'Oh, Paw's the same. He can't do without, and

we both know that's how police solve crime: chugging coffee.'

'How is Rory? I haven't seen him in a while.'

'Same old, same old. Complaining about politicians and getting glitter all over himself when he plays with my nieces.'

Aileen grinned, knowing the man who led their local police team cared a lot about his family, no matter how hard-nosed he could be as an officer. 'Well, Isla and I, we, er—'

'You're looking into Dr George Erwin's death? It's not a surprise, Aileen.'

She tilted her head. 'We're not really looking into his death. We wanted to know if there's a connection between him and Linda McCloughan?'

Eric frowned, wiped off a crumb, and gazed out of the window. 'Linda… Oh, aye, she was a nurse, wasn't she?'

'And he a doctor.' Isla stabbed a finger on the table. 'And we wanted to know if there was any connection between them – unrequited love, a vengeful colleague, a scorned patient or an angered family.'

'It's before my time, you see. But there's a nurse in the hospital, Jackie. If there's anything, she'd know. Give me a day to ask her?'

'That's great, but aren't you Pluto McCloughan's doctor? You could ask him.'

He grinned, balling up the used napkins. 'And that's when client confidentiality comes in.'

Isla waved her hand. 'Oh sure, he's a nice man. And he loved his wife.'

'Sure did. They both have… had… very generous hearts. She's the star in the local nursing community. I was interning at the hospital when she passed, and well, it was a sad day. The nurses were weeping – the ones old enough to have worked with her.'

'She made an impact.'

'That she did, aye. And cared deeply for her patients.'

Isla intertwined her fingers, rested her elbows on the table. 'What a selfless soul! Always working for the benefit of others.'

Eric scratched the side of his lips, a frown corrugating his forehead. 'You know what? Now that you mention it, I remember what Jackie said about her that day. Jackie talks a lot, but I remember it because, well, Linda was like the Florence Nightingale of Loch Fuar. She studied autism too. For Ricky, of course.'

Aileen blinked. 'Ricky?'

'Ricky Ridge, aye. He's autistic, although Pluto refuses to acknowledge it.' Like a true Loch Fuar local, Eric forgot about time and leaned in to tattle. 'The story goes that Aaron Ridge, Ricky's father, wasn't around a lot. Pluto and Linda took it upon themselves to raise the boy.'

'Wow! That must have been difficult.'

'Took it in their stride.'

Aileen cupped her chin with the palm of her hand. 'What about Ricky's parents?'

'I don't know about Aaron or Ricky's mother. But Linda took courses to learn about autism and how to tutor autistic children. She invested a lot of energy in that boy. Jackie said Linda nursed Aaron in the McCloughan home, too, but I can't remember the specifics.'

'And Ricky's schooling?'

Eric shrugged. 'Pluto refused to enrol him into a special school or let anyone label him as autistic. Linda didn't like that, so she took matters into her own hands. A selfless person. I remember it because I told myself if I can be even a wee bit as dedicated as she was, I'll be successful enough.'

Isla squeezed his forearm. 'You're a fantastic doctor, Eric. No other doctor willingly volunteers at a senior citizen centre filled with nosy old ladies. And you enjoy tea parties with them.'

Eric's smile lit up his eyes and propped dimples on his cheeks. 'They're wonderful people, and they tell me stories about my childhood. That's weird, but when you grow up in a small town… And well —' His phone dinged. 'Oh crap, is it five already? Sorry! I'm late. Sorry. I'll see you around?'

'Of course! Thank you for taking the time.' Aileen waved him off and turned to Isla. 'You are a genius. Aaron Ridge. Linda—'

'Nursed him at their house. But there's no mention of this man in her obituary.'

'Nor is he anywhere in the household. Maybe if you go through all those family pictures, but otherwise…' Aileen pursed her lips. 'And Ricky, he… No wonder he is the way he is. I wonder why Pluto didn't want to send him to a special school.'

'Pride?' Isla shrugged. 'Well, now you have a lead. Linda nursed Aaron Ridge in their home. And Eric says he doesn't know what happened to Aaron.'

'And how is Aaron connected to Erwin?'

'I don't know! Maybe Erwin was his doctor?'

'Erwin worked on a lot of patients in his time. Perhaps all of Loch Fuar.'

Isla rubbed her eyes. 'All this work for nothing?'

Aye, nothing. All they had was gossip and no new information on Erwin or her father. And certainly nothing on Jack McCloughan. Aileen was back in the town of No Progress.

Aileen huffed. 'It's time for me to head back, too. Hell! I don't want to!'

'Best of luck. It's a matter of a few days. They'll grow tired of hassling you and leave. Once they're out the door, it's you, me and a tub of ice cream.'

'Make that plural.' She'd need several to feel even a smidge of normality again. If someone existed up above and had any mercy to dole out, she needed it. Before her parents browbeat her into doing something stupid, like leaving.

❄

CHAPTER TEN

'Are you sure?'

'We processed it. I examined it myself.'

'What about the rest of the papers?'

'There are so bloody many of them. You know we can't process them in hours.'

'But you studied this?'

'It was in a darned safe! Behind the cash!'

'Go home, get some rest.'

'I could say the same thing of you, Detective. But—'

Callan stared at Mr Halston sitting in his visitor's chair, a mug of coffee by his elbow. Callan's shift had ended a long time ago. All he wanted to do was check up on Aileen. But a man was dead and now Halston had found something disturbing.

The tall leather-bound book was as mysterious and important as it appeared. Its surface seemed polished with care, and its ochre pages were frayed at the edges to indicate years of use.

Halston handed Callan a pair of gloves. They'd cleaned Callan's desk to create space for the huge tome, shoving papers onto the floor.

For the first time since he moved in, Callan saw the pale blue surface of his desk. A rather depressing colour, but he'd cover it up with heaps of paper again soon.

Halston arranged the ledger on butter paper, and with gloved fingers lifted the front cover. The page was mottled with brown spots, and the rough feel of the paper told Callan it was handmade.

A logo was embossed on the first page – one he'd seen before on Gerald Erwin's belongings. The crest of the Erwins.

If the emblem wasn't enough, Erwin had had his name printed in calligraphy in the centre of the page.

'Fancy, eh?'

'You saw the house.'

Halston chuckled. 'Sure did. But this has to be important.'

Callan flipped over a page and frowned. The page had four columns, something similar to the accounts Aileen loved to pour over.

In the column on the left was the date, and the one on the right had a pound symbol. and listed out sums of money in the rows below. On the column beside it, Erwin had written fractions. For what,

Callan wasn't sure. The column in the centre terrified him the most. Sitting next to the date, with a heading of 'particulars' it listed:

Kidney. Liver. Heart. Brain. Right Lung. Left Lung.

And so it continued, listing out parts of the body, some repeating and others appearing just once.

Unease rumbled in his stomach, erupted bile into his throat. 'What the hell is this?'

'What do you think?' Halston settled in his chair. 'Read one entry at a time.'

He scanned the first page. It had two hearts, a right eye, skin, three tongues…

The vomit soured on his tongue and he wrenched his eyes away from the page and onto the whitewashed wall in front of him.

Two breaths steadied him, and he took in the first entry on the page again.

On 1 July 2019, *Tongue* fetched Erwin a few hundred pounds. In the fraction column Erwin had scrawled '1/5'.

What was the sum for? Was it for what he had assumed it was? Did they have a Burke and Hare out there?

And the fractions. Why were they written against each body part?

To think Erwin would be into something this sinister…

They had run him through their system and his records showed the man had retired after an honourable service in the NHS. And after his son's conviction, he'd clung to the shadows.

'Hand me a piece of paper and a bloody calculator.'

A bead of sweat emerged on his forehead, pregnant enough to trickle down his face and disappear into the mask. Seconds later, another one followed.

Callan stabbed at the keys of the calculator, cursing when his fingers found the wrong button. His hands shook as he noted the amounts. He sucked at maths, and in the next fifteen minutes he figured out he needed help. 'This is not adding up.'

Halston sighed. 'We need time to study this.'

Did they have the time? Callan didn't want to wait.

Erwin had a business, something to do with body parts and heaps of cash. This was not good news. He needed someone to crunch the numbers for him on priority. Ah…

'Could you send me the scans for this?'

'Sure. We'll get back to you with more.'

'Thank ye.' Callan picked up his phone and speed-dialled his girlfriend. He had a task for her.

It took her five minutes to barge into the police station, pens and yellow notepad peeking out of her satchel, and a gleam in her eyes.

Callan glared at her while she shook hands with Halston. 'You seem prepared, for someone who only just got a call to get to the police station.'

She shrugged. 'Isla and I had plans.'

He flashed another glare when she didn't elaborate.

One wide smile and Callan let it go. Sap. He guided her towards his office and shut the door behind them.

'Jeez! What have you done to this place? It's wrecked!'

He glanced at the papers everywhere. She was right – it looked like a paper mill had exploded in here. 'I cleaned it.'

Aileen pointed to a bag in the corner. 'No, you didn't. I gave you those folders to file.'

'I'm not a secretary.'

'You're impossible.' She plopped into a chair. 'What do you want me to do?'

'Grunt work.' He explained it all to her. Aileen was smart, and it took her two minutes to catch on. 'You think he sold body parts? I hate him, but would he do something this horrible?'

'Something bought his fancy cars. Just work on the numbers and tell me what the business model is.'

'I can do that.' She tapped his desk, her stance confident. 'It's my field of expertise, after all.'

He waited for his emails to load and forwarded the scans to her. 'Are you sure you don't want dinner first?'

'Later, perhaps. Thanks for saving me from a family dinner.'

Callan eyed her, and dropped his voice. 'You can't avoid them forever.'

'That's what Isla said. But I can stay away. And perhaps they'll get bored and leave.'

Callan sat back, watching Aileen retreat to the closet-like room opposite his office. Somehow he doubted Eean Mackinnon ever gave up on things.

For now, all Callan had to do was work this case. He faced the murder board and scratched his chin. He had a lot of information, all too fragmented to join the pieces together into anything coherent.

They couldn't trace the filing cabinet. The neighbours had seen no one and nothing suspicious, the report noted.

He worked through the information until his stomach let out a loud protest. Callan had missed lunch. It was time to fill himself up with something more than coffee.

He'd get to this tomorrow.

He shrugged into his jacket and wondered if Aileen'd had any luck with the data.

AILEEN STRAIGHTENED, GRIMACING WHEN HER muscles begged for mercy. The library's chair earlier that day and now this one mingled with the stress would turn her hair grey.

A moan slipped from her lips, and she clasped her right shoulder.

She stared at the scans. What was it with Loch Fuar's men and paper?

George Erwin had maintained a ledger. His records worked for someone who knew what they were searching for.

She'd struggled to look past the gruesome names, some so deeply entrenched in biology textbooks she couldn't pronounce them. As of now, she had shortlisted twenty body parts and created ledgers for each of them. How many pay-outs from each? On what date?

Her mind had latched onto a pattern, but she still had to cross-check. It would take a while.

Aileen grabbed her phone and informed Nancy of her delay. A trickle of guilt slid into her heart. Her gran had come here to rest. And Aileen had shirked her responsibilities as innkeeper to avoid facing her parents.

Aileen twirled the pen in her hand, eyes back onto her laptop. It was time to find patterns in the numbers.

She checked Erwin's entries for January. Then February. She deciphered monthly pay-outs, and some quarterly. Was he selling something, or was this a guise for another operation? She could tell very little without the key to decode this.

She let the numbers tell her the story, cut the fluff out and traced the trail.

Aileen then tried to make sense of the fractions. More number crunching led her to believe this was not a stock ledger but a cash one. Each fraction represented the amount of payment each, er, body part had made. So 5/5 meant their debt was paid.

Did Erwin run an illegal loanshark business?

Tongue paid out quarterly instalments − Erwin hadn't mentioned what for. *Heart* paid monthly, and the *Large Intestine* handed Erwin the cash once every two months.

All payments went like clockwork, better than the loan payments at the bank.

She applied the pattern to a bunch of more body parts.

Who was *Tongue*, *Heart*, etc? They needed the key to decipher that.

'Hungry?'

Aileen dropped her pencil. 'Gosh, Callan! You scared me.'

She rubbed her forehead where tension strummed like a loud electric guitar. She had to get up, move, and eat. 'I think I cracked it!'

'Already?' Callan swished his hands. 'Sorry, of course you did. What did you find?'

'This is a cash ledger, not a stock ledger. You need the key to figure out who *Tongue*, *Heart* and the rest of them are. Mostly people Erwin lent money to, or… or this is a blackmailing operation.'

'If that's the case, the filing cabinet must be the key. No wonder someone stole it.'

'But they didn't take the logs?'

'Not if they wanted to prevent sensitive information from reaching the police. This is useless without the key, isn't it?'

'One without the other won't make sense unless the person who stole it is one of these body parts.'

'Let me add this to my board. Are you hungry?'

Aileen followed him to his office and grimaced again at the mess. If Erwin's office was anything like Callan's, she pitied the officers processing the scene.

'You know his cash ledger is very meticulous for the picture you painted of the man— a messy study and all.'

'Priorities, I think.'

She stretched out the tight muscles of her neck and plopped into the visitor's chair. 'Did you make any headway?'

'We need the filing cabinet to narrow down the suspect list. How many body parts were listed in the ledgers?'

'Close to twenty.'

'In Loch Fuar, that's a substantial number.'

'It is.' Aileen narrowed her eyes. '*If* that is Loch Fuar. He could have fished elsewhere.'

'Not if it's blackmail done the old-school way – threaten to expose them in the community. As a doctor, he had sway. Looking elsewhere would mean legwork for him.'

Aileen sat back. 'What is that list you've pinned there?'

'I had Robert go through the list of people who hold firearm certificates, particularly antique firearms. Dr Brown says the bullets were .44 calibre from an older revolver.'

'You know, there are people who know how to drive but don't have a license?'

'I know, damn it! This is a lead, isn't it?'

'It's an awfully large pool.'

'Once we find the files in the cabinet and get names, I'm sure it would narrow down. Until then, we have Jack McCloughan and Julian Wagner fighting for the top spot on my suspect list.'

'The councillor? What did he say?'

'I'm paying him a surprise visit tomorrow. That way, he has less time to prep. These politicians…'

Aileen walked up to the board, squinted at it, then faced Callan. 'So now that you have Erwin's body, you can work around that area?'

'Aye.'

'Strange, isn't it, that you have to stop the excavation and then a man dies on the peatlands?'

Guilt and anger flashed in Callan's eyes. 'Someone's halted the search for Blaine Macgregor purposefully. What gives politicians the right to play with the fate of murdered eighteen-year-olds?' He stabbed at something he'd scrawled on the board. 'That's one of the things I want to question Wagner about. This order could benefit Gerald. And Eloise Wagner and Melanie Erwin are friends. I wonder if there's a connection between the order and his death.'

Aileen crossed her arms, scepticism swirling in

her blood. She didn't like politicians either. Or sleazy lawyers. 'What makes you think Wagner won't lie to you?'

Callan's grinned like a lion preparing to attack. 'Oh, in that case, I'd know the man has something to hide, and then I'd find out what.'

She squeezed his arm. 'Best of luck. But every lion needs food. Care to take me out for an impromptu date?'

'You just want to delay going home.' He intertwined their fingers. 'Come on.'

ANN MACKINNON SLAPPED THE FILE CLOSED AND scowled. 'You've gone too far this time! This is a serious breach of privacy, and you know it!'

'I have my reasons.' Eean said.

'You are being a controlling arse. And you know where that takes you.'

Ann didn't understand. Men were sleazy arseholes. Him being one, for example – shattering other's dreams, stomping on husks of promises and killing hope.

'Police officers cannot be trusted. They think they're the law.'

'This man worked the Lewis case. And covered all his bases. You can't seriously think—'

Eean stabbed a finger on the desk. 'So what is

he doing in a dump like Loch Fuar? Why did he transfer here out of Edinburgh?'

'People have their reasons.'

'They have *agendas*.'

Ann snorted and wiped her eyes. 'You're cynical. And we're making a mistake. It's time to step back.'

'No, it's time to push forward.'

'That'll only drown us in hate! And she'll loath us. Honey, you're just repeating patterns.'

'I'm doing what I must. Everyone might hate me, but in the long run, the pain will have made things better, stronger. You know that.'

'Not in this case.'

Eean picked up the thick file, spelling out the life of Detective Inspector Callan Cameron.

An amputee, a hardworking police officer without a single blemish on his record. Except for reprimands for speaking out of turn towards his superior officers. The man didn't pull his punches when it came to justice. Not a stickler for rules, either. He knew how to walk the tight line and get the job done.

He didn't like the man from their brief encounter. He was just too… just too…

'Why are you having second thoughts about this?' Eean asked his wife.

'Because when we came here, *he* wasn't in the equation. Now he is, and he's a force to reckon with.'

'You like him?' he spat. How dare she?

Ann lifted her chin. 'Very much. And you're making a mistake.'

He sighed. Never mind. 'I have work to get done.'

'It's midnight.'

'Ambition demands hard work to turn dreams into reality. You know that.' He stalked to his laptop and dropped into the chair. Work always fulfilled.

She sighed. 'Think things through again, will you? Good night.'

'Night.'

CHAPTER ELEVEN

The sun twinkled on the water droplets clinging to the leaves.

The Erwins and Wagners lived within five minutes of each other, in similar estates. Wagners' house was three storeys, with a loft on the fourth floor. Politics paid well.

Callan cursed at the empty driveway, as winding as the Erwin's, with the road splitting off in two: one towards the porte-cochere near the main entrance of the house and the other towards a garage.

The doorbell sounded through the house, echoing through the open doors on the first floor. A light breeze tickled the drops of water from the arbour, creating the illusion of a drizzle.

'Yes?'

Callan frowned at the woman wearing an apron and a hat. Was this a regency drama?

He flashed his badge. 'I'm here to see Julian Wagner.'

'He's out, I'm afraid.'

'And Mrs Wagner?'

Heels stalked towards them. 'Martha, who is it?'

Martha opened the door further.

Mrs Eloise Wagner startled. 'Oh, Detective! We-we weren't expecting you.' She adjusted the bracelets on her wrist and flashed a smile. 'I was just heading out.'

'I have a few questions regarding George Erwin's case. It'll only take a few minutes.'

Eloise pursed her lips and rubbed her palms on her thigh, allowing him to study her.

The dark purple dress, transparent heels, and diamond jewellery gave off a chic look. But where was her car? Or her purse?

And she hadn't looked him in the eye when she'd said she'd be going out. Did she want him gone?

'Please, come in.' She said instead, and opened a door onto a living room, as big as his entire flat. A fireplace glimmered on their right, a stark contrast to the whitewashed walls.

Jewel toned pillows were scattered on the eclectic sofa. Was Eloise a creative, or was this the magic of an interior decorator? He settled on the latter.

'Would you like some coffee?'

Callan shook his head and produced his

notepad. 'Why don't we get on with the questions so you can head out?'

Her smile and laughter were as fake as her eyelashes. Eloise folded into a chair opposite Callan's and smoothed her dress. 'What would you like to know?'

'Where were you the night of George Erwin's murder?'

'Sleeping in my bed.'

'How well did you know George Erwin?'

'Not very well, though I know his wife. Mel and I are close; have been for a decade, almost. It's a tragedy what she's been going through these few months.' Eloise relaxed her shoulders, but her lips shivered. 'It was quite a shock for me to hear the news. She's broken.'

'I'm sure, Mrs Wagner. What did you make of George Erwin?'

She waved her hands and rested them back on her thighs. 'Nothing much. He retired a few months ago and spent all of his time in the study. Melanie was always upset about it – he hardly spent any time with her, especially after Gerald…'

'He wasn't a loving husband?'

'I wouldn't say that, Detective. He bought her a lot of things or told her to buy them – designer clothes and her car. George Erwin adored his wife, but… I can't say the same about Mel.'

'What do you mean?'

'Perhaps it was the stress of the trial, or maybe

before that, too. She never once did things for George – she hired a cook, never asked him what he'd like to eat, she… she… Oh, you know how it is! She didn't go out of her way for him.' Eloise licked her lips and leaned in, ready to tattle on her best friend. 'When I was over at their house, I often thought to myself how cold she was towards him. Hardly ever smiled at him.'

'Maybe they'd had a fight?'

'I'm sure that's what it was. But Melanie isn't a very warm person; she tells it like it is.' A door shut outside, and Eloise jumped up from her seat. 'Oh, that must be Julian. He said he'd be here soon.'

The man entered, dressed in a suit and a red tie. His polished shoes gleamed despite the puddles outside. Like his wife, his smile was fake.

'Detective!'

Callan shook his hand with a firm grip. 'Mr Wagner.'

'You're here about Erwin?'

Eloise patted his arm. 'Why don't you gentlemen have a chat and I'll get Martha to bring us some tea, coffee?'

'Sure.'

The man's salt and pepper hair sat neatly combed on his head, as if ironed and starched with the same material that held his suit together. He walked over to an armchair, adjusting his suit buttons. 'Please, take a seat.'

The man's face didn't so much as twitch. He

had a poker face, a must for his occupation, but one look at his wife and she understood him.

She said, 'I'll get the coffee. Excuse me.'

Wagner dropped into the armchair and rubbed his forehead. 'It's a tragedy about George. A good man, a brilliant doctor…'

A good man? Politicians had strange standards.

'So? How did he die?'

'I can't divulge the aspects of an ongoing investigation. But shots were fired on the McCloughan's land in the middle of the night. When we answered the call and carried out an inspection, we found his body.'

'Tragedy… tragedy. And I warned him about this.'

Callan raised an eyebrow. He hadn't expected this. 'Could you tell me what you warned him about?'

'Ah, there's Martha!'

Martha bustled into the room, a white apron fixed on her black dress and a tray in her hand.

Wagner adjusted his shirt again. 'That'll be all, Martha.'

'Would you care for some coffee?'

Callan shook his head, imploring the man to get on with things. He hadn't dragged his feet when signing off on the order.

Wagner leaned forward, used tongs to plop a sugar cube in his coffee, not noticing the drops that splashed on the table. 'George had a successful career as a general practitioner, but he wanted more.'

The china clinked as the liquid formed a tornado in the cup.

And still he didn't elaborate. The hallmarks of a true politician. Why couldn't the man just talk?

'What more did he want from his career?'

Wagner sighed. 'He wanted to run for the councillor's office. And compete with me.' He spread his fingers. 'I know that incriminates me in a way, but I'd never hurt a friend. We weren't bitter towards one another.'

Erwin wanting to be the councillor was news. Not because Callan didn't bother keeping himself up to date, but because he doubted anyone knew of Erwin's plans. Anyone except Isla and Siobhan. Those two would've known, somehow.

He'd crosscheck with them. Now, he watched Wagner bend at the waist, use both hands to lift his cup and saucer and sip.

'When did he express his wish to stand for election?'

'Last week, I think. Days seem to roll into each other. And now he's gone. We'd only just come to grips with his son's conviction and now this. Have you considered, Detective, this could be a crime of rage? A hate crime?'

Callan shrugged. 'You should know, as always, we have all lines of enquiry still active.'

'Of course. The case is still young, I suppose.'

His cup clanked on the saucer. 'Sorry, talking about Erwin… What a loss.'

'Were you in touch with him?'

'As neighbours, aye. The occasional "hi, how are you?" in passing. We didn't specifically call each other as you might your close friend or family member.'

Not according to Erwin's call log. A smooth liar, wasn't he? Callan was sure he suited George Erwin just fine.

'Yet he told you about running for the councillor position?'

'I'm the current councillor, after all.' Wagner laughed, rubbing his palms on his thigh. 'He just informed me, that's all.'

'What did you warn him about? Not running for councillor?'

Wagner shifted in his seat, crossed his legs, and stared at the wall next to them. 'Hmm, he called me.'

'Regarding what?'

'The work, the official responsibilities.'

Callan frowned. 'That's all?'

If not a politician, this man would've succeeded as the broody hero in a film. 'No, Detective. And I hope you forgive me for keeping this from you. It was his idea.' He met Callan's eyes with a faux soulful look.

'What was his idea?'

'The environmental rally.'

Callan's muscles stiffened. Erwin had a connection to the order. For all his talk about not supporting murderers, he'd been in the thick of it. Did the man have no sympathy for Blaine?

'Could you elaborate on that?'

'George Erwin called me one day, out of the blue, and he told me Melanie had run into my ex-wife. My ex-wife and I co-parent our children. Erwin and I spoke about our children, and he told me the boy his son murdered had to be somewhere in the peatlands—'

Hope flickered in Callan's heart. 'He didn't remember where?'

'Sorry, Detective. He didn't specify. But he told me how, as a former member of Loch Fuar's EPC – the Environmental Protection Committee – it saddened him that his son's actions were uprooting our environment. Peatlands are essential for our environment. And so we devised a rally—'

'George Erwin wasn't a part of these rallies.'

Wagner sat back, spread his hands. 'How could he be? If he'd been anywhere near them it would have looked like he was trying to keep the police from finding evidence against his son, that he stood behind the heinous act his son had committed.'

'So he asked you to do it?'

Wagner's lips twitched. 'Aye. As a current member of EPC, I rallied our members to protest. And our petition was passed.'

Erwin and Wagner had rallied for the police to

halt their excavation, and Wagner's office had signed off their petition and convinced the police chiefs.

Two-faced bastards.

'Is that the last time you spoke to him?'

Wagner nodded. 'I believe so. If that's all, Detective, I have to head out with my wife. And then I have business to get to. Death or not, my duties call me.'

Callan stood. 'Thank you for your time.' He'd sure learned a lot.

AILEEN EMPTIED HER TROLLEY ONTO THE CHECK-out counter: beans, condiments, far too many egg cartons, and loads of veggies.

'Morning, Ms Aileen.'

'Hey, Sonja! How are you?'

Sonja partly owned the supermarket. She always had a smile for her customers.

Aileen popped the items in her carrier bag and realised she didn't have enough muscle to carry them to her car. 'Could I—'

'Just leave the trolley by the door, Ms Aileen. I'll get it later.'

'Thank you so much!' She lugged the trolley, stocked with five bags, to the shop's front door. Her car was right outside.

Aileen gritted her teeth and used all her might

to get the first two bags to her sedan. Mud spots still splashed over it – another task on her to do list. Clean the car.

She placed the bags on the ground, fiddled with her car's lock, and hefted the bags inside while ensuring the mud didn't brush her clothes. She shut the door and went back for the other two. Her fingers hurt. When she fetched the last bag, her arms felt like noodles. She was lifting it with both her hands, trying her best not to drop it when—

'Ah!'

'Crap! Watch where you're going!'

Aileen startled at the voice, mouth gaping. 'Ricky?'

A brown stain was spreading over his overcoat. He held up the cardboard file, saving it from the coffee splatter.

'I'm so sorry!'

His lips turned down, eyes dark. 'Doesn't look like it! Don't you look where you're going?'

She dropped the bag, dug into her satchel for tissues. 'I am sorry. This bag was really heavy and—'

'Excuses!'

'Are you hurt? Was the coffee hot? I—'

'It's summer! Who drinks warm coffee?'

Why was he wearing a jacket, then? Aileen huffed. Ricky was in a sour mood. She didn't dare goad a pissed man.

Ricky stalked over to the dustbin to their right

and dropped the to-go cup in it. 'Stupid woman! Think she can just dump coffee on me, like… like…' He plucked the tissues Aileen held up.

'It was a mistake. There's no need to be rude.'

'Rude?' Ricky dabbed himself. Then he took his thick winter jacket off and plopped onto a bench. 'Pluto said I needed to wear my jacket. Helped, didn't it?' He patted his chest. 'All dry.'

'Yes, lucky.'

'It's nothing to do with luck! All I wanted was a few peaceful moments and now you've gone and spoiled my coffee treat!'

Aileen set her bag on the bench and sat next to it. 'Could I get you a new coffee? And a treat? From Isla's Bakery? Whatever you want.'

'Why?'

'As an apology.'

He studied her from top to bottom, then shrugged. 'Okay.'

Aileen smiled. 'Let me just get this into the car. Alright?'

Ricky stalked towards the bakery without another word, leaving Aileen to stumble over to her car and dump the bag inside. She groaned, happy she'd accomplished one job. Now all she had to do was get the bags inside Dachaigh.

Isla's Bakery bustled with customers, especially with people craving something sweet with their lunch.

Aileen found Ricky huddled in the far corner of the café, head bowed over a file. 'Ricky?'

He didn't look up.

'Ricky?'

He startled, banging his knee on the table. 'What is your problem?'

'I called you… Never mind. What would you like?'

'Chocolate truffle pastry and a cold brew.'

She tried a smile, but, autistic or not, this man was just rude.

Aileen stood in the queue as any other respectable customer might and Andrew greeted her by the counter. 'Hey Aileen! What can I get you?'

She rattled out the order and ordered an Americano for herself.

'Anything else?'

'No thanks, Andrew.'

He handed her a tray over with their coffees and pastry. Her hands still trembled from the weight of the bags, but she carried the food to their table and smacked it next to the file.

Ricky startled again, flapped the file closed and frowned. 'What is it with you?'

She plopped onto the opposite seat and handed him his order. 'What are you studying?'

Ricky took a sip of his coffee, nodded, and then bit into the pastry. 'Why are you here?'

'Thought I'd join you?'

'You thought wrong.'

'Come on, Ricky.'

'Jack hates you.'

Aileen swallowed the warm liquid. 'That he does.'

'Why?'

'I don't know.'

Ricky ate another bite, downed some coffee, and then sat back. 'You must have done something rude! Like spilled whisky on him. You're capable.'

'I—'

He stuffed the rest of the pastry in his mouth. 'Horrid woman!' He said through the food. 'You come home, and a man dies! A bad omen, you are.' Ricky picked up the cup and shook his fist. 'Stay away from my family. Stay away from Pluto. He's a nice man, and all you do is taint his reputation. Bad woman, very bad.'

He banged the cup on the table.

Aileen gaped, wondering what she'd done to deserve Ricky's ire. 'I've done nothing of the sort. You set me up in the loft with no electricity! Where were you the night Erwin died?'

'I was asleep.'

'Through all the commotion?'

'Are you pointing the blame at me, at Pluto? You're horrible!' Ricky pushed the chair back with such force it slammed into the wall. He turned and marched out the door, leaving behind a stunned Aileen.

'Hey, you okay?'

Aileen nodded at Andrew. 'What a strange man.'

'I've never seen him in here before. Who is he?'

She gave Andrew a gist, said her thanks and got up. She had a few guests checking into the inn today, so she'd better get back. Aileen wiggled her arms, adding more strength training sessions to her task list. Her gaze fell to the floor and to a cardboard file. Ricky had dropped it in his anger.

She groaned, knowing if she followed him to hand it back, he'd just bite her head off. The boy had too much rage pounding in his veins.

Aileen picked it up and papers scattered. Just her luck. She shoved them into the ochre cover and stood, flipping her hair over her shoulder.

The file had no label on it, but it smelt musty, like something recovered from deep storage. *Don't peek, don't peek, don't—*

Her curiosity won, and she pulled open the thick card covering. Aileen settled back down on the table, made space for the file, and hunched over it.

An image of a man with a thick scruff and a narrow face – much like Ricky's – stared back, unsmiling. The headline over his picture said:

Aaron Ridge missing.
Reward of £5,000 for information about his whereabouts.

The next page had a form with Aaron's name on it – a medical report of sorts, dated back to

2004. It listed his birth date, blood group, allergies, and personal information.

Aileen flipped over and found a writeup in an illegible hand. She cursed, before pulling her phone out and using the magnifier app.

Aaron Ridge, she made out… then found the word *alcoholic* and…

Aaron Ridge is an alcoholic and chain smoker. He fell down the stairs, and has a fractured limb that isn't expected to heal fully. But he will walk again.

He has refused hospital care, often behaving violently towards the staff. Pluto and Linda McCloughan have decided to take him to their house and nurse him.

A line cut across the report, and below it was a section dated 2005. There it read:

Mr Aaron Ridge passed away from a heart attack. Mrs McCloughan has found missing a dose of morphine. Did she kill him? After all, he had been bed ridden for over a year and the responsibility of taking care of him and his son rested solely on Linda. Did she snap? Pluto thinks so.

Aileen gasped. No matter, Ricky was upset to read this. Where had he found this file? How did he know it was legitimate?

And… she checked the date on the missing persons poster and then the year of the entry… the same year.

What was this about? What was Pluto hiding?

She went over to the last page of the report. The writer of the report continued:

However, Linda couldn't have injected the morphine into

him. Chances are, the man swallowed the tablets himself. Why would the glass of water have shattered on the floor beside his bed otherwise?

Why had they filed a missing person report if the man had died in his bed?

Aileen bit her lip, wondering what to do. She stood up and walked towards her car, eyes still on the file.

'You stole it?'

She jumped, clutching the file to her chest. 'Ricky! What are you doing here? I was just about to—'

'Nosy bitch! Stay away from us!' He snatched the file from her, glared, then stalked away.

She blinked at his back. Was he standing here all this time?

An interesting turn of events, this was.

Could Linda have murdered Aaron Ridge?

CHAPTER TWELVE

'Someone's here to see you.'

Callan blinked up at Police Constable Robert Davis. 'Who?'

'Er… I'm not sure if this is case-related or personal.'

Suspicion niggled at his mind. 'Who, Robert?'

'Ann Mackinnon.'

Callan gripped the edge of his desk. What did she want? To ask him to stay away from her daughter?

Robert bit his lip. Was the eejit hiding a smirk? 'Ann… That's Aileen's mother, isn't it?'

'Aye.'

'Best of luck. I know what it's like when the parents want to talk to you alone.'

Callan's heart skipped a beat. 'Eean Mackinnon's here?'

Robert shook his head. 'Just her mother.'

Sometimes fate worked on his side. Callan had been thinking about having a go at Eean Mackinnon again. There was a thin line between being harsh to your girlfriend's parents and being a detective interrogating a person of interest.

Callan stood up and caught himself smoothing out the wrinkles in his shirt. Wimp. He cleared his throat, gulped and, well…

Get a move on.

Callan tugged his shirt sleeves and walked towards the waiting room.

Her bob of ironed hair had frizzed, giving her face a more approachable look. She sat twiddling her fingers, and Callan was struck by the contrast of the trousersuit-clad woman he'd met previously with this jean-wearing one.

Ann popped up the moment she saw him and gave him a close-lipped smile.

What did that mean? Was she here to tell him off?

'Detective!'

'Mrs Mackinnon.'

Her eyes flitted around the space and landed on the coffee machine.

Callan pointed to the machine and said, 'Coffee?'

Ann's bark of laughter caught him unawares and by the pinking of her cheeks, her too. She covered her lips. Her skin looked paler today. Her eyes, too. No makeup.

What was going on?

'Sorry, Detective, I'm not used to this. I've never been in such a situation.'

Callan lifted one eyebrow before heading over to fix coffee.

'I… I hope I'm not disturbing you?'

'No, ma'am. I was just about to head to Dachaigh myself.'

Her footsteps treaded over to him and she waited for the cup of coffee. 'Smells divine.'

'We prefer good coffee. My boss, Rory Macdonald, says we need real coffee if we're to solve cases accurately and efficiently.'

'You've one of the best track records in the country.'

Callan froze, his hand in mid-air, still holding the coffee. How did she know their closing rate was one of the best in the country? Maybe it was a wild guess. 'Aye, it does.'

'Could we sit?'

Better than making small talk. He shivered. Callan never made small talk; he believed in dashing straight towards the point. But talking to your girlfriend's mother made you rethink your opinions…

Ann sat in the waiting room which was adjacent to the main entrance and front desk. As usual, Loch

Fuar's police station was a haunted house in the dead of winter, albeit warm.

The seat creaked under him.

'I'm sorry for encroaching on your time like this, but you see, I'm not in agreement with my husband. And I had to speak with you.'

'About George Erwin?'

She waved her hands. 'Erwin, Aileen, you name it.' She huffed. 'If you know Aileen at all, you'll know the Mackinnons are a stubborn bunch. And no matter what you say, they just won't listen once they've set their mind to anything.'

A smile tugged at his lips. 'I always thought she gets it from Siobhan.'

'So does my husband, Detective. There is no changing that; it's in their DNA. I…' She shook her head. 'I've always wondered how Aileen kept that part of herself hidden.'

Ann turned away from him, eyes glazed over with memories. 'I waited for adolescence to hit, then the teenage phase where she'd rebel. It never came. We forced her, and she flowed with it. Always. Eean, of course, didn't realise it. He's grown too accustomed to having his own way. We enrolled her into French classes, piano lessons, etiquette lessons and yet… She never was herself apart from the time when we brought her here. Only once. And now…'

Callan waited for her to elaborate.

She swished over to face him again. 'I'm rambling. Perhaps I should go. I'm not even sure why I came here. I'm sorry—'

'No, Mrs Mackinnon.' Callan wasn't sure what to make of this situation. But he felt it in his gut — she was here for something. And if her husband won't talk, chances are she would. 'Please, I'd like to know more about Aileen.'

Ann pulled her handbag close, clutching it until her knuckles turned white. Ready to bolt…

Then she set the handbag aside and cleared her throat. 'You must have questions about Eean.'

'Aye, I do.'

'Why don't we talk about those? You see, I'm better at discussing facts than emotions.'

Callan understood that. A year ago, his skin would've been twitching like a Richter scale at a hint of small talk or emotions.

He rested his elbows on his thighs. 'Had you heard about George Erwin before you came here?'

'No. I know little about Loch Fuar. Just what Eean's told me.'

'Has he ever mentioned George Erwin to you?'

'Not that I can remember. We discussed Gerald Erwin when he… when he hurt Aileen, but we didn't hear details about what he'd done to her until much later. We weren't in the country.' Ann shut her eyes, trying and failing at hiding her guilt. 'I've never hated myself more for prioritising my career. My daughter was dying, and I didn't even know! After that, Eean and I decided we won't take off-the-grid clients.' She stopped, a blush tainting her cheeks again. 'Sorry, I'm rambling.'

Her muscles hunched up, corded tight. Ann Mackinnon still wasn't comfortable.

Callan braced, wondering when the shoe would drop. When she'd straighten her back and tell him to stay away from Aileen.

He swung the conversation back to the case. 'Have you ever met George Erwin?'

'No, Detective. He wasn't on my radar even after what his son did to Aileen. Not until we came to Loch Fuar and you told us he was dead. My husband has nothing to do with him, either.'

'You say that with conviction.'

'My husband and I are a team, and we don't keep secrets. I spoke to him after you left the other day. He wasn't in touch with George Erwin. And I believe him.'

'So who did he speak to on the phone the entire week?'

'How can you say it was him? What if someone spoofed his number?'

'I'd say as his wife, you know better.'

Ann swatted a strand off her face. 'Yes, he was on the phone with someone. Every night last week, the phone rang like clockwork. And Eean's mood would sour. Contrary to what you've seen, Eean's not that ill-tempered with me. And that call would put him in a mood. He'd end up working late into the night and avoid me.'

'Who was it on the other end of the call?'

'He wouldn't say. It still drives me crazy. So much for not keeping secrets.'

'He didn't give you any hint?'

'He's stubborn. Told me at first it was nothing of consequence, just a pesky client. Now, since we've been here, and you asked him about the calls, he says its best I keep out of it, for my safety. I told him I can take care of myself, thank you very much. But that man!'

I told him I can take care of myself, thank you very much.

Callan had heard that phrase so many times, said in such a similar tone… He grinned. 'Sorry… Why does your husband not like the Mc-Cloughans?'

'It's the first time I've heard about them.' Ann stood and walked over to the only window in the room. The day was bright outside, and a slight breeze had the branches dancing. 'My husband…' She pivoted to face him. 'I feel like I'm ratting him out, but if he's being bad-tempered… My husband and I share everything, but there's a time of his life he hasn't told me anything about. Thirty years of marriage, Detective, and a healthy marriage too. And I doubt even Siobhan knows anything about it and she—'

'Knows everything.'

'Yes, she does. But she had her hands full with an inn to run and Earl, Eean's younger brother.

Eean, he grew up too soon. Their father passed away when Eean was only five, and he took over, watching out for Siobhan. If Siobhan knew, she'd have his head. But that's Eean. He cares too much.'

Callan wouldn't call the man 'caring' from first impressions, or from what Aileen said. But if there was anything he knew from a decade of being a police officer, it was that people were complicated creatures.

'He hasn't told me why he left Loch Fuar in a hurry or why he never thought of coming back here. Yes, he has ambition, in spades. And I've supported him through it.' Ann sat down again, spread her arms. 'When we met, I begged him to holiday up here. We didn't. He invited Siobhan and Earl over. Then we came once after we'd wed, only for a day. When Siobhan insisted Aileen spend a summer with her, he gave in, but we didn't stay with her.'

'He avoids this place.'

'Yes, at all costs. So when he suggested we travel to Loch Fuar... I've had my doubts. Even if he said it was to convince Aileen.' She huffed, spoke before Callan could respond. 'He's trying to kill two birds with one stone. I just don't know what he wants to achieve besides dragging Aileen back. That's all I can tell you about my husband.'

'That's a lot.'

'I don't support him in this venture, at least not anymore. I wanted to tell you that.'

That wasn't what Callan had expected at all, no matter Ann's appearance. 'His venture?'

'We planned to convince Aileen to return with us. You weren't in the equation then. We didn't know… And Aileen… She refused. I say that in awe, Detective. She's never stood up to us, and I like this new Aileen. Now when I poke her, she hisses back. It might sound silly, but I'm so happy to see the fierce Mackinnon in her finally shine through.' Ann shrugged. 'And you sealed the deal for me.'

'Me?'

'I didn't know she had a beau. And she loves you. She leans on you and you care about her. Liam… They weren't right for each other. And I was glad when she broke it off, no matter what I said to her about him. Now, she has you and, er, the baker… Isla? She has a support system here and I won't let my husband drag her away from this. He will try, I know he will. I want you to be prepared. He's hard to please. I can say, however, he doesn't have much to hold against you.' Ann cracked a smile. 'But he's a Mackinnon. He'll come around, but it will take time.'

Callan's mouth opened in surprise. He wondered if he was dreaming. Why was Ann Mackinnon so forthcoming? Was this some sabotage plan? And Eean Mackinnon…

Ann stood, picked up her purse and held out her hand. 'I've taken too much of your time, Detective. Thank you.'

He watched her walk out, still reeling from all that she'd said. Had she just given him her blessing?

AILEEN DUCKED INTO DACHAIGH, WELCOMED NEW guests, stuffed the groceries in the larder and rushed out before her parents caught a whiff of her presence.

Now her sedan groaned and jostled as it trundled down the road, no match to the rocks jutting out from the mud.

Something hit the car hard and pushed Aileen out of her seat. Thank goodness for seat belts. 'Oh!'

She steadied herself before hitting the accelerator hard enough for the car to fly out of the ditch with another jump. 'Hell!'

She had spent a fortune on this thing, and now she risked breaking down in the middle of the road.

Aileen signalled to turn into the distillery and let out another curse.

Cars were littered across the car park, including vans and buses. Summer was the tourist season. God help her weed through this mess. She slowed down when she reached the row of cars and craned her neck to find herself a spot. Nothing.

Aileen checked the next row and smirked. One spot.

She bit her lip, swinging her car to the left,

inching it to the right, and slotted it into the space between a bus and another tourist vehicle.

Her parking space was so narrow, the car door didn't fully open, so she squeezed out, sucking in her stomach and gritting her teeth as her arse swiped the mud off her car.

Now she had to get her satchel out. Just her luck.

This time, her back swiped some mud, but her left hand caught the satchel's handle and tugged it out.

Aileen patted the dirt out from her jeans. When a child saw her pat her arse, he mocked her, wiping his own. She grinned at the cheek and walked over to Pluto's.

The brigade of tourists marching towards the distillery drowned out her knock.

Perhaps taking a distillery tour would assist her in her audit. But so far, she'd done nothing productive apart from arranging the receipts in chronological order.

Aileen banged the barrel door knocker, smacking it against the wood with force. Another few seconds passed until—

Wham.

The door opened so fast it hit the back wall and rattled.

Aileen jumped back. 'What the hell, Ricky?'

He grinned at her and gestured her in, then he turned his back and walked down the corridor, ignoring her. What happened to all the anger from before?

She made to follow him when a burr said, 'Leave him be, lassie. He's off to lock himself in that room for the rest of the day. Lord knows what he does in there.'

Aileen shrugged. 'I was wondering if I could continue my audit?'

Pluto grinned and gestured toward the staircase. 'You're one tenacious lass. One mention of murder and it'll have most people running for them hills.'

She took the steps ahead of Pluto but angled herself so she could speak with him. 'Your wife had excellent taste in décor. She seemed tenacious, too.'

He didn't reply for a long time. Aileen slowed down to match his ascent. Without his walking stick Pluto gripped the railing like his life depended on it. His cheeks pinked with the effort of the climb.

They halted on the mezzanine, Pluto's breaths echoing in the dark.

'Not as fit as I used to be. But aye, my Linda, she'd hop up these steps like a ballerina if she were here.' His eyes glassed at the memory. 'My beautiful Linda, her taste in décor, food, zest for life – everything she touched turned beautiful.' He wheezed out a laugh. 'Look at me. I went from a hooligan to a semi-respectable man!'

He ushered her on. The smile on his face remained, but his mind was light years away.

Aileen needed answers about Aaron and Linda. 'Was she a decorator?'

'In our days, we didn't have the luxury of following our passions, especially where she came from. She trained to be a nurse like her mother. Her patients needed that gorgeous smile. She wore one even if the grind and stress took more from her than it gave. Like you, she was determined.'

He placed a hand on the wall when they reached the first floor, eyeing Aileen. 'Aye, you remind me of her. Beautiful and tenacious, although Linda wasn't a wee thing like you. Tall. Aye, tall enough that those eyes could see into mine, as if mine were transparent. Could never pull one over on her, ever.' Pluto shook his head. 'I'll let you be, lass. I need to rest.'

He left her standing alone on the landing, disappearing into the room on the left. If she knew right, that was his bedroom.

Pluto loved his wife, after all these years, to see such strong love made her doe-eyed and her heart sing. Once in a lifetime. That's how rare such love was.

She wound her way to the library and to the desk where she'd arranged the receipts and ledgers the other day. This time she'd comb through the data with a fine-toothed comb. And she'd—

'What the—!'

On the desk below the window lay a huge, disordered heap of receipts and ledgers, the clips she'd used to file them were missing. Light glittered in through the panes.

Had a cat walked over all her work? Somehow, she didn't think Pluto owned any pets.

No, he had a lad with enough rage to go through all that trouble.

She huffed. This was going to be a long night and she wouldn't leave until she'd made more progress than this shitload of grunt work.

Her satchel fell onto the carpeted floor. Aileen had to segregate the receipts again, figure out what was wrong with these accounts, and find a connection between Linda, Aaron and Erwin.

She bit her lip, groaned, and fell into the chair. She'd spent too much time in chairs lately and now this.

At least, the McCloughans lived big and believed in semi-comfortable furniture, especially in the library.

Aileen pulled one ledger to herself, scowling at the papers lying everywhere. She'd need a deep tissue massage after this. Callan better study up on massages and long, warm baths.

Why hadn't the McCloughans digitised their records? Which distillery welcomed all these visitors, boasted mechanised security systems to care for their whisky — something Isla had mentioned — and didn't have a digital accounting system?

And if Pluto wasn't the owner, why did he have these records in the first place?

She'd known this audit was a farce, even when she accepted it. Why did Pluto want her to dig dirt on his own son? That question hit home…

And why did her parents want her to leave Loch Fuar behind?

Aileen grabbed one receipt and set it on top of the corresponding ledger. Here her efforts go again.

CHAPTER THIRTEEN

Callan frowned at the mud splattered sedan parked opposite his own car.

After running a background check on the Mystics and More Self Care shop, Callan was sure they had nothing to do with Erwin or his murder. He'd asked Robert to dig into any past cases involving the McCloughans or their land. The IT team had still not found the spoofed phone numbers and was moaning about how tedious the task was. Callan had hung up on them, and since the McCloughans were the most forthcoming amongst the other phone numbers on his list, he'd come here.

But what was Aileen's sedan doing here?

She could never steer clear of trouble, and this time, she was hiding from her parents. Her parents... Callan didn't want to ponder over his conversation with Ann Mackinnon. It was still too strange.

The sun blazed overhead at 6 p.m., and a breeze tugged at Callan's light jacket. He side-stepped a couple of children jumping into puddles and slipped past Pluto's house. He quenched the temptation to head in there and hover over his girl-friend. She'd skewer him, and he had work to do.

A group of tourists walked back up the road towards the car park, carrying bags stamped with the McCloughan name and logo. Families, couples and single travellers all ignorant about the horror that had stained the peatlands behind this distillery just a few days ago.

The exposed brick matched the walls of Pluto's house, but the two structures appeared different. This one held influences from Asia – a pagoda roof used to release the steam that heated the malted barley to make whisky. With no entrance on this side, the building had a huge McCloughan logo in the centre.

He backed up and followed the path around the side of the distillery. Pluto's house stood to his right, and Callan checked the windows: no peeking faces.

Callan nodded at a bunch of tourists who emerged from a glass door up ahead. It had translucent glass with the McCloughan logo on it and a plaque on the frame that read 'Shop'.

He pushed inside.

His eyebrows shot up at the timbered floor and

matching shelves full of glittering bottles. Golden lights shone overhead, placed in such a way that the whisky bottles stood in partial darkness – a forbidden mystery.

The McCloughans didn't just sell whisky. They also sold non-alcoholic single malt fudges and a huge range of branded merchandise. On the shop wall, a poster announced daily distillery tours and whisky tasting.

Something told Callan all this was new, thanks to the younger blood in the business. Didn't Pluto approve?

Footsteps smacked against the floor, drawing Callan's attention to the till.

Jack McCloughan stopped. 'Detective.'

Callan walked up to the counter and leaned on it. 'Mr McCloughan, I hope you're not too busy.'

The man's lips turned down. 'You shut us down, and now that we're finally allowed to open we've had to deal with twice the crowds we're used to. It's summer, in case you forgot, and most tourists can't enjoy the complete Highland experience without visiting a distillery.'

They hadn't shut the distillery for kicks or to sabotage the man. Had he forgotten about the dead doctor in his backyard? 'Do you own a firearms certificate?'

'I showed the certificate to your colleague, as you probably already know. I have a permit to carry my .44.' As did plenty of Highland folk, especially those who lived in such remote areas. If they couldn't contact the police, they had to protect themselves.

Callan pulled out his notepad and recited the McCloughan's phone number. 'Is this yours?'

Jack dragged a brochure towards Callan, scraping it against the wood of the desk. He tapped the address and phone number on the page. 'Aye.'

'Know this one?' Callan recited Erwin's phone number.

'Modern technology allows us to save people's numbers on our phones. I don't make it a habit to learn everyone's numbers.'

He hadn't denied contacting Erwin. Callan made a note of that. 'Who had access to your land-line number here at the distillery?'

'We have a single line and it's connected to five points.'

'Could you show me these points?'

Jack narrowed his eyes, studying Callan. Finally, he shrugged and nodded. 'Whatever you can do to solve this damn case quickly and not trot your badge around here. It raises a few eyebrows and taints our name.'

As if his badge was one of shame.

Callan ducked over to the other side and followed Jack through a door in the back wall. Malt fumes tickled his nostrils.

They climbed a stepladder until they stood on an iron grill-work platform. Callan moved closer to the balustrade, and a loud clang echoed through the room. 'Will this thing hold?'

Jack chuckled, sauntering ahead, not caring for the loud bangs his footsteps made.

Three large copper stills heated the wash below, each one shaped like a bulbous funnel set face down on the floor. Their thin necks curved until they disappeared into the wall on the other side. Callan studied the other barrel-like large containers that fermented the barley.

At the end of the iron platform, Jack pointed Callan towards a door to their right. A plaque stated it was for 'staff only'.

Taking one last look at the distillery, Callan stepped through and blinked.

The office was decked out in vibrant light, with whitewashed walls, white cabinets and grey carpet which didn't match the overall McCloughan look. It had none of the mysterious aura of the shop.

'We like our office space more utilitarian than fancy.' The room was a slender rectangle, running parallel to the distillery's building. Jack hobbled over to a machine in the far corner of the room. 'Coffee?'

'Don't mind a cup, thanks.'

Jack pressed a few buttons and the machine filled two cups. Callan almost groaned at the aroma – pure coffee, as blissful as can be.

They walked over to a desk facing the coffee machine. The desks were a mess of wires, computers and CPUs, along with a landline phone propped against the far wall to the other side.

Chairs lay discarded, facing anywhere but at the desks they stood in front of. It looked like an office on a Friday evening.

'Our staff just called it a day. And we've had a big one. Sarah should be finishing up the last tour of the day at the shop. So, er…' Jack pointed to the desk at the other end of the room. 'That's one of the landlines. That's where our marketing manager sits. The second's on my desk.' He pointed to the desk they were sitting beside.

'The shop has one, of course. That's three. The fourth one is in our house and…' Jack tipped the coffee down his throat in one go. 'The fifth is at the main house.' Jack's facial muscles tightened, and not because of the scalding coffee he'd just gulped. Jack McCloughan didn't like his father having access to the distillery's line. Why should he, if he's retired?

'Father insists on maintaining the line as it is, at his place. Even if it's buzzing all day with calls. He says it doesn't bother him. In fact, he loves being close to all this.' Another squeeze of his facial muscles. 'Old habits.'

The nervous laughter didn't hide the undercurrents between father and son. Business tensions, a clash of opinions and trouble with letting go – those were the issues in the business.

'Who has access to these lines?'

'That's a tough one to answer, Detective. We

have a policy on what the lines can be used for. No personal calls, of course. But employees use this line to contact vendors, business associates or online customers.'

'You have an online shop?'

'Aye, we started it up three years ago. Online business is good, and we have the required permits.'

Callan waved it off. He wasn't here to check permits. 'So who can access the line?'

'Any office employee working in here. Sarah, me, or anyone in the shop has access. The ones working in the distillery's primary operations have a different setup. We don't allow personal phones on the floor for safety reasons.'

'And who has access to the line at your house?'

'Just Sarah and me. And because of all the tourists, I lock the front door.' Jack huffed. 'There's also a line at my father's and he doesn't lock his door.'

'So anyone in his house could use the landline?'

'Aye.'

'Was George Erwin a frequent shopper here?'

Jack's back straightened, erasing any trace of the man's easiness. 'As far as I'm aware, Erwin didn't come down here to purchase anything. I'll need to check our online logs, but I don't think he shopped online either.'

'Did you know him, personally?'

'No.'

'Your father?'

'Can't say.'

'Mrs McCloughan?'

Again his facial muscles contracted. 'Sarah isn't from Loch Fuar. And I'm not sure she's ever met the doctor. He retired before we moved down here.'

'So what was Erwin doing here that night?'

'Hell if I know! If it were up to me, I'd barricade our property with high fences topped with barbed wire if it prevented eejits from using our land to kill someone. Murder is damned inconvenient for business, not to mention harmful for the brand. Tell me, Detective, why would any of my family members risk that?'

Callan shrugged. 'People kill out of rage and aren't very rational when they go about it. And it's my duty to dot every "i" and cross every "t". If you think of anything at all regarding Erwin or who might have misused your landline, give me a call.' He smacked his card on the desk and stood up. 'Thank you for the coffee and the information. I'll contact you if there's anything else.'

COULD SHE SPRAWL OUT ON THE CARPET?

The last time she'd tried it, the bristles stank and pierced her skin. But with her muscles ready to atrophy, Aileen considered just melting onto the floor. Her limbs hurt worse than she'd ever imagined, and she didn't want to think about the throbbing in her neck.

'Ouch!' She pushed up from the chair and stumbled to the other end of the library. Pacing would get the blood flowing back through her body, perhaps bring her dead arse back to life. She felt like a drunk with no control over her whole body, and the pain... Spending all those hours in a chair, then hefting grocery bags and now stuck to a chair again...

Look on the bright side, Aileen. She had the Highland scenery for company. That wasn't the case in her old job as a forensic accountant.

Aileen halted her pacing to peer at the stacks she'd made for each of the five ledgers. Five thick ledgers for five years... There just weren't enough transactions for a distillery of this size. Where had Pluto acquired these receipts? They were genuine, she knew that. Or really good fakes.

Aileen blew a raspberry. Whatever they may be, they did not correspond with the actual transactions for a distillery. They couldn't.

Why, then, had Pluto asked her to look at them? If not to sabotage his son, what for? What did he have to gain?

And why had Ricky messed up her work, so she'd have to start all over again? Was he impulsive or just angry at her? She'd done nothing but read his file, a personal file...

Aye, she'd been a fool to leave stacks of papers

without paperweights on them, but it wasn't the wind which caused this mess.

Aileen stretched her arms up and worked the cricks in her neck. She let out a sigh, imagining a hot bath. *One day, sometime soon.*

Now she had to make some headway, find out what was going on here.

She worked through the 2017/2018 ledger, which contained no mention of a takeover. It looked as if Pluto stepped away from the business with no compensation at all.

She found cash entries: transactions where the customer had exchanged cash for their bottle of whisky. And similar cash entries for when the company purchased raw material to distil the whisky.

Aileen chewed her lip. The cash must truly be cash because she didn't find a mention of a bank account. Nor did she find any other ledgers with entries for reserves, provisions, or depreciation. This could not be the entire set of accounts.

She combed through the following year, the one after that, and then reached the fifth one at about midnight.

The entire landscape had grown silent, unbeknownst to her. Now she blinked at the long shadows, the sunken sun, and the twilight sky. Half past ten.

Aileen's stomach let out a growl. She'd come prepared this time. The homemade granola bar burst flavours into her mouth – chocolate, peanuts and coconut. Bliss.

She sucked down some water and let her stomach settle.

The wrapper crunched into her satchel, and Aileen pulled out her trusty yellow notepad. She had to paint the whole picture now.

The whisky, five barrels of it, based on the cost per barrel she'd calculated, lay somewhere in the cellars on the McCloughan lands. If each barrel produced about 200 bottles of 750ml each… That was a lot of money. And these accounts showed they had that kind of money in cash. Like customers had purchased bottles in cash, without the taxes…

Goodness. This wasn't the distillery's accounts, this was the second set of accounts. Bootlegging. Whisky's history was entrenched in such operations, but doing that now? It shouldn't be possible at all.

Aileen pulled out her phone. Nothing like good old research.

She huffed out a breath when she saw the one bar of signal and punched in what she was looking for: how someone could bootleg a whisky selling operation in the 21st century.

Was this what Pluto had been worried about when he said Jack was messing with the quality of the whisky? A bootlegging operation?

Still safes, the search engine told her, were a carryover from the excise duty in the 19th century and remained a part of the whisky distilling process at every distillery. A hydrometer calculated the quality of the spirit and helped the distiller to craft the perfect whisky. Still safes were locked using a padlock and until 1983 only the local Customs officer held the keys to it. But now the keys sat with the distillery manager.

Who was the McCloughan's distillery manager? And…

She stared at her notes. It wasn't about *now*, was it? For a product to be called Scotch whisky, it had to be finished in barrels for three years, minimum.

Dread washed over her. Pluto had handed over the reins to Jack five years ago. So either Jack or Pluto could have distilled the whisky. She'd never know until she found those illegal barrels.

Thud. What was that? Aileen's skin leaped and smattered with goosebumps. Her heart pounded in her chest.

Her watch told her it was close to midnight. She'd been here longer than she'd intended.

'How dare you?' A bark rang through the room.

'How dare *I*? You played me!'

The walls shook at the sound of the two male voices. Pluto and Jack. Her prime suspects were having a go at it, at midnight. Goodness.

Callan was right. She did have a penchant for attracting trouble. How could she get out now? Aileen shut her notepad and dropped it into her satchel. Her stationery followed.

She had information, even though she'd have to leave her hard proof behind – the receipts and ledgers. It was best she contacted the police about this.

She wouldn't get into it. No.

But right now, she had to get out. Aileen tiptoed to the library door. Pluto's study stood on the other side of the thick walls to her back, squashed between the library and his room. The door was cracked open, enough to carry their voices to her ears, and her tiptoeing to theirs. Hell.

'You gave it to me, remember?'

A scoff. 'I had to. Linda wished it. Badgered me into giving it up to you! You're a useless eejit.'

'If I'm so useless, why didn't you hand it over to good old Ricky?'

'He's not ma blood, is he? Even though I'm ashamed to say *you* are.'

A long pause burned Aileen's eardrums.

'No, Father. You're ashamed because they nominated my whisky. Something they never did for yours.'

'Ha! Like I care. For all I know, you paid them off! For all the bottles you sell, where is the profit?'

'You know as well as I do: we pay 70% tax on every bottle we sell. And our profits are similar to our competitors.'

'I was better. And try as you might, you'll never measure up. Linda coddled you into a wimp. Be a man. But you can't. You'll run this legacy to the ground just like I knew you would!'

Footsteps pounded on the carpet, and the door creaked. Aileen slunk into the shadows when she saw Jack framed in the doorway. 'It's mine now. What's done is done. Just stay out of it.'

'How can I?' Pluto's roar vibrated through the walls.

Aileen slapped a hand over her mouth, but neither man heard her gasp.

'I can't let you spoil our name!'

'Being called one of the best Highland whiskies is hardly a slap on our name, Father.'

'Forget about the glory, boy. The bottom line's what matters. And it's slipping lower and lower under your ownership. We'd be eyes deep in debt and you'll still be blind to it.'

Crack. The door slammed shut and shook the walls. A slew of shouts and curses followed, now all muffled by the door and walls. And these walls were thick.

Pluto hated his son. She didn't need a better demonstration of that fact, and as far as she could tell, Jack had done nothing wrong. Except maybe let profit margins drop, which was in tune with the added technology he'd invested in for the distillery.

She slinked away in the darkness, one step in front of the other. The air seemed to freeze, the hair on the backs of her neck rose.

Aileen drifted down the staircase and—

The door upstairs crashed against something and footsteps cascaded down the stairs. She plastered herself to the dark, but too late: Jack saw her.

Aileen swallowed, and the words tumbled out, 'I'm sorry.'

Jack waited a beat, another second. She waited for him to yell, to wake up the entire neighbourhood. He tapped down the stairs and halted right next to her.

His eyes glinted in the dim light from upstairs, highlighting his sadness. 'He doesn't believe in me, never has. And I know he never will.'

'I know,' she found herself saying. 'I know how much it hurts.'

Jack looked away.

She thought she'd felt hostility in him before, but she was wrong. 'My parents've come here to Loch Fuar to take me back to the city and force me back into my horrid job. And not because I'm miserable here – I'm the happiest I've ever been – but—'

'It's about their reputation and their wants. Not about yours.' Jack nodded. 'Aye, it's always about them. You're the one who messes it all up, like a lit matchstick to gunpowder.'

'They came here on a Saturday morning and expected me to pack up my life by Sunday.'

'My father has never once tasted the whisky I've made. Never appreciated it. Never looked at the changes I've made to bring his legacy into this century. He just doesn't care.'

Aileen gripped his forearm.

'That's how it's been all my life, Aileen. I look back and think, "where did I go wrong?" And I realise I prolonged it for too long. I became the water that slides around a rock, only the rock turned into a dam and never let me flow. I should've confronted him a long time ago, but I didn't.'

His eyes bored into hers. She felt them more than saw them in the dimness. 'Don't make the same mistake. Stand up for yourself. Your dreams matter.' Jack stepped onto the stair below and before she could digest his words, he slipped out of the door.

Stand up for herself against her parents. It was the toughest thing to do. No matter what Jack said, she'd prolonged it until her default to her parents' commands was a "yes".

She was at least thirty years younger than Jack. Would she let her habit remain? Would she let herself stagnate?

She had people in this life who believed in her, unblocked her enough to flow, to be free. Aye, it was time she fought for herself.

Aileen jumped onto the ground floor landing and hurried over to the door. She gripped it and—

Whack. Something smacked against her skull, her eyes smarted, and everything turned black.

Help.

❄

CHAPTER FOURTEEN

Callan rubbed his eyes. His brain wasn't functioning, but he had work to get done… and no desire to go home to his cold bed.

He groaned, knowing he sounded like a sap. But his mind was still abuzz from the conversation he'd had with Aileen's mother.

It seemed so unreal. And he wasn't sure what to make of it. Who could he talk to? Isla? Isla's husband and his best friend Daniel?

If he told either of them, the news would make its way back to Aileen. He didn't need that to happen. And he couldn't tell his mother. No, she'd bake a cake and take it to Dachaigh just to meet Aileen's parents. Aye, his parents were tamer versions of Siobhan regarding his love life, especially his mother. And sister.

Callan shuddered. He was a magnet for attracting crazy women, currently he had three in his life. How he survived was beyond him.

He pushed off his chair, knowing he should hit the gym. It was almost 1:30 a.m. – in two and a half hours he could head to the trail for a run, get blood pumping into his dead limbs again.

Callan stretched, blinking the sleep from his eyes, and focused on the case instead.

Dr George Erwin, an influential doctor, had been murdered in the peatlands, shot to death with an antique .44 Smith and Wesson Russian, so the report he'd just received said. Erwin had no outward connections to the McCloughans except he'd been in touch with someone there for the past two weeks before he died.

And he'd also been in touch with Eean Mackinnon. And according to Ann, those calls had put her husband in a bad mood. So the history between Eean and Erwin was bad. Enough for him to not confide in his wife.

No way would Eean tell Callan – a detective and his daughter's boyfriend. The man couldn't distinguish between those two roles, for all his professionalism.

Next there was Wagner. Callan hadn't yet been able to verify his claim of Erwin wanting to run for councillor. Or that Erwin was the one who'd instigated the stay on the excavation.

And finally, the key to the cash log and all that cash in the victim's safes…

Dr George Erwin had his hands full with too many affairs. What were those cash logs for?

Callan stalked over to the board, put his hands on his hips, and tried to search for the big picture. Any one clue that could point him towards the killer.

Eean had an alibi.

The Wagners… well, they were each other's alibis. And the man had a firearms certificate too. If Erwin had really wanted to compete against Wagner, that was a motive for Wagner to kill his neighbour. But Rory didn't want Callan to prod into a politician's personal life unless he had to, unless he had more than a 'maybe'. Things got itchy otherwise.

The McCloughans… their alibis weren't very robust. Jack and Sarah were in their house, and so was Pluto. Ricky was another matter entirely. That chap had been missing, because Callan didn't remember seeing him anywhere when he'd arrived.

Where was Ricky?

Such hullabaloo in the house would wake everyone up, especially in the middle of the night. There was something about Ricky that just didn't add up.

The SOCO team had calculated the distance as being about a kilometre between Pluto's house and where they found Erwin's body. Trudging a kilometre through the soggy peat in the dark would take longer. Perhaps twelve to fifteen minutes. If it had been Jack, he'd cut it close. Aye, not enough time to do the deed, go home, change into different shoes, and find a new revolver before barging into his father's house.

Because the police had checked Jack's revolver, and it wasn't a .44 Smith and Wesson Russian. But where there was a will, there was a way.

A ping sounded through the room, pulling Callan from his thoughts. His email…

Callan peeked at the screen and saw the subject: *List of cases around McCloughans' land.*

The officer mentioned they hadn't found any serious cases that took place on or near this land, save for one missing person's report filed by the McCloughans in 2005.

Callan's heart missed a beat when he saw the year. 2005 and missing persons cases had him sweating. That was a lethal combination. Blaine Macgregor had died in 2005 when he'd stood up for Callan against Gerald, unbeknownst to Callan. It had been a stormy night, and Blaine's missing persons case had sat unsolved for fifteen years.

And here was Aaron Ridge.

He clicked open the file on Aaron Ridge, collating all the information the police had on him.

Aaron Ridge had one son, Ricky, who was twelve at the time of the report. Aaron had no other family – no parents, siblings, spouses, partners or cousins. Just a minor son. The report said Ridge went missing on 24th July 2005.

Callan's blood froze.

24th July 2005 was two weeks before Blaine Macgregor was reported missing. Coincidence? Callan hated that word. His skin prickled. This case was too close to home. Training helped him focus on the case at hand.

Aaron Ridge was last seen by a member of the distillery staff at 10 p.m. two nights before, deep into a bottle of whisky. He was an alcoholic and under medication – not the best combination.

They never found him, despite an offer of a reward. Vanished, according to the report, without a trace.

His bank accounts hadn't been operated, nor his phone. The police found no financial withdrawals in the run-up to his disappearance. Nothing hinting at him hoarding cash to make a break for it. Just like Blaine but without the alcohol and medications. Callan clenched his fist. What would Aaron Ridge have run from?

A few clothes were missing, but not a bag.

Strange.

He hit print on the report and waited for the printer to spit it out before tacking it onto his board.

The whole thing was so crowded, he didn't know where to look. A complicated case.

What connection could Aaron Ridge have with Dr Erwin?

Callan squinted, mind whirled, and it hit him—

Linda McCloughan had been a nurse, George

Erwin a doctor. Aaron Ridge had been on medication. Was there a connection there?

Had Aaron been admitted to the hospital?

Somewhere a door thudded, and footsteps strode over to his office. PC Robert Davis appeared, eyes swollen, hair a mess. 'What the hell are you doing here at 2:30 a.m.?'

'Dancing?'

Robert rolled his eyes and entered the room, eyeing his board. 'Mrs Mackinnon stomped over your sensitive heart?'

'Buzz off.'

He smirked. 'Or are the future in-laws keeping you out of the inn?'

'Nobody said anything about in-laws!'

The eejit laughed, wandering into the room. He planted his arse on the chair. 'Want my help?'

A ring interrupted Callan's retort. He frowned at the phone.

'Gee, looks like your girlfriend can't live without you.'

Callan picked up his phone. Terror found a stronghold in his gut when he saw the caller ID: 'Dachaigh.'

'Hello?'

A garbled response came down the line. His heart pumped harder.

'You aren't making any sense, Siobhan. Slow down. What happened?'

'I had my Horror Nights on and I drifted off in front of the telly.'

'It's okay, you're okay—'

'Shut up! I'm not bloody okay. Aileen left this evening to get away. She promised me she'd be back by ten at the latest. She isn't answering my calls.'

'She's not with me.'

'And her car's not at Dachaigh.'

Oh heck. His legs crumpled, shoving him towards the chair. 'Are you sure? Perhaps—'

'I'm old, not dumb. Her phone's switched off. I wouldn't call you otherwise.'

He knew that, but… 'I'll trace her phone. Hold on.' He cursed, stabbed at the screen and pulled up the tracker app Aileen had installed on her phone so he could keep tabs on her. The app pinged saying her phone was out of range.

His fingers shook when he hit the last seen icon and the app retraced. The location pin bounced, moved, and landed on a top of the McCloughan distillery. Shit.

'Aileen's location shows she was last at the distillery. I'm going to call you back, Siobhan.'

Robert was already out the door. 'I'll get the car.'

'Hell no!' Aileen had put him through this several times. And in times of trouble, he would be the one driving.

Callan gritted his teeth, remembered his jacket at the last minute and jumped into his car. The Mc-

Cloughans better beware, because they'd just un-leashed the wrath of DI Callan Cameron.

Pain stung her forehead, like being pricked by thousands of needles.

Aileen fought to open her eyelids, and gasped. 'Ouch!' Her eyes prickled, and a tear escaped. Everything hurt.

She breathed, remembering an important lesson Callan had taught her: handle every situation with calm.

Once she'd schooled her thoughts, Aileen's brain kicked into gear. She mentally scanned her entire body. Her head hurt, eyes hurt, and her mouth was dry. Her throat was as parched as a person lost in the Sahara.

As for the rest of her body, nothing felt off except maybe something sticky near her foot.

She was horizontal, perhaps sprawled out on mud or at least something equally cold. Her jacket kept her from freezing, but barely.

Phone.

Aileen patted the ground, aware of the moisture coating her palms, and pushed up from her elbows.

A moan slipped out and she twisted, fighting the vomit rising in her throat. 'Urgh!' She took a deep breath, swallowing as much oxygen as she could. No use.

Vomit retched out like Mount Vesuvius erupting over Pompeii. Her stomach rumbled, reminding Aileen she hadn't eaten in a long time.

She scrambled away from the mess she'd made, grimacing at the bitter taste in her mouth and nose.

The vomiting must have helped, because she found the strength to pry her eyelids open. Darkness painted the room a deep brown, much like peat. She sat on a mud floor, exposed bricks encasing her into a cellar.

Odd shapes appeared as her eyes adjusted.

She shoved the sting from her mind and took it all in.

A wooden cabinet stood against the opposite wall, with a well-worn bureau next to it. More scraps of furniture emerged, towering over her. A table, a chair missing its leg, a bin, a cupboard to her right covered in a cloth dotted with holes.

She twisted her head to the side and a recent memory trickled in: her discovery of either Jack or Pluto running a bootlegging operation, the argument she'd witnessed between father and son, Jack's words to her before she left and then the pain.

Her hands slipped to the back of her head and felt liquid. Blood.

How long had she been here? Where was she?

Phone. She tugged at her coat, patting herself for her phone, keys, purse – anything.

Hell. Whoever had hit her wasn't stupid. They'd

emptied her pockets. And now she was stuck in this hole.

How soon would someone realise she was missing? Given it was Callan, he'd notice by the morning when he didn't get her usual good morning text. Hopefully.

She didn't have her watch on her either, nor her earrings.

This was not an average burglary, because who'd hold her hostage like this? Was she being held hostage?

She remembered the skeleton and the note. *You shouldn't have come.*

Someone holding a vendetta against her father?

Aileen shook her head and immediately regretted it. Her vision swirled like someone had dropped her in a whirlpool.

She had to get out of here before she lost consciousness. Jacket or not, the cold was slipping in and so was the dampness. And both could kill her.

Aileen staggered to her feet. She used the furniture to find a way, leaning on it. Aware of the throbbing at the back of her skull, Aileen walked the perimeter of the room.

A draught of cold air soaked into her bones.

She paused.

A draught of cold air… If there was a draught of any sort, there had to be a way out. She only hoped it was big enough to fit her.

Aileen took a step ahead to hold on to the next

piece of furniture under the cloth and almost planted her arse on the floor.

That was not a table. It felt circular to the touch, like a… barrel. No way—

She pulled the sheet up and gasped. Aye, her five barrels were right here. Carrying 200 bottles of pure Scotch whisky. At least she wouldn't go thirsty…

The wood felt rough to the touch and a scent of smoked peat and barley tickled her nostrils. Better than the stench of vomit.

This meant she was still on McCloughan property.

Where Erwin had died a few days ago. Hell.

Callan had every right to rage at her. If he found her breathing, that is.

Get moving.

Aileen flipped the sheet to cover the barrels.

She continued her investigation around the room, this time with a beat of urgency. She'd crash later.

When nothing yielded at first sight, Aileen held up a hand and tried to deduce the origin of the draught.

She moved to the left and felt the intensity of the cold increase. Another step forward, to the right. No, left. Diagonally ahead, then a step back—

Aileen found herself in front of a bureau with a

table stacked on top of it. It had to be somewhere here.

A shiver zipped through her, and her teeth clicked.

Aileen clenched and unclenched her fists, hoping to pump some blood into them. Breath in… She had to get a move on, right now.

Her palms flat on the bureau, Aileen hefted herself onto its surface, not caring if the table would collapse on her.

For once her petite-ness worked in her favour. She fit, head kissing the bricks above. Her hair fluttered, revealing the source of the air: a gap behind the bureau and the table.

A door? A tunnel? She didn't care, as long as she got out.

She had to push this table out of the way and squeeze through.

Aileen pressed her back against the thick wood and pushed with her feet. Nothing budged.

She tried to push the table with her arms. Still nothing.

Her inspection told her the table wasn't only heavy, it was wedged between two cupboards with no space to move sideways.

She'd have to push it to the floor while keeping her fingers intact. And if her kidnappers came in search of her, she'd run like a lunatic.

Aileen hopped off the bureau in search of

something to push the table, something like a crowbar.

She tugged the doors of the cupboards, tried to find something that could work…

Nothing. Nothing except the wooden leg of a desk that had come apart.

She had to try.

Aileen leaped onto the bureau again. She pressed her back to the brick wall and wedged the wood in the slight gap between the air duct and the edge of the wall. The wooden leg stuck out at an angle in front of her.

She gripped it as Callan had taught her to hold her dumbbells while doing a bicep curl, and pulled.

'Urgh!' She used her might so much that the force dragged her to the edge of the bureau. The table inched ahead. Success.

She tried again, and nothing moved… except her arse.

Aileen slid from under the wooden stick, praying she didn't snap it. It was her last hope.

She pressed her back to the stick and tried again. Her feet skidded on the ground, but the table didn't move.

Gritting her teeth, Aileen shoved her entire weight on the stick, her muscles tensed, face scrunched and—

The scrape of wood on wood echoed through the room. The table had moved another inch.

She tried again, and another scraping sound. More air blasted on her face.

Progress. One more push and she should be able to squash herself between the gap and escape.

The table moved and—

'Oh shit!'

One leg of the table slid off the bureau.

Aileen leaped into the gap and—

Boom.

The crash burst her ears, and at the same time her palms connected with the splintered wooden stick.

'Ouch!'

Just her luck.

Draughts of frigid air smacked her face.

She was in a tunnel of sorts. Damp and musty, it itched her skin. But she was no longer in that cellar.

Aileen turned to find a heap of wood. The table had fallen off at an angle, dragging the bureau with it and almost crushing her.

That knowledge crumpled her limbs. The echoes of her palpitations swirled towards a crescendo.

Move, Aileen.

A memory of Callan's voice rang in her ears, followed by an image of his hard eyes. Every time he dragged her to his self-defence sessions and glared at her, her limbs moved. His voice made her do things she'd never instructed her body to do.

And now the memory worked. She stood, and her leg stepped forward. The other one followed suit.

Soon she was jogging through the narrow tunnel, barely wide enough to fit her and tall enough to scrape her head.

She ducked out of the way of rocks encased in concrete. Not a single cobweb smashed against her face.

Someone used this tunnel often.

The cold grew icier, and the air turned lighter.

She pushed; her limbs felt like they'd been infused with lead. Her eyes drooped. A yawn tore at her lips. Darkness hung at her side like mist.

Her body was shutting down. But she continued, knowing she had to get out. Out to the end of the tunnel and into fresh air. Then she'd crumble. Not now.

Her vision blurred, and her shoulder caught onto a chunk of concrete. What was more pain in a reservoir-full of it? Her legs gave out, but she caught herself from crumbling to her knees. *Just a bit more, one step…*

And she continued.

Nothing registered; she couldn't see. The prickles at the back of her eyes felt like piercing swords.

Finally, fresh air trickled through her hair and jacket. She took a step, her foot caught onto something and—

'Oomph!'

She fell, and—

Thwack.

Her cheek connected with sludge.

The cold, and now the water, seeped through the front of her clothes.

She'd landed on her stomach and her fingers caught onto something bristly yet soft: grass. She was outside.

The moment that thought entered her mind, her body gave up and unconsciousness swallowed all of her.

CHAPTER FIFTEEN

Callan slammed the brakes. His body's momentum yanked at the seatbelt.

He leaped from his car, took a cursory glance at Aileen's, and took off down the path to where Robert was banging on Pluto's door.

'Police! Open up!'

Callan cupped his mouth and used his entire lung capacity: 'Pluto McCloughan! Open the door.'

He turned to Robert. 'Locked?'

Robert nodded. 'We'll have to break in.'

A door slammed somewhere, and feet scampered over gravel. He pivoted on his heels, readying himself for whoever it was.

Jack McCloughan skidded to a halt beside Pluto's house, his robe flapping and hair in disarray. 'What the——?' He wore combat boots, unlaced, and the barrel of his revolver pointed at them. 'It's 3 a.m.! What do you want?'

Callan pointed to the car park. 'Aileen Mackinnon. She's missing.'

He braced for Jack's spitting match, but the man frowned, walking closer. 'Aileen Mackinnon? She left at about midnight.'

'Her car's still here and she's not home, nor is she answering her phone.'

'Perhaps she's spending the night with her lover?'

Callan growled.

Robert saved him from answering. 'Seeing as he's here, that's unlikely.'

'That's not possible, Detectives. I saw her leave.'

'Where's your father and Ricky?'

'In their beds?'

'And they don't respond to the police banging on their door? Open the damn thing. I want to check.'

Jack hustled forward, tugging a key from his pocket. 'She was fine when we spoke last. She had her satchel with her and was heading home. I went out the door before her, but I'm sure she followed me. Are you sure she couldn't have gone anywhere else?'

The moment the door opened, Callan pushed past Jack and hurried into the living room. He scanned the wall where the artillery hung above the throne.

A revolver was missing.

'Aye, I'm sure she hasn't left your property.' And he silently prayed he found her with her pulse still beating.

Robert flew down the stairs. 'No sign of Pluto McCloughan or Ricky. And Pluto's room is a mess, bedsheets on the floor and things knocked over. Signs of an abduction.'

They had to move. 'Jack, use your cameras to clear the distillery. We're heading for the peatlands.' Callan ran out the door.

Icy wind tugged at him yet sweat clung to his brow as images flashed in his mind. A beast, a bludgeon, the stench of iron: blood. Callan shook off his overactive imagination. He wasn't in a horror movie.

He flashed his torch, losing the game to the mist swirling around him. His heart pounded in his ears, and his lungs pumped oxygen in and out of his nostrils.

'Aileen!'

'Aileen!' Another set of footsteps joined Callan's. 'Ricky's doing?'

'I'm not sure.'

'And Aaron Ridge?'

'I don't think Ricky's father ran away, Robert.'

Robert squeezed Callan's shoulder, obviously thinking about Blaine's case. 'Whoever it is, they couldn't have taken Aileen that far. It's difficult to tread these peatlands with a victim in tow.'

Callan swatted at the picture that formed. Aileen was smart. She'd get through. 'Let's split.'

'No way! These lands are treacherous. You can barely see past your nose. Besides, I've called in the cavalry.'

Callan didn't care about any of that, as long as he had a warm-blooded Aileen in his arms in the next minute or so.

Soon. Patience. But Callan didn't heed his own gospel right then.

He ran straight ahead, compass in one hand and his torch in another. 'Let's go to where Erwin was murdered.'

Robert joined him and— 'Callan!'

Callan flashed his torch to where Robert pointed.

A shoe. A lady's boot.

Dread washed him to his knees; he doubled over.

'Aileen!' Robert called again. He flashed the torch around.

Her shoe. Why would her shoe be here?

'Get up, Callan. This is just one shoe. We need to find a trail.' Robert gripped his collar and pulled him to his feet.

Callan summoned his training but failed to clear all his thoughts like Old Brun had taught him. This was Aileen.

A victim he needed to protect.

He gritted his teeth and searched the area

around the shoe for any other clue. His meticulousness and focus erased a smidge of fear.

They searched until Callan found a tuft of uprooted grass. 'Drag marks.'

Placing one foot in front of the other, they checked the area for more clues or markers.

They progressed, albeit too slowly. But they found nothing else.

If she were unconscious Aileen wouldn't leave breadcrumbs like Hansel and Gretel. A possible reason her abductor had dragged her, especially if they'd also taken Pluto. He'd be easily subdued with a gun and perhaps too terrified to leave crumbs.

Time dragged on. They didn't see the flash of red and blue, nor did they hear help arrive. Callan and Robert jogged, following the drag marks.

Damp mud left a trail and when grass or weeds cut it off, they searched the area for uprooted fronds or disturbed soil.

A raindrop smacked Callan's face. They didn't need the rain to wipe away any clues. Nor did he want Aileen soaking wet in this cold weather.

'Hurry up!'

'Haven't we reached the end of the McCloughan land?'

Callan had no clue. But they'd been heading west for a while now, right towards where Loch Fuar curved inwards. 'If I'm correct, there's a patch of peatlands, then a hillock separating it from the loch.'

Mist wound a cyclone around them, and an image flashed again: a giant with a bludgeon, blood dripping from it. The giant looming above, dampness clinging to his limbs, and pain, so much pain.

Red eyes, the numbness drowning the pain, darkness closing in – Callan begging. *Not me, monster, please.*

A laugh like the cackle of thunder.

'Callan!'

He blinked. What was that?

Focus, Cameron.

His shirt was soaked, part rainwater and part sweat. What was happening to him?

Trees hovered behind the mist, silent silhouettes. Why wasn't the sky lightening? How many more hours until dawn?

Callan stumbled over a block of stone, steadied himself, and rushed ahead. The low wall demarcating McCloughan land ran beside them. 'Their land tapers ahead. Right behind those trees.'

He quietened his heart, shoving aside images of blood and a red-eyed giant.

Rain pelted in white sheets. Callan's clothes weighed him down, but he held a finger to his lips. 'Hear that?'

Robert lifted his head. 'A voice?'

Aye, it was a male voice shouting over the rain. They rushed towards where the trees formed a barricade.

Someone was right behind it.

Callan and Robert clung to the foliage, not caring about the rainwater soaking through their clothes and turning their bones to ice. The rain muted their shuffle forward and the moment Callan crouched behind the last tree, he was grateful for it.

The low wall of the McCloughan's farm continued to the right, flanked by a line of trees. Dried pine needles cushioned their footsteps, and the damp mud sucked at their feet.

The scene in front of him had Callan almost weeping.

Ricky brandished the revolver at a prone figure by his feet. He recognised the petite form with dark hair, unmoving and unresponsive.

Beside her, writhing and pleading, was Pluto. The man's larger-than-life persona had diminished into a mess of tears. 'You can't do this! She's innocent.'

'You killed my father! I was twelve.'

'I didn't.'

'Linda did! Admit it!'

Pluto sucked his lip as if that would stop the trembling. 'No, boy.'

'She did! She killed my father. He didn't run away and leave me. The proof is right there!'

Callan followed the lad's finger to two small stones on his left, dwarfed amidst the trees.

Stones? Tombstones?

McCloughans didn't have a family chapel or cemetery here. But if one stone was Aaron's…

Disappeared two weeks before Blaine Macgregor.

Callan swallowed against the thumping in his chest and the bile which rose in his throat. He stuck to the trees and slid to the left. Silently, Robert made his way to the other side, where Pluto lay.

It was up to Callan to disarm Ricky.

Two tombstones. Aaron Ridge disappeared two weeks before Blaine Macgregor… Could one of the tombstones be… *Focus, damn it.*

The rain covered them up, thank god. Callan hurried to the other end. Right then, Ricky threw the revolver up in the air and caught it, just barely. With a flick of his hand, he aimed the barrel straight at Aileen. Callan's heart jumped at the callousness of the moment. He clutched a tree in terror.

Callan's breath puffed out. *Full focus, Cameron. Aileen needs you.*

Holding that thought in his mind, Callan leaped out of the shadows and barrelled towards Ricky.

The lad turned towards Callan, eyes wide in horror and pointed the revolver straight at Callan's chest.

Callan didn't hesitate. He lunged.

Ricky was so light, he lost his footing under Callan's weight. The lad fell to the left just when Robert hefted Pluto aside.

Crack.

Mud splattered around them.

'Police! Stop!'

Callan grappled with the lad, disarming him in five seconds. He twisted the eejit over and cuffed him. Ricky writhed, shouting over the pounding rain.

Callan spat the mud from his mouth. 'Stay. Got it?'

Ricky bobbed his head.

A growl ripped Callan's chest apart. 'Where the heck are our reinforcements?' Holding Ricky by the collar, he dragged him to a tree and leaned him against the trunk. 'You just came after my girlfriend. You'll be sorry if you try to run. Yeah?'

Another bob.

He ran back to the prone figure and sagged to the ground in relief. She lay on a soggy piece of cloth. A bullet hadn't hit her, nor had it scraped her. He cupped the back of her head and felt the warmth of blood on the palm of his hand. 'We need paramedics.'

'On their way, Callan.'

Aye, he heard the sirens through the rain now. Callan wanted to pull Aileen into his arms and run towards them, but if Ricky had struck her with too much force, he didn't want to risk moving her.

'Callan?'

'Hmm?'

'You need to see this.'

Callan caressed Aileen's cheek.

'It's important.'

He faced Robert and didn't like the tears

shining in his eyes.

Trepidation flooded Callan's blood. 'What is it?' He crouched next to the two stones and dread mixed with hope in his soul. They were six inches tall and twelve inches wide, made of cheap stone. Etched words traced the name *Aaron Ridge*.

The one on the right ripped through Callan. He sagged, pressing his palm against his heart.

Blaine Macgregor.

'PLEASE, FATHER, CAN'T THIS WAIT?'

Eean crossed his arms, glaring at Aileen like she was a speck of mud on a floor he'd just cleaned. 'As soon as you're out of here, we're taking you back to the city. If you want to continue with the inn, out-source it to someone. You should be able to afford that with the salary from your job.'

Aileen groaned. Her headache had subsided, but the doctor insisted she stay overnight for observation. She didn't want to spend a night in the hospital when all she'd needed were a few stitches.

The soggy peat had saved her from scratches or deep cuts. She had a few that burned, but it wasn't all that bad.

Almost as soon as she arrived, her parents had descended into her hospital room with their noses up in the air and a glint in their eyes that said, 'I told you so.' Now they wanted her back in the city, for her safety. And, according to her mother, so they could keep an eye on her.

What was she? Eighteen-years-old?

The door to the hospital room – the best of the best for Eean Mackinnon's daughter, her father had demanded of the nurses – cracked open to reveal a pink-faced old man.

Pluto wore pyjamas, not hospital scrubs, and looked meeker than the usual gusto he surrounded himself with. 'Hope I'm not interrupting.' He walked in and nodded at her father. 'Eean.'

Her father bobbed his head without cracking open his mouth.

Then Pluto smiled at her mother, who was sitting on the sofa. 'You must be Ann.'

And her mother, unlike her father, smiled at Pluto.

Pluto patted Aileen's hand. 'How are ye, lassie?'

'Ready to break out of here.'

His laugh filled the room with cheer. 'Aye, me too. But I know the moment I step out, the authorities will be nipping at my heels. And before that, I have to apologise.'

Aileen reached out to grab his hand, which was soft yet calloused. 'What Ricky did was his fault. You're as much a victim as me.'

'Bet yer boyfriend wouldn't see it that way.'

Aileen puffed out a breath. Callan hadn't visited her yet, but had sent a police officer to take her statement. 'He's a good detective.'

'Hence, I have no doubt he knows about the bootlegging. And I know he will pass on that information to the tax authorities. And I'm sorry, lassie. I'm sorry for lying to you, for involving you in something so dangerous. If Linda was here, she'd have ma hide.'

'Pluto, I knew. I knew there was something amiss from the moment I saw the ledgers.'

'Yet, it's my fault for getting you involved. I'm so pig-headed.' Pluto's gaze met Aileen's parents. 'As a parent, you want the best for your wean. But when your wean excels, does better than you'd ever expect… I never thought I had the green-eyed monster in me. Apparently, it thrived inside.' Pluto thumped his chest. 'And more so for my own blood. So much that I wanted to sabotage him. I made a set of illegal books and wanted you to audit them. Ricky made a mistake. He gave you the bootlegging ledgers instead of the false ones.

'Ricky… he's… er, special. I know he can never surpass my talents as a distiller, because he isn't gifted with a mind such as ours. Linda wanted to send him to a special school. We raised him after Aaron…' Pluto swallowed the words he was about to say, and sighed. 'But I knew his classmates would pick on him. And he'd think he was less. So I stuck him in the same school. My wife wasn't happy about that. I did my best by him and I take responsibility for his actions.'

Pluto gripped Aileen's hand. She let him talk, to

get it all out. 'My father raised Aaron Ridge, too, after his father passed away having worked for us all his life. Aaron was a close friend, but he liked the bottle far too much and it drove him to an early grave. Linda tried to help him fight it. Aaron's wife left Ricky. The lad looked the spit of Aaron, but it wasn't enough to bring him out of his drunken stupor.

'And one day he died. Linda was frantic. She thought he was doing better. Aaron had taken a tumble after a drunken night, a few broken bones. Linda was a nurse, so she cared for him and knew he was getting better. And in the morning, he had no pulse. We called Erwin, and he said Aaron had likely died of a heart attack after pumping more doses of morphine than necessary.

Linda had been caring for him after his fall, giving him the medication. And Erwin picked up on that.' Pluto breathed in and a muscle ticked in his jaw. 'He made it seem like my sweet wife had… had given Aaron the extra dose because he was a burden to us. It was my word over a doctor's. My sweet Linda would not do that, would she? But she'd been tired lately, working so hard. I didn't know what to do, so I begged him to say Aaron had run off. That under the influence of alcohol he'd taken off.

We buried him in the peatlands, and I thought that would be that, I really did. Linda didn't ask questions, I didn't tell her. I didn't ask her if she'd done it. It was stupid of me, but I paid Erwin for his silence. Then…'

Pluto hung his head, his breaths puffing out. 'Then he came to the house in the middle of the night two weeks later, soaking wet. Said it was time I repaid my debt. He-he had a slip of a lad in his back seat. Dead.'

Aileen's heart pounded. She knew who the lad could be. Had Callan found Blaine's body? And here she was stuck in a hospital. When she'd thought Pluto was lying about the audit, she never imagined what the old man was truly hiding. A connection between Pluto and Erwin didn't get any more illicitly robust than that. 'Pluto, you need to tell this to the police. To Callan. Why didn't you come forth with this information before?'

He rubbed his face. 'A few weeks ago, Erwin said he was done. He was telling your boyfriend where his friend was buried. But that would mean everyone would know about Aaron and suspect Linda. I love her still. She was the sweetest creature, and I didn't want anyone to suspect otherwise.'

'So you asked Erwin to keep it in the past?'

'Aye, but he wouldn't listen. I think he was there that night to prove the tombs existed. Every year since the day Erwin brought the boy, I lay flowers on his tombstone. I knew very little about him and… I want to say I did it for Linda's reputation but that's an excuse for cowardice. I'm sorry.'

Pluto's shoulders drooped, and he didn't meet

Aileen's eyes. She didn't know what to say, what to feel. Pity for the man, or anger about the secret he'd hidden? Tears stung her eyes.

She just wanted to hold Callan until his old wounds no longer stung. He'd speak to her. If only she'd—

As if conjured up by angels, the door opened to reveal a man, pouches under his reddened eyes and rumpled black clothes. His gaze cut to Aileen's and frowned.

He nodded at the rest of the people in the room before stalking over to her. 'Don't cry.'

'I'm not.' Her words came out garbled.

'Is she on pain meds?'

Ann nodded.

Why was Aileen crying? She needed to comfort *him*.

A hand landed on her forehead and caressed it. She met Callan's eyes, but was too tired to tell him she knew, and she'd always have his back.

He leaned over and pressed his lips to her forehead. 'How are ye?'

'Fit enough to not be in the hospital. Blaine—'

'If you're complaining about the hospital, that's karma.'

'I didn't jump from a racing car—'

'We can't understand you, darling.'

Aileen glared at her mother, who still sat on the sofa, hands crossed over her chest.

Callan pecked her cheek. 'Head hurts?'

No, her heart did. She glanced at Pluto. 'I would've spoken to my spouse, been open about it. If Linda was a nurse, as sweet as you say she was, she wouldn't have taken a life, no matter how wasteful it was.'

Callan straightened, still caressing Aileen's head. 'Considering the kind of man Dr George Erwin was, he probably played you like he did several others.' His gaze switched to her parents. 'And the sooner people speak up about him, the sooner we can decipher what kind of person he was.'

He didn't elaborate on that comment, and her father paid him no heed. Callan squeezed her shoulder as gently as one touched a butterfly.

'I need you to come down to the police station, Mr McCloughan. I need your statement and I have a few questions for you.'

'You're saying Linda didn't kill Aaron?'

'We don't know, we never will perhaps. But you hid a body.'

'I was a fool.'

Callan huffed. 'In love, we often are.'

Aileen reached over and held his hand like she had when they'd first ventured into the peatlands in search of Blaine. They'd face this together too.

He nodded as if he understood her.

CHAPTER SIXTEEN

Callan forced the fumes of hope away. Several months ago, he had stood in front of yet another tombstone, just as inconspicuous, bittersweet that he'd found what happened to his best friend yet couldn't save him. And all that had come crashing when the body hadn't been Blaine's.

He let the door slam behind him, cutting off those thoughts and the guilt they carried. He focused on the man in the room, who bowed as if in prayer, muttering words, his shoulders trembling.

The metal of the chairs glinted under the white light. Grey walls surrounded them on three sides and on the other the one-way mirror was a pool of dark mercury. Enough to drive a sane human to Bedlam, eventually.

Callan's boots echoed, and the slap of the file

exploded in his ears like the thunder raging outside. 'Ricky.' The chair scraped and groaned when Callan dropped into it. 'Have you been read your rights?'

A bob of the head.

'Do you understand them?'

Several nods. Ricky continued to lean over, shoulders drooping, head down. A curtain of damp hair covered his face. 'Aye, I understand.' He sounded like a child being reprimanded. 'They lied to me.'

'Who lied to you?'

'The bloody McCloughans! They knew! They knew, and they didn't tell me!'

Ricky's head jerked up and bloodshot eyes glared at Callan. Tears ran down his pale, bony face. 'Why didn't they tell me?'

Callan tilted his head. He knew too well the kind of pain that ripped through you when someone you thought had run away was, in fact, dead. You grieved for that person once again. And nothing prepared anyone for that pain. It had been Blaine in Callan's case, a friend. For Ricky, it was his father.

In Callan's line of work, he wasn't allowed to show softness towards a possible criminal, no matter the circumstances. So now, if he wanted the right answers from Ricky, he had to ask specific questions especially because the lad was autistic. Callan swallowed his sympathy. 'What didn't the McCloughan's tell you?'

'That Daddy died. They said he'd run away, and I thought it was because of me.'

'And—'

'I was twelve! Linda and Pluto pulled me out of my Year Six class and told me he'd gone. Disappeared. They said they'd care for me like they did before. Everything would be fine. That's all I remember.'

'Have you seen the two tombstones at the edge of the McCloughan's property before last night?'

'No.'

'That area is a part of the McCloughan's property. Didn't you ever play there while growing up?'

'Pluto said I wasn't allowed to go off alone that far away, it was dangerous. I could fall and hurt myself or get lost.'

Callan took a deep breath, coming to grips with the situation. Ricky Ridge's file didn't state anything about his autism. Pluto had made sure of that. Talk about protecting those you love.

'When did you realise your father had died and not left of his own accord?'

Ricky intertwined his hands and uncrossed them again. 'The evening I opened the box. I wasn't supposed to, but it sat there and I really wanted to go through it.'

'What box?'

'The box from the dead man's office.'

'Where did you find the box?'

'In the room behind the stairs in the main house.'

'Do you know who brought it to the main house from George Erwin's?'

'Sure. I did.'

Good god. Ricky had confessed to a crime.

'Pluto said now that he was dead, we had to get the boxes he kept all the important stuff in. He told me to go down there when the dead man's missus wasn't around and grab a cabinet. I did everything I should have. I even gave the other woman, the brown-haired one, the wrong set of accounts!'

Ricky's eyes widened, and he slapped a palm against his mouth. 'I wasn't supposed to say that! I take it back!'

Callan leaned in and said, 'Ricky, did you kill the man?'

'Aye, I did.'

His pulse pounded. Callan placed a copy of Erwin's photograph they'd found in his study. 'This man, did you kill him?'

'That's the man Pluto was upset about. Nay, I didn't kill him, I killed the bad man in my video game.'

Callan pointed to Erwin's photo again. 'Do you remember what happened the night this man died?'

'I had my headphones on, playing my games. Pluto says I'll get deaf in a day listening at the volumes I do. I have still got my ears, haven't I?' He tugged at them. 'The other girl shouted so loud I heard her over my game.'

'Why didn't you rush towards the girl, I assume that's Aileen Mackinnon, if she was shouting?'

'I hate her.'

'Is that why you hurt her last night?'

'I didn't hurt her! I messed up the work she'd done, the brown-haired girl. Roughed it up, so she'd have to start again and get bored. So Pluto would think I'm so smart. He never said I was smart.'

'If you didn't hurt Aileen Mackinnon, what did you do last night?'

Ricky crossed his arms, set them on the table. He kept repeating the pattern. 'I emptied the cabinet, dumped it in the cellar, and moved a few tables to the entrance of the tunnel. She wasn't supposed to get out. I put the files that were inside the cabinet in the other room.'

The SOCO team had found it all. Aileen's satchel tucked under the staircase, along with her phone. She had filled it with notes about a bootlegging operation at the distillery. And they had also found Pluto's cellar entrance filled with barrels of illegal alcohol, Erwin's now empty cabinet, and the tunnel leading out to the peatlands, the exit exactly where they found Erwin's body. And in one of the back rooms they'd found boxes filled with notes, all filed and segregated by names.

Callan hadn't studied those notes, but by the looks of it, Erwin maintained information about his patients he had no business storing years after his retirement.

The SOCO team had found Aaron's medical file wide open.

'What did you find in the files, Ricky?'

'My father's name.' Ricky swiped a tear away. 'I believed them! But the file said he died. And Linda. He wrote that. But… but… Why…?'

Callan placed his palm on the table, hoping to calm Ricky down. 'Why did Pluto ask you to get the cabinet from Erwin's office?'

'Dunno.'

'Did he know what was in the cabinet?'

'Aye, it was the treasure chest of cash. I got it for him.'

'Did Pluto ask you to get anything else?'

'Anything else?'

Callan shook his head at the frown of confusion on Ricky's face. 'Do you know what Erwin was doing on the McCloughan property?'

Ricky widened his eyes and nodded. 'Aye, he was troubling Pluto. I didn't like him much. He wouldn't go away. He'd come at all times during the day and fight. Loud noises. And then I'd have to go get the doctor. For Pluto.'

'What did Erwin want?'

'The truth, he said. Tell them where *they* were. I don't know what *they* he was talking about.' Ricky scratched at an almost invisible mark on the table. 'Pluto said he was being unreasonable. Er, out of line. That he should leave the past in the past. But he wouldn't listen.'

'Do you know about Blaine Macgregor?'

'Nope.'

'Do you know what a .44 Smith and Wesson Russian is?'

'A revolver. I use it in video games.'

'The real weapon. Do you know how to use that?'

'Pluto said I wasn't allowed to learn because it's dangerous. He knows. Jack knows. They're not fair. He said it wasn't for me.'

Ricky didn't know what he'd been doing. The revolver he'd pointed at Aileen was empty. And it didn't match the one that killed Erwin.

'What happened before you took Pluto and Aileen to the tombs?'

'I was angry. I heard Jack and Pluto arguing. And then heavy footsteps running down the stairs. It was the brown-haired girl. She had worked too much. The files were organised again, and she knew. I knew she knew about our business. We could only survive if we bottled our own whisky, Pluto said.' Ricky fell silent for a long time.

Callan gritted his teeth. 'What else did Pluto say that night?'

Ricky wound his fingers together again. 'Something about Jack not being smart enough and profits falling. And Pluto not getting paid. We had some casks I'd transferred to the main house before Jack took over. We bottled it and sold it, sometimes an entire barrel.'

'And you didn't pay taxes for it?'

'Only bad businesses pay tax, Pluto said. We did good business.'

'I'm sure Her Majesty's Revenue and Customs would be interested in your definition of taxation, Ricky. What did you do after you realised Aileen had found out?'

'I waited for Jack to leave and then I hit her.'

Callan's fingers itched to connect with the eejit's face. Autistic or not, he shouldn't hurt someone, especially not someone so close to Callan's heart. 'Did Pluto ask you to do that?'

Ricky shook his head. 'I wanted to make him proud.'

'So she fell unconscious. What did you do after that?'

'I took her to the cellar and dragged Pluto downstairs to show him. He shouted at me! For helping him! He said I was stupid. So I used the gun like in my games, so he'd keep quiet. He didn't.

'We left the house, like I told him to. I said I wasn't stupid; that I knew he'd lied. I knew about my daddy. I wanted to meet him. Pluto said he'd show me. So we went out. I still had my gun. I wasn't a fool. I am not.'

'What about Aileen Mackinnon?'

'Found her lying there playing dead. But she knew, so she had to come along. Pluto told me to carry her. Like he could dictate. She's heavy. I lugged her.'

After that, Callan had seen what he never wanted to. How lucky were they that Ricky's revolver was empty?

But if the lad couldn't operate a revolver, he couldn't have killed Erwin. He had committed other crimes and had been smart about it, too. Like an actual criminal. But he hadn't killed.

Erwin's killer was a steady shot.

Callan pushed away from the table, eyeing the desperation in Ricky's eyes. 'That's all, Ricky.'

And he walked out.

EEAN MACKINNON SLAMMED THE LAPTOP SCREEN shut and gritted his teeth. For the first time in decades, he found his mind straying from work.

Work had been his life ever since he'd left Loch Fuar behind.

He ground his palms against his eyes. The last time he'd been this distracted was when Ann was expecting their child. They'd both been like children on Christmas Eve, for nine whole months. The image threatened to pull his lips into a smile and he tuned it out.

He'd let her down. He really shouldn't have come.

Ann wasn't happy with him, or at his persistence in dragging their daughter back to the city, especially now that she had a beau. Something Eean hadn't ever expected – his daughter in love with a police detective.

A decent police officer. That was the first thing Eean saw to since he found out – a background check told him DI Callan Cameron was as tenacious as they came. That had put a damper on his plans and drawn a wedge between him and his wife.

Aileen had such potential. Why couldn't she see that? The potential to be the best of the best, enough to get her international fame. She'd achieved more than most at her age. What lunacy had driven her to Loch Fuar? His mother, no doubt.

Eean sank into the chair and pulled out his wallet. Two families, same blood. One in black and white, the other in colour.

He traced the coloured photograph, him without a grey hair in sight and his beautiful wife, radiant as she was to this day. Both grinning at the screen like they'd won the lottery. They'd won so much more: a daughter.

This one time, the ice floe slipped from his face.

Eean studied the four faces in the other image in black and white. He clung to his mother's apron and his brother had his arms around her neck. And all three of them were encased in a man's embrace. Edward Mackinnon. Eean remembered his father like a splash of colour hidden behind the mist. And somehow he remembered the man's belly-deep laugh. Gone too soon, aye, but his mother had some of that spark, the zest for life.

And Eean had decided to bury it all when he left. Turned himself into an unfeeling block of ice.

In retrospect, it was the correct choice. He'd have suffocated here. And he'd never have met Ann. They loved each other today more than the day they'd said, 'I do'.

But the heaviness rested in his gut, the feeling remained.

You shouldn't have come.

He'd let people down, he'd lied and shattered promises. Scared, lost and cowardly enough to never return, not really, except maybe to drop his daughter off for a holiday with her grandmother. Once had been enough for him. And it killed him to never see his daughter like that, laughing her grandfather's laugh. She'd burrowed into herself in the city, he'd known that. But her potential… She couldn't stay here. Should she?

You shouldn't have come.

They must leave. It was wrong to come here, especially at such a time.

The bastard was dead; somebody'd finally pulled the trigger on him. So close to where his daughter had been.

Eean stood from his chair and went to peek out of the window.

Lush heather, the glittering Loch Fuar with the

backdrop of the mountains. Those mountains had watched him grow up, stumble and flee.

Ann had once commented that his laugh was so deep, it lit up the entire world. His father's laugh.

But now an ice floe on his face hid the laugh. How long would the ice remain frozen? It wasn't him, but it had stayed on for so long, Eean no longer knew who he was behind it.

Carefree, like his parents? Passionate?

The proof resided in his last name. There never was a Mackinnon born without a fire in their blood, and thirst for the wind in their hair.

He'd let her down again. He could barely face himself. But he needed the mask on now more than ever. And—

A hand squeezed his shoulder. Ann.

'Honey.'

He wrapped his arms around her, held her.

'You know, Aileen and you are two peas in a pod. Just like you and your mother. You hide under the cold, and they burn in the fire, but you each have stubborn in your DNA. And it's for the rest of us to wonder what we should do with you.'

'I love you.'

'And I you, Eean, and so does your daughter.'

'No, she doesn't.'

Ann patted his chest, cutting off his comment. 'She does, just as fiercely. Aileen's a Mackinnon. Speak with her, listen to what she says.'

He couldn't talk to her. He'd only let her down again.

He thought of his mistakes, the suffocation he felt here when…

You shouldn't have come.

Shit. He pressed Ann to his chest, protected in his arms.

Was he aiding history to repeat itself?

AILEEN PULLED THE HANDBRAKE AND SIGHED. SHE'D made a run for it at 6 p.m., when her mother answered a client's call.

Ann had hovered around all day, as if waiting to lay it on her – how Aileen had almost been killed. Her mother had hinted at them leaving Loch Fuar, asking Aileen to stay with them for a couple of days – not permanently, she'd emphasised. What was her mother playing at? Aileen could never understand her parents.

She stepped out of the car and headed into the police station. The aroma of coffee hit her, followed quickly by Robert's smile. 'Glad you're doing good.'

'Thanks. Callan?'

She found him cursing at the murder board, a pile of papers mounting around him. Despite his height, in a few days she wouldn't find him among the huge amount of paper in his room.

'Did you even sleep?'

'Hell! What are you doing here? The doctor said—'

'I should be careful about the head wound. And I am being. Nothing's wrong with me.'

'You need to take care. This is not taking care. What are you doing outside Dachaigh? Did you drive yourself here?'

She raised an eyebrow. 'Do I have to sign a permit every time I step outside the house?'

'Aren't you lucky I had the tracking app on my phone?'

'We've talked about this, Callan. That app is meant for you to find me in times of trouble. It worked, and I ended up solving your case.'

'You didn't!' Callan prowled to the board and stabbed at it. 'You bloody didn't!'

'But Ricky—'

'Doesn't know how to use a real weapon. And Eric Macdonald certified Pluto cannot be our man either – he has arthritis in his right arm. He can't aim a revolver as precisely as Erwin's killer did.'

Aileen dropped into a chair, as did her hope. 'So we didn't solve the murder?'

'No, but we solved a case – a bootlegging operation we didn't know existed.'

She waited a beat for him to bring it up. He didn't. So she forged ahead, addressing the elephant in the room. 'And we found Blaine Macgregor.'

Callan plopped into his chair and dropped his

head back. 'We can't be sure it's him, not after the wild goose chase we went through last time.'

He was hurting, she deciphered that from his facial features. And she'd wade through these messy emotions with him before they swallowed him again. 'This time you have a witness; Pluto was there.'

Aileen went to his chair and gathered his hands in hers. 'Talk to me.'

Callan didn't move but a muscle in his jaw twitched. Finally, he met her eyes and straightened. 'I had reconciled myself to the fact that I'd never find him. That order made sure of that. And now… He was right there under my nose all along. Pluto knew and yet… Goodness Aileen, I might actually find Blaine this time, still fifteen years too late to save him.'

And there in lay the issue. Callan blamed himself for what Gerald had done to Blaine.

She bent until they were on an eye level, wanting to throw her arms around him. She resisted, knowing she had to get her point across. 'You found justice for him and worked tenaciously to find him. It's not easy to pursue a cold case like Blaine's when it's so close to one's heart. You worked it despite all the hurdles, the threats to your career and the emotional pain. And now you've found him, fifteen years later. That's commendable, Callan. You've never given up on Blaine Macgregor, that's what he expected from you. You didn't let him down.'

'I hope it's him this time. It would be difficult for us, me, but…' He squeezed her hands still entwined with his. 'It would feel complete if we could bury him properly.'

'I'm here for you.'

'I know…' Callan sighed, and pursed his lips. 'Until the forensic team responds with a report, I have a murder to solve.'

Knowing he needed a change of topic, Aileen asked, 'What about the filing cabinet Ricky stole from Erwin's office?'

'It stored files belonging to Erwin's patients. SOCO's still processing them.'

'And the person who threatened my father?'

Callan gritted his teeth like a wild animal pacing in its cage. 'Makes no sense, damn it! We found the same paper in Erwin's study, with two sets of prints on it: his and Melanie's. Makes sense that we'd find her prints in there.'

'And she could've stacked those papers on the printer for her husband.' Aileen tapped her phone. 'All they had to do was connect a device to the printer's network and hit print.'

'Or, apparently, you can email the printer too, to print out the page. And Erwin had left the printer on.' Callan shook his head. 'It's a mess. I don't think Ricky has a motive to hurl that stone or want your father gone.'

'What about Pluto?'

'We'll find that out as soon as your father tells us how he's connected to them. All that remains is Wagner. He has the motive and the means. Is he the one who wants your father gone? Why? I've to go down to his house again, perhaps ask to see his firearms certificate. That's the only stone left unturned. Damn politics.'

'You have that, and the possibility of it being someone from Erwin's files.'

'They are medical files belonging to his patients. I have to follow up with Halston as well. If they find something tangible, or something that builds the case against Wagner...'

'Or Jack.'

'Aye, or Jack. He's the only one left. And he hates your father.'

Aileen approached the board. 'You need to clear this up, as much as you can. Pluto and Ricky are off your list now.'

'And I have over three boxes of suspects to add.' Callan huffed. 'Let's go through this case from the top.'

He found the duster, cleaned up the side of the board he'd dedicated to Pluto McCloughan. 'Not him. But it could be Jack.' He drew a line. 'What's Jack's connection to Erwin? We don't know if there is one.'

'Maybe...' Aileen tilted her head. 'Maybe like

Pluto, he wanted to keep his mother's secret hidden?'

Callan pulled out his phone, calculated how old Jack might have been in 2005. He'd be old enough to have moved out of the house, but still pick up on a possible murder. If Pluto the devoted husband suspected his wife, a son could too. 'Aye, that's a possibility. So he shoots Erwin in rage.'

'And he hates my father enough to throw that stone.'

'Would the hate be so harsh? A murder and a stone through your library window – how does that connect? A hate-induced rampage?'

Aileen leaned her hip on the desk and thought of Jack McCloughan. 'What if he's all bark and no bite? That night, he could've kicked me out of his father's house. He was raging, seeing red. But he talked to me.'

'Perhaps his behaviour is unpredictable.' Callan shook his head. 'But he's acted level-headed, apart from when we shut his business down. Right now, he's right up there with Julian Wagner as a suspect though.'

Aileen's phone buzzed. She let it ring out, thinking about the case. Then the buzzing started up again. 'Urgh!' She whipped it up, frowning. 'Hello?'

'Aileen, where are you?'

'Mother—'

'Are you at the police station? Is the detective with you?'

Aileen rolled her eyes. 'Yes.'

'Tell him to drive you back.'

'I—'

'I'll see you soon.' And the call went dead.

Aileen groaned. 'What's got into her?'

Callan checked his watch, and then the board. 'Halston should be here with the files soon. And you should head back. I have to see what he's got. Need me to drop you off?'

'I can drive!' Aileen gripped Callan's arm, waited until he gazed into her eyes. 'Keep me posted. About Blaine, too.'

He nodded.

She pecked him on the lips. 'I've got to get back before my mother chops my head off.' She walked out, hoping they really found Blaine and for once Callan wouldn't blame himself for what happened.

CHAPTER SEVENTEEN

'Mr Halston wanted to discuss the files found at Erwin's.' DCI Rory Macdonald said the moment he saw Callan.

Rory greeted Halston and ushered him into his office.

The man straightened his tie before plopping onto the chair. His feet kissed the ground, short as he was. This was perhaps the first time Callan had seen Halston without his scrubs or a mask. Yellow teeth, as dented as an anthill, flashed at Callan. 'After my colleague worked on the files, we discussed them. Our forensic accountant hasn't found the pattern in the logs.'

'I hear a "but", Mr Halston.'

'But the files – the ones in the cabinets that you found – they seem to be a patient repository of sorts. And instead of ailments, the files contain family secrets.'

'You think Erwin used the files to blackmail his patients?'

'Depends on the logs.'

'They're cash logs, Halston, not stock registers. My… My forensic accountant found the pattern.'

Halston raised a grey eyebrow but didn't ask more questions. 'Your accountant must be a smart one.'

'She is.'

Rory typed for a moment and turned the computer screen to face them. 'These are the logs you found in the safe?'

Callan nodded.

Rory pointed to a box resting against the wall. 'Those are the files Ricky stole from Erwin.'

Halston launched up from the chair, waddled over to the box to retrieve a handful of files. His dark eyes flashed with victory. 'See this.' He slapped a file onto the table. 'That's a Mr Halliday.'

Callan swallowed. Taylor Halliday, former teacher. The man who'd called Callan's mother to school for his misadventures.

Callan peered at the page, not wanting to read something he'd never forget. 'These are Mr Halliday's medical records.'

'Aye, they are.' Halston nodded. 'It's unethical to keep records of your patients after you retire. And these are private records.'

'My forensic accountant said we need a key to understand those cash logs.'

Callan's eyes landed on the information box titled 'nickname' in another file. 'Tongue' it said. The same *tongue* which had fetched Erwin part of his revenue.

'Oh no! Erwin's nicknamed his patients based on body parts.' Callan pointed to the files. 'Each patient file should have their nickname. And the entries in the cash log correspond to each patient.'

Rory massaged his head. 'What a bastard!'

Halston plopped into a chair. 'It's a lot of names, but not everyone has a nickname. I think they were his future, er, *clients*.'

His boss cursed something fierce before glaring at the two of them. 'Callan, do you have a list of nicknames mentioned in the cash log?'

'Aye.'

'Then work through those files. I want you to do it. The fewer officers involved with this, the better. If it's all of Erwin's former patients, I fear it'll be the majority of Loch Fuar's population. So find the people Erwin was blackmailing. We'll start there.'

'I'll help you out.' Halston popped up again. 'Shall we start now?'

Callan had all the time in the world. As long as he didn't have to think about finding Blaine Macgregor and the guilt mixed with relief that came along with it.

They hefted the files to his office — all two hundred or so – and set them on another pile of papers Callan hoped weren't important.

'You need to get a cleaning company in here.'

Callan shrugged, before moving another stack of files from the visitor chair and dropping them on top of the printer. 'Don't start.'

Halston dragged one pile towards himself. 'These files are organised by patient name. You give me their nickname and we'll hunt through each file.'

Callan plucked the list of nicknames from the murder board and handed it to Halston. 'Pull out any files you find with a nickname. I'll start with these.'

He pulled another set to himself, starting from the surname 'M'.

Lieutenant General Matthews. Callan's sensors tickled. He squinted at the list on his murder board, the firearms certificates. Matthews featured on the list. The man would be eighty-five now, based on the birthdate in the file. As old as Pluto. Could he have shot Erwin?

His file didn't have a nickname, though. Callan set it aside.

Callan found a lot of popular names of older Loch Fuar citizens. Not his friends or his family, he was glad to know. But people living on his street, those he'd grown up with.

He worked until his eyes drooped. Then he stretched and clomped towards the coffee machine.

The machine spit out a fresh brew, the fumes tickling his nerves.

Robert had switched off the brighter lights in the waiting room, and Rory's office door remained shut.

Silent night – a phenomenon unique to Loch Fuar. Although with added tourism, things were changing. What was it with the human race? They went on holidays to relax and commit crimes they thought they'd get away with.

Like the eejit twenty-five-year olds who'd broken into a shop, too many bottles deep to even make a run for it when the police cruiser showed up.

The dark sludge sloshed into two cups, and Callan plodded over to his office and set one in front of Halston.

They worked until Callan was cross-eyed and counted twelve files with nicknames. Halston slapped an eighth file on his pile and looked up. 'That's all twenty. Ready to match them up?'

Callan didn't want to. It was late. But he wasn't looking forward to another night of restless sleep plagued with strange images.

They set the files on the table and pulled the first one towards them. Councillor Alfred Heath was the first person on their list.

'This one is "Liver"?'

Callan nodded. 'He was the councillor before Wagner. It's said he loved the bottle.'

Halston shrugged. 'Hence the nickname. Who else is on there?'

'Spine. That's Cartwright. Local school principal. Last I heard, he's rolling in it after winning the lottery.'

They went through Aileen's notes on the cash logs and realised Cartwright paid one of the highest rates to Erwin.

'Has motive, but he doesn't have a gun license.'

'Those are fickle, Detective.'

Callan pencilled Cartwright onto his suspect list. And so they continued, from the minutest of body parts right through to the large ones, until they were down to the last one, without a mention of Jack McCloughan.

'Who's the brain?'

Callan opened up the file and cursed. 'Julian Wagner.'

'And based on what your accountant's mentioned here, he was Erwin's highest paying client.'

'That's his motive doubled. It's time I paid the man a visit.'

Halston checked his watch, grinned. 'Try it out tomorrow. He has some big conference to attend. He should be nervous about it. Best to attack them when they're at their weakest.'

If Callan didn't want Wagner to sue them for harassment, he best not visit him at 11 p.m. Tomorrow. First thing tomorrow. He'd ask Julian Wagner the straightforward questions.

❄

AILEEN LOCKED THE BACK DOOR AND SLUMPED HER shoulders. Sleep tugged at her eyelids, and fatigue clung to her muscles. The time on her phone read 11:30 p.m.

Some cases bled the energy out of her, but justice and the chase always left her salivating. And now this case had led Callan to find his best friend's body. She'd be damned if she didn't hold his hand through this trial.

Aileen eyed the dim light in the library and knew who sat there, perhaps slumped in front of his laptop like she'd been not ten minutes ago.

She tiptoed to the library's entrance. Who in their right mind worked in a room with a broken window? On a cold night? Eean Mackinnon, apparently.

Aileen had boarded up the window, vowing to replace it as soon as she had time.

She poked her head in and froze. The ply had vanished, replaced with transparent and gleaming double-glazed glass. How…?

'Since I put you through all that trouble, it's the least I could do.'

Aileen didn't dare breathe. Her father fixed her window without asking her?

The chair creaked when he stood up and stared outside. 'We broke it so many times while playing as children. Gran would turn red like her tomato plants next to that hedge, every time.'

Was he drunk? Why was he talking to her like *that*? In all these years, Eean Mackinnon had only spoken words that slashed across her heart.

Aileen couldn't see an empty bottle of alcohol, nor a half-emptied one.

'It's time I fixed things up.' His words weren't slurring.

What if this was some sort of simulation?

He wasn't looking at her. Eean turned, and his eyes were sharp as his mind. 'Where were you?'

'Working in my study.'

'Helping with the case?' The anger vibrated off his body. 'Does that bloody boyfriend work you to the bone?'

Ah, he'd fixated on Callan this time. Her father wasn't about to pick on her.

Eean crossed his arms. 'Some police officer he is.'

She wouldn't let him slander Callan. 'He saved me, in case you forgot. He tracked my location via the app. And we're putting all this work in because of you.'

'That's enough!'

Aileen narrowed her eyes. 'You don't want to hear your misdeeds, do you?'

Eean's face contorted with rage. 'Someone hitting you over the head wasn't enough, was it? You call *that* good police work?'

'I got out okay.'

'You were injured and would've died of hypothermia if your gran hadn't figured you weren't home!' His eyes flashed through the faint glow, burning Aileen's temper.

'I'd've got away, as I have several times.' Times her father hadn't even called to ask about her.

'Like when Gerald Erwin pumped you with drugs?' Eean roared.

Her skin prickled at the memory. 'That was once!'

'And when a biker ran you off the street? Or when you went running into a house to face a mad-woman with a gun?'

How did her father know about her adventures? She'd never told either of her parents about her sleuthing. Did they keep tabs on her?

'You think I'm a blind fool, Aileen?'

She crossed her arms. 'I'm helping him out, no matter what you say.'

'You don't seem to care about what we say.'

'I'm twenty-nine.'

'Act like it.'

How had she got into an argument with her father this late at night? Her head throbbed with fatigue. 'I'm going to bed.'

'In the morning, pack up.'

Her foot stuck in mid-air and she exhaled sharply. She enunciated each word. 'I said I won't leave.'

'You don't understand—'

'Oh, I do understand. I understand your need to control me.' She spat.

'Aileen—'

'Tell me, *Father*, what business did you have with Erwin?'

'Nothing got to do with you.'

He still wouldn't tell her. After everything that had happened. Why didn't her father understand? 'The man was murdered!'

'And I was in the city.'

She jabbed a finger at the window. 'Who threatened you? Why don't they want you back here?'

His laugh shot icicles across the room. 'Ah, about that… Not every nugget of information is found at the library, Aileen. All of this is nothing to do with you.'

Aileen's rage froze. 'The *library*?'

'Aye, I know about your little snoop-fest the other day with a friend – what's her name? Isla, aye. Isla the baker. Do people here abandon their business for kicks?'

So he knew more about Aileen's life than he let on. But he wouldn't share information about his. Aileen persisted. 'Why is someone threatening you?'

'I didn't kill anyone. Leave it at that.'

'Help the police.'

Eean crossed his arms, mimicking Aileen's posture. 'I have nothing to say.'

'Father, why won't you co-operate? Or do you just want to be difficult?'

'I'm sure you knew the kind of man George Erwin was.'

She did, but that didn't excuse his killer.

'He cared only about his family's name and reputation. The man turned his back on his son. And under that façade, even as a student, all George did was haggle with the teachers and charm them. He got away with bullying, not getting his homework done, and failing exams. His father paid his way to medical college, pulled several favours. Why do you think he never left this bloody town? He hid behind his family name.'

'Were you in the same grade?'

'Yes. And I have always been determined and focused on my work.'

'Stubborn' came to mind for Aileen. 'Why did you want to leave Loch Fuar so badly?'

Eean made a sound, somewhere between anger and exasperation. 'What should I have done? Stay here to bake cookies and smile at the entitled arses you call guests?'

'You'd rather slave away in the city.'

'Polluted air makes you stronger and opens doors for you. The same reason I'm making you see sense.'

'Yet you can't see beyond *you*. You didn't like George Erwin so you won't help catch his killer. You don't like me having a happy life here so you want me back to the drudgery of the city. I hate it there!'

Eean's footsteps echoed in the room, thundering over her loud breaths. 'Aileen, you're not the police. Whatever your boyfriend wants to question me on, he can do that face-to-face. And I'm not obliged to answer him.' He waved a hand as if flicking the questions away. 'I say whoever killed the bastard rid the world of a malignant rat. So I'm not very concerned about his death. It might be selfish, but I have little to do with that man.'

'Why did you speak to him, then?'

'Good night, Aileen.' He stalked past her without a glance, let alone a smile.

'Father!'

She watched him thunder up the stairs, then turned to stare at the glass reflecting her face. Where they barking up the wrong tree? What had come into her father to act like that? To not only install a new window but to let it slip that he kept tabs on her. *Tabs on her as a loving father might…* Yet staying tight-lipped on Erwin?

Humans were as strange and contradictory as butter and bruises.

And she hadn't a clue how to uncover answers about her father's involvement with Erwin or the McCloughans.

Aileen fought off yawns while making breakfast the next morning.

Siobhan clicked her tongue, too cheery for 6 a.m. Her sundress matched her mood.

'I trust you had a good night?' asked Aileen.

'And I trust yours didn't include a good romp between the sheets with your beau.'

'Urgh, Gran!'

'What's got your knickers in a twist this morning?' Siobhan popped a strip of bacon in her mouth and leaned against the counter. 'This is finger-lickingly good!'

'Did Father have enemies here?'

Siobhan grunted, understanding the reason for Aileen's sour mood. 'He left when he was eighteen.'

'Gran—'

'He hated the McCloughan boy because they were both good academics and fought for the top spot in the school rankings. At least, that's what I think. But they were friends, too. I don't remember when the relationship soured. Your father and you are similar in this way – you both need to be liked.'

'If so, he wasn't very likeable towards Callan.'

Siobhan giggled, nicking another strip.

Aileen swatted her hand away.

'He's afraid. He asked me too many questions the night he met Callan. And he also called some friends to ask about a DI Callan Cameron.'

Aileen gaped at the version of her father Siobhan described. She'd never known he'd kept tabs on her. 'He... why would he be *afraid* of Callan?'

'He is a criminal attorney and has his contacts. And he asks the right questions. But as a mother, I know where he was leading with those inquisitions.'

'He wants to find dirt on Callan to convince me to leave with them.' Aileen huffed. 'Why is he so infuriating?'

'Darling Aileen. You're thick about love. He's afraid to lose his daughter to another man.'

Aileen put the lid on the pot and used a spatula to flip the salami sizzling in the pan. 'You mean he doesn't like me having a boyfriend? What about Liam?'

'Liam Darlington, ah… You were never in danger of falling in love with that fool. Your father knew Liam and somewhere in his heart he knew you'd never truly love him. But Callan? You go together like fish and chips with the perfect drizzle of vinegar.'

Siobhan could be a wee bit delusional about love. Aileen veered the conversation back to the case. 'So what about enemies other than the McCloughan's? Like Erwin?'

'George Erwin? Dim as a light, wealthy as a king. Not a great combination but unfortunately found too often in society.'

'Do you know anything about Father's connection to the two men?'

Siobhan raised her eyebrows and huffed out her breath. 'This was decades ago. Me and academics, even when it concerned my children, never got along. I didn't know what the two tykes did. I put them in uniforms and marched him off to school. Fed them later. That's where my job ended.'

'So you don't know who they hung out with?'

'As long as they did their chores, helped with the inn and I didn't hear a bad word from the teachers? They were free to do whatever.' Siobhan held up a finger. 'Except stay out after curfew. And, when they hit their teenage years, to knock up a girl and abandon her.'

Only her gran would have such rules.

But a nugget of information fought to the forefront of her mind. 'But if you say he disliked George Erwin and Jack McCloughan, do you mean they were in the same school together? At the same time?'

Siobhan nicked another strip. 'Hmm.'

Not every nugget of information is found in the library, Aileen.

Her father was mistaken: in her library at Dachaigh she had a copy of a school newspaper dating back to 1974 — the year her father graduated.

Maybe it was time to take a step back in time to solve this mystery.

CHAPTER EIGHTEEN

The day was as sour as his mood: it was pouring drops of icicles. Callan huddled into his jacket, unable to prevent the rivulets trickling down his face and knocking a shiver through him.

It was 7 a.m., and too early for Callan after a night of tossing and turning. He'd parked his car down the road thinking he'd walk up the driveway and surprise the councillor. And then the rain had picked up. Fickle summer.

Callan stepped under the porch and shook himself like a dog, uncaring if he looked silly. His finger pressed down on the doorbell with more punch than necessary. And no one answered.

He tried again, waited.

He was about to try for a third time when the

door swung open to reveal a heaving Mrs Eloise Wagner.

'Detective!' She adjusted her dressing gown. 'What brings you by this early?'

Callan crooked his elbow with a flourish and peered at his watch. 'It's 7 a.m. I was told the councillor's busy today.'

'I'm afraid you just missed him. He left five minutes ago.'

Just his luck. Callan swiped off the water beading on his jacket and flicked a stray drop off his neck.

'Please come in, Detective. Let me fix you some coffee.'

Callan followed her inside and took his jacket off. It had kept his clothes dry, at least.

'Let me get you a towel. Please take a seat.'

She walked off, called for Martha and returned with a Turkish towel, gleaming white and scented. The best for the councillor's house, he supposed.

'I'm sorry for barging in on you.'

Eloise took a seat, adjusted the robe again. 'I believe you have more questions?'

How much would the wife know? Callan thought of Ann. A wife knew.

'Do you know if your husband was in regular contact with Mr George Erwin?'

A frown marred her face, unpainted today. She hadn't awoken with her husband – the sleepy haze in her eyes told him that.

She tucked a strand of hair behind her ear. 'My husband would say he wasn't.'

'What would you say?'

'I'm not sure. You see, my husband is in contact with a lot of people. But recently… The order about the excavation in the peatlands… Melanie was upset about it, said that was George's idea. If it was, he must have been in touch with my husband.'

'Were they close?'

'I won't say close, but they weren't acquaintances either. Melanie and I often tried to arrange double dates, but we both felt our husbands weren't very keen.'

'Would you know why that was?'

Eloise twisted her fingers, staring at them for a while as if formulating an answer. 'I don't see how this helps you with George's murder.'

'I'd like to have a better clarity about the man George Erwin was.'

'According to my husband, he wasn't much.' Eloise rubbed her forehead. 'Julian isn't very fond of the man. And based on what Melanie says, George didn't make friends. He had very few friends, almost no family he was on good terms with.

'George worked hard as a doctor, according to Melanie. And he has a good reputation in town, as you may know. But whenever I'd go over after his retirement, I always found him holed up in his study. People, after retiring, often pursue hobbies.

The Erwins have such a lovely garden. Melanie was livid when he hired a gardener to do up the place instead of getting his hands dirty. And he hired plumbers and stuff. No holiday for George, not even when his wife begged him to take her on a cruise.'

Interesting, wasn't that? The man had enough cash to afford several diamond studded suites on cruise ships.

Eloise leaned ahead, charging forward with her gossip. 'I thought that was so contrary. He was always lavish with Melanie. Bags, clothes, shoes, furniture, jewellery – you name it. And let me tell you, that woman's a big spender. Nothing short of pure leather and diamonds for her.'

'Did she tell you why he refused to take her?'

'Said he was busy. Ha! Busy after retirement? But he wouldn't listen. And I felt so bad, because Julian got us a nice big room. And he took the week off. It's so rare for him to do that.'

'What do you make of Melanie and George's marriage?'

'Oh, it was as any marriage is after a few decades. Or at least I imagine so. Julian and I will be married for ten years next month. That's hardly as long as the Erwin's.'

'How do you imagine a decades old marriage?'

'A wee bit sour? Not really carving the time to hang out with each other. But too comfortable to make any changes.'

Callan had seen how decades old marriages worked first hand: his parents. And they weren't as Eloise described them. Not his parents, at least. And his mother wasn't easily pleased.

'So they didn't spend much time together?'

'That's my take, based on what Melanie says. That's the real reason George made excuses for the cruise, I'm sure. He didn't want to spend all that time with his wife. He was a weird man, not very social for a GP.'

'But he was on the Environmental Protection Committee?'

Eloise waved her hand with an eye roll. 'Wasn't Julian surprised when George came up with the idea for that? Two years ago, that was. He said how it was imperative to save our peatlands.'

'The EPC was George Erwin's idea?'

'Of course! We never knew he was that concerned with the environment. But he's an old soul. I haven't met him much, despite being friends with Melanie.'

'Did Mrs Erwin mention any sort of disagreements, stress or conflict about her husband's work?'

Eloise frowned, settled back, and toyed with the strap of her gown. After much deliberation, she shook her head. 'No, I'm not sure Melanie would know if there was such an issue.'

'Mr Erwin didn't confide in his wife?'

'It was the other way around with Melanie, Detective. I... I always think she'd have been better suited in the Victorian age. She's never had much ambition other than purchasing expensive items. She…' A blush tainted Eloise's cheek. Her gaze flitted around the room before she leaned in. 'The other day Melanie came crying to us, Julian and me, saying she didn't have a clue about their finances, that George managed everything. She didn't even know where to get the money to arrange his funeral. Who does that in this day and age?'

It wasn't lost on Callan how effortlessly the answers rolled off Eloise Wagner's lips. But he could sense the truth in the last bit of it. Melanie Erwin could very well be blind to her husband's business affairs.

'She never worked, ever. First, it was her father – she's still his little girl. And then her husband. George, as I said, took care of everything. Always. She's never wanted for anything.'

Except maybe peace of mind.

'So it was a love match between them?'

Her laugh whipped through the room, devoid of humour. 'I hope not! The Erwins have always been influential and revered in our community. George fell for her. Melanie? You'd think if she was the traditional sort, she'd do the cooking and cleaning. She made George hire help. Said she wasn't waiting on him. Now *that* is all tattle, of course.'

Callan smiled. 'Sure.'

'Oh, Detective. I feel horrible talking about my

friend like this. But this early in the morning? My brain's hardly awoken enough to function.'

'This is part of an investigation, Mrs Wagner. I won't pass the tattle on. You've been very helpful. Thank you.'

Now all he had to do was somehow cross-check whether what she said was true. And he had no clue how to do that.

Siobhan had bound the 1974 edition of the annual school round-up, a supplement of the student newspaper. For all her talk about keeping her children fed and staying out of their academics, Siobhan sure was proud of her sons. She had tucked countless scrapbooks and memorabilia from their wonder years into the upper bookshelf of the library.

Aileen clung to the last rung of the ladder, shuffling through each scrapbook. If her father wasn't about to tell her, she would find out. The issue wasn't a lack of information; it was wading through the bunch of books to find the information she wanted.

Hugging three books to her chest, Aileen descended and dropped the books in one of the high-backed chairs. She hiked up again and picked four more books, praying she didn't find herself on her arse and the ladder on top of her.

It took four rounds to get the ones she wanted. There were still more photo albums, and others belonging to her uncle.

Aileen stared at the twenty books and huffed. Her only reprieve was the ability to go through them sitting in her study, in her pyjamas if she wanted. There were no planned check-ins today. Her inn was full, and she'd hired a team of three to clean up for the duration of the summer months.

After surviving the debt debacle, she had put her business knowledge to use. That being said, she had yet to plan the menu.

She'd rather dig through her father's past. And uncover details she'd never be able to forget.

Aileen plopped into the other chair, toed off her shoes, and plucked out the first book – the annual supplement of the school newspaper from the year her father graduated.

The first page was a half-page picture of five pupils, their uniforms starched within an inch of their lives. Aileen recognised the boy in the centre with a small smile and straight shoulders. He stood an inch taller than the one next to him. Her father with Jack McCloughan. Bingo. Jack had his hands on his blazer's lapels and beamed at the camera, a smile reminiscent of Pluto's.

Aileen didn't recognise the other three girls.

The five of them stood behind a huge trophy with a globe on it, held afloat by two criss-crossing metallic fronds.

Her father had been the team captain when they won the national debate competition. Their arguments on the positive outcomes of change in British society had floored the judges, as well as their opposing team.

According to the article, the finalists had been called to tea at the Palace of Holyroodhouse in Edinburgh, and then packed off to Europe for the next leg of the competition.

Aileen frowned. Her father had never mentioned going to Europe for a debate competition. He'd left for the city the month after graduation to study law.

Did he not go to the championship? Did they lose?

She could hardly ask him, not after the words they had exchanged last night.

Aileen read the rest of the paper and found her father had also topped his final exams. And submitted an essay in French for another essay writing competition and bagged first place.

She shut the paper and pulled out the next book. And the next. The more she read, Aileen realised why she'd been such a disappointment to him. The man wasn't just an overachiever, he'd done more in his eighteen years than Aileen had accomplished in almost thirty.

Stacked with a room full of trophies and certificates, the man had interned under the best lawyers and taken over that firm and soared it to new heights: more international awards, and high-profile cases followed.

In some of the later snippets her gran had pinned to the scrapbooks, Eean Mackinnon in partnership with Ann Mackinnon had won over juries and overturned false convictions. A true power couple.

And their daughter? Here she sat.

The disappointment her parents must feel about her flooded her system. A colossal failure she was. But…

She wanted this life. Aileen bit her lip. Now wasn't the time to wallow in self-pity. *Find the clues.*

She leafed through more, and didn't find any mention of George Erwin. But Jack McCloughan was right up there with her father. Why the man had left it all to become a distiller, Aileen didn't know. With grades like his, he'd be as successful as her father. Perhaps the man wanted to become a distiller, despite Pluto's resistance.

His passion, he'd said to Aileen, the night Ricky struck her. He hadn't stood up for himself but toiled in another distillery because he'd wanted that.

It was all about choices.

Why did her father leave this town in a hurry? Was that the dream?

Had there been a catalyst?

Aileen cracked open a velvety photo album and her smile bloomed at the first picture. Her father and mother in a tight embrace with her squashed in the centre. She didn't remember this photograph. Her parents had swaddled her in blankets and she'd shut her eyes, ignorant of the world as only toddlers were.

The love in her parents' eyes, for her and each other, smacked her upside the head. That love would drive her father to keep tabs on her, to pull favours, and to run a thorough background check on Callan.

He's afraid. Was he?

She moaned at the barrage of questions woven with emotions, as heavy as an elephant.

The next pictures were of her parents, clutching her against their chests, peppering her with kisses and cooing at her. A tear trickled down her cheek, and she swiped it away. She was being silly. There was no need to cry. None at all.

She flipped through the rest of it and found the entire album littered with pictures like that. The second album was all about her parents. Them on some beach holiday, then somewhere in the lush wilderness.

Aileen didn't remember her family ever taking holidays but there her parents were, most surely not photoshopped, holding hands and grinning at the camera.

She snapped the album shut and went for the last one, hoping it wasn't more sloppy stuff. Idiot as she was, dampness still prevailed in her eyes, the pictures stamped on the backs of her eyelids.

She breathed out in relief. This album was only of her father, before he had a ring on his finger or a baby in his arms. Him in Loch Fuar.

Aileen smashed her lips together, leaning in now for some information.

A page in and she wished she'd braced herself.

Her father, grinning like a drunk, bottle in hand, shoulder to shoulder with Jack McCloughan. Her father and uncle lounging in front of a car, gleaming under a blue sky. She knew the car couldn't be theirs.

Mugshots of the two of them. Only Siobhan would treasure those.

And several happy moments: her father at his graduation, him with the trophy, and several more with people she didn't recognise.

It hit her then, how little she knew of her father or his life before her.

Scary, wasn't it, to think that she knew her parents for only half of their life? The other half lost to the past, stuck in photographs.

She saw the carefree, laughter-struck version of Eean Mackinnon. A smile she didn't recall him cracking at her, but he had, based on these previous albums.

Aileen got to a picture of her gran, her hair fluffed around her in a tapestry of gleaming blond and brown, eyes glowing, arm in arm with her eldest.

She flipped through more photographs and

landed on one. It sent a feeling of deep sorrow through to her bones.

The image, barely four inches tall and three inches wide, black and white with some warm tones, its edges frayed, and some parts faded to white.

She recognised Siobhan in her wedding dress, flowers blooming in her cascading hair. The glint in her eyes just as it was today. The dress accentuated her vase-like figure, just like a movie star, and a face to match.

Siobhan had been a beauty. And the man next to her, Aileen had only ever seen in photographs her gran treasured: Edward Mackinnon. The love of Siobhan's life.

Beside this photograph was the same couple, the smiles on their face more indulgent and a baby in Edward's arms. Her father.

Aileen gnawed on her lip to keep her emotions from fizzing over the surface. What was it with her? Dammit.

Love and loss were a part of life. But to argue when that love existed between people who breathed? It was a waste of time.

She moved on to the next leaf and frowned at a plain image of the sky. No family here. She traced that photograph and frowned. Something wasn't right.

The plastic crackled when she dipped her hand in between the sheets and gasped. There was another photograph stuck to its back. She plucked it out and blinked.

Colours splashed in this professionally staged picture; a backdrop of pink flowers, green grass and yellow sunlight meshed together to give it a dreamy feel. The photograph had slightly washed out over time, fading the two people in the image.

She recognised her father, although his posture wasn't as relaxed as in the photographs with her mother in his arms. He looked almost restless.

And Eean Mackinnon wasn't looking at the camera. His gaze was riveted on the woman in his arms. It wasn't her mother or her grandmother. She had blond hair nipped at the chin, and red lipstick on her stretched lips. Her blue dress matched the pocket handkerchief in her father's suit's pocket. They embraced each other and…

Aileen gasped.

The woman had a ring on her ring finger.

Oh god. Her father had a fiancé here. At eighteen? The woman didn't look much older. And who hid this photograph in here?

Her father had been right. Some things were better left in the past.

Oh shit.

CHAPTER NINETEEN

Aileen hefted the bag from the back seat and slammed the car door. The smell of warm bread and molten chocolate loomed over the street. Isla was baking. The intensity of the aroma doubled when the door to the bakery shut behind her.

At 2 p.m., it wasn't crowded yet. And Aileen planned to borrow some of her best friend's scant time.

Isla popped up from behind the counter and frowned at her. 'Where have you been? I haven't seen you for days. Where is the menu?'

Aileen held up a bag. 'I bring sleuthing work.'

'If it's anything like that library, that's hardly a peace offering.'

'It involves good old gossip.'

'I'm not helping you.'

'Please? Pretty please? I'll babysit Carly, so you and Daniel can have the evening to yourselves.'

'Babysitting Carly is not a chore for you. All you do is eat chocolate and dance like lunatics.'

Aileen held up the bag. 'Some Mackinnon gossip? Pretty please?'

'Urgh. My office!' Isla followed behind her, muttering curses. 'I give up too easily.'

'If you did, you wouldn't be the Queen of Gossipmongers.'

'And proud of it, too.' Isla plopped into her chair. 'What do you have for me?'

Aileen grinned at Isla's flushed face and flour-stained cheeks. 'Were you rolling around in sugar?'

'I don't kiss and tell.'

Aileen opened the zip to reveal a set of books. 'In the library at Dachaigh Gran has an entire shelf dedicated to family memories. These all belong to my father, and include my mother and me. I went through them, but I need a fresh perspective.'

Isla pulled a photo album towards her. 'These don't look like the parents who'd force you to do anything.'

'Don't go there. Jeez, Isla, those pictures… Just go through them and find a clue. Something for me to dig into.'

'If you clear the air with them, things could work out.'

'Father won't answer any of my questions.'

'And your mother?'

'She's been hovering over me since I came home from the hospital. It's strange.'

Isla flipped a page. 'This shows a family in love.'

'I know.' Tears threatened her eyes. 'I'm such a stupid fool! Gran says Father's afraid of Callan.'

A giggle burbled from Isla's lips and she laughed until tears leaked from her eyes. 'Siobhan hit the nail on the head.'

Aileen blinked, baffled. 'What?'

'Who is this?' Isla held up the picture of her father embracing that young woman. Aileen had tucked it into a fresh leaf so it wouldn't fade further.

'Is that an—'

'Engagement ring. And that's not my mother.'

'You know your parents had a life before they met each other. You can't be upset over something that happened before they met.'

'I know that, but he's never mentioned an ex.' Not that she had to Callan either…

Isla stabbed at the picture. 'Why is it faded?'

'I found it hidden behind this other picture.'

'That's strange. Maybe your father regrets the relationship. It looks old, and the couple's standing far off from the camera. Siobhan might know who that is.'

Her gran had been in bed today after sipping a finger or two too much of her beloved whisky. She was incorrigible. Aileen had left her snoring.

Next Isla picked up the student annual supplement and raised her eyebrows. 'Your father's sure handsome. And smart.'

'In that sense, the apple fell too far from the tree.'

'I disagree. But, Aileen, isn't this Jack Mc-Cloughan?'

Aileen nodded. 'He's everywhere – the debate competition, elocution competition, next to my father in the merit list, them arm in arm in one of those photographs.'

'And you said they hated each other.'

A lightbulb switched on in Aileen's head. 'Oh, ooh. Gran said they used to be friends!'

Isla leaned over, stabbing at the front page of the newsletter. 'Look at them, shoulder to shoulder, grinning at the camera. The last month of school before graduation.'

'And father hightailed it out of here a month later.'

'Why did he wait a month?'

Aileen shrugged. It was anyone's guess. 'Perhaps he waited to help Gran through the summer months and settle matters.'

'Or fight with a friend and leave, never wanting to come back here.'

That would explain why Jack didn't want Aileen at his property. The two best friends had had a major fight. 'I should go talk to Jack.'

'Not alone!' Isla shook her head. 'After last time – don't be ridiculous.'

'Jack didn't hurt me. Besides, it's afternoon. The distillery will be swarming with guests.'

'Aileen…'

Aileen massaged her forehead, trying to soothe her swirling thoughts. She couldn't see straight anymore. It was a lot of information to process. It would all be made easier if her father just talked. Damn him. 'I have to talk to Jack.'

Isla huffed. 'You know you are the spit of your father, personality wise: smart, stubborn and determined?'

Aileen pushed off from the table. 'Thank you, Isla.'

'Keep tabs on your phone! And stay safe!'

Aileen huffed. She would. Perhaps she'd even tell Callan and demand a ride. Lord knew her car wouldn't survive another ditch on the McCloughans' roads.

EEAN SHOVED CLOTHES INTO HIS SUITCASE, WANTING nothing more than to flee. The noose was tightening around his neck, as it had so many years ago. He'd been eighteen, gasping for breath. The intensity of it had him leaving everything behind.

And his daughter had found the books. Smart. She was too brilliant. And he had given her the clue. Some answers were in the library alone.

He didn't have the strength in him to answer

her questions, to speak to her about the past. The past should lie in history, as unseen and unheard as the dark ages.

Eean's breath puffed out, and his heart palpitated. He couldn't inhale enough oxygen. His hands trembled.

He dumped his laptop in his work bag and zipped up the suitcase, not caring if clothes got rumpled.

'Ann! Ann!'

Her footsteps raced down the corridor, muffled and familiar. But even she couldn't loosen this noose. He needed to breathe.

She burst through the door, panting. 'Eean! What are you—'

'We're leaving.'

'Now? Without Aileen?'

'She can stay here and rot if she chooses to.'

Ann paused, seeing through his façade. His cold poison never worked on her. 'What happened?'

'I said we're—'

'Didn't you argue with me the other day that Aileen had to come with us? That's why we stayed. You had your PA change your schedule!'

Eean waved his hands. 'I've changed my mind.'

'Eean, that's not like you.'

'I'm not me here. We've to go!'

Ann's eyes crinkled, the wrinkles making her appear so much more beautiful. 'Sweetheart, not everyone's raised amongst green meadows. It's beautiful here. I found a brochure on the reception counter. They have trails that—'

'Stink of cattle dung.'

'What's put you in a sour mood?'

Did he have another mood besides sour? He needed air.

'Did Siobhan say anything to you? Did Aileen?'

'I let them down. I let history repeat itself. I have to leave.'

'What are you talking about?'

She didn't know. He'd never told her; never wanted to. Why? To keep her safe. To never give her a chance to see how out of her league he was. He pulled her closer and buried his nose in her hair. It became a tad easier to inhale.

She wrapped him in an embrace. 'What is it?'

'Complicated. It's anything but easy when the past comes back to haunt you. I graduated with dreams, Ann. And no one was allowed to come between them and me. Not morals, not blood, nor love. I bulldozed everything and left disaster in my wake. Yet here I am, with more than I deserve.' Eean burrowed into his wife until not even a hair could slip between them. 'I'm once again too late to help. Too late because I was busy chasing my own dreams. I haven't changed. We weren't here when our daughter fought for her life. No, I was too far away to get here to her—'

'We tried everything. If it wasn't for the storm—'

'Those are excuses, Ann. If we aren't here for our baby, what's the point? Why are you smiling?'

'She's almost thirty.'

'Still our baby.'

'You have to tell her, you know, from time to time. That you love her. And so do I.'

'I've let her down. The one I should have put above everything else. I let her down.'

Ann pursed her lips. 'We have time yet. Running away won't solve anything. You say you don't want the past to repeat itself. So unlike the past, don't run away. Stay and fight.'

'I can't.'

'You can, sweetheart.'

Eean caressed his wife's back, seeing the love in her eyes. With her on his side, he had overcome so many uphill battles. This was the biggest of them all and here she was, willing to stand by his side even when she knew little, so very little.

He had to start small. Begin with apologies. And this bit that tied to his past, he had to overcome alone. Eean nodded. 'Fine, we'll stay. But first I need to head out, start repairing my wrongs.'

'I'm here.'

'And I'll need you when I talk to our daughter.'

Ann kissed his lips, muttered her love for him, and stepped aside. 'Best of luck.'

CALLAN SCRATCHED HIS CHIN AS HE STUDIED HIS murder board for the thousandth time. He'd etched the thing on his mind with permanent marker and yet he couldn't find the pattern.

Halston's team had done a thorough sweep of the cellar in which Aileen had woken up. It had three entrances: one connected to each house and a tunnel leading out onto the peatlands.

Callan stabbed at the diagram he'd drawn of the cellar, the houses, and the tunnel. It bothered him that the tunnel led to the same spot where they found George Erwin's body. And the fact that they'd found the tunnel with minimum cobwebs, in use for the bootlegging operation. Ricky had blocked its entrance the afternoon he'd assaulted Aileen, other-wise anyone had free access to the cellar.

Could the killer have used it?

But they had also found the footprints, two sets from the layby to that spot: one belonged to an ex-pensive shoe and the other as ordinary as you could find. The ordinary shoes had retreated to the layby.

Who was that? If it wasn't Pluto or Ricky, that left Jack or Sarah. Why would they hike to the layby and back, and then rush over to Pluto's? He had timed someone running over from the house, and it hadn't worked. But if someone had used this tun-nel, they could make it in time to find Aileen hiding under the sofa.

Was he looking for two killers? Or a witness?

Callan's ears perked up. Footsteps, light and familiar, strode towards his office. He turned, a frown at the ready for Aileen. Think of the devil…

'Jack!' She didn't give Callan a chance to talk. She threw a bag as big and heavy as Santa's onto the visitor's chair. Aileen panted, hands on her waist. 'Jack and my father. I found the link.' She pointed to the bag. 'They were friends. And then something happened the month after they graduated.'

'Show me.'

She laid out the books, spluttering without inhaling a breath. Something about her father, his fiancé, Jack McCloughan, their competition, friendship, and then her father's break for the city. 'So you see, they were friends!'

'And you think Jack still holds a grudge against your father?'

'Didn't he spit at me for being a Mackinnon?'

Callan pressed the bridge of his nose. 'Be that as it may, it doesn't explain why he might kill Erwin.'

Aileen paused, eyes wide, hands hanging in the air. 'But… but he has a .44, and Erwin threatened to expose his family's secret. And now he has a connection to my father, and could have printed that sheet of paper and thrown that stone through the window. He is strong enough.'

Callan plucked the annual supplement and stared at Eean Mackinnon's name at the top of the merit list.

The local school still published such a supplement. Callan's mother had his tucked away somewhere in the attic. Callan remembered the exuberance with which Blaine had shown him the paper. Being smart, Blaine had topped the merit list, like Eean, and also won first place in a national piano competition.

Callan sighed at the memory. He had plenty of those. They popped up once in a while to pile on the guilt and to remind him of the life Gerald Erwin had robbed from Blaine. It hurt, always.

He moved his attention to the supplement dated 1974, predating him by almost a decade and a half. The school paper listed out every student who had graduated that year. The list was long. Callan skimmed over the familiar names:

Eean Mackinnon, George Erwin, Jack McCloughan...

And then a small snippet listed Jack Mc-Cloughan, Charles McCool, Lucia Smith, Melanie Matthews, Meredith Lincoln, and Derrick Johnson as the school's rifle shooting team who'd won second place in a national competition.

Jack was the team leader. Goes to show that he was good at that too. Good enough to shoot in the dark and hit his target perfectly.

'I have to go chat with Jack McCloughan. I have questions.'

'I THINK YOU SHOULD DRIVE SLOWER.'

Callan pulled the handbrake and jumped out of the vehicle, not waiting for Aileen to follow.

She scampered after him. 'Hold on!'

'I think *you* should wait in the car.' He couldn't understand why she insisted on coming. She'd found a connection between Jack and her father. Her work was done. But the woman was a Mackinnon: stubborn.

He shot her a glare before circling Pluto's house to head to the cottage at the back. Both houses were dark, the windows shielded with curtains.

Callan's fist connected with the door. 'Jack Mc-Cloughan!' He waited a beat before hammering on the door again. 'Open up!'

'Hey!' Someone shouted from behind them.

Callan swished around. 'Hell!' He pulled Aileen behind him.

Jack held a revolver. The clouds gathered in the sky above his head, making him appear like a superhero about to avenge a victim. Callan wasn't sure the man was a superhero.

'We'd like to have a word.'

'Goodness!' He dropped the revolver. 'You startled me, banging like that. We're wrapping up for the day.'

Callan stepped aside so Aileen could see. 'We have questions.'

Jack huffed and stepped up to unlock the door. 'Fine. It's about to pour, so make it quick. Darned summer!'

If Jack knew why they were there, he didn't give it away. He invited them in, cranked up the radiator and led them to the sitting area.

'We're here about George Erwin.'

The sigh that left Jack's lips was a reminder of the nuisance Erwin's murder had been for the Mc-Cloughans. A split-second mistake or premeditated murder? 'What about Erwin? I thought we answered all your questions.'

'Did you know about the files Erwin maintained about his patients?'

'No. Isn't that illegal?' He frowned. 'You should investigate that. His patients won't be happy to hear he kept their private info.'

'Private data evokes powerful emotions in others, Mr McCloughan.'

'Were you in talks with George Erwin?' Aileen said.

'I told you, anyone in the company could have used our landline number. It wasn't me. I didn't like the man. And even in death, he's nothing but an inconvenience. Why would I have anything to do with it? Perhaps Father was trying to dissuade Erwin telling everyone about the tombs.'

Callan jostled Aileen's arm and pointed to her satchel. He wanted the folder she'd tucked in it. He snagged it from her. 'You have a firearms certificate?'

'I already told you I do.'

'Do you use your .44 revolver regularly?'

'Yes.'

'Do you own any unregistered weapons?'

Jack waved at the revolver where it now rested against the wall on its stand. 'That's the only one I have.'

'Have you used your father's revolvers recently?'

'I didn't kill Erwin.'

'Please answer the question, sir.'

'I didn't use any of my father's because, as Aileen will tell you, we don't get along. And he doesn't like me touching his things.'

'But you have a key to his house.'

'He is old and Ricky, as you might know, isn't capable of caring for him.'

Callan jotted it down on his notepad. 'What about the cellar?'

'It's been there ever since I can remember; sans the whisky barrels. It used to be a cellar to store alcohol bottles, but Mum had it converted into a dump of sorts. She loved redecorating and when she removed pieces of furniture, she stored them there for later use. I haven't been down there since she died.'

'Is the cellar also connected to your house?' He knew the answer, wanted to know if Jack would lie.

'I think so. This used to be the old servant's quarters and was connected to the main house via a bridge. When the Ridges moved in, Father had the bridge taken down. But we still have the door that leads to the cellar.' He clomped over to the wall behind Aileen and crouched where the carpet ended.

Aileen's eyes lit up. 'Is that a trapdoor?'

'Bolted from here and not used.'

'Hold on, Mr McCloughan.' Callan peeled the carpet back, studying the trapdoor. Twenty-four inches square. Enough to fit a human and his revolver. 'This leads to the cellar?'

Jack pointed downwards. 'Into the tunnel first. The other trapdoor is at the main house and leads straight into the cellar. Aaron had this one remade for kicks back when the cellar was nothing but a furniture dump.'

Aileen tilted her head. 'Didn't the wooden furniture spoil in the damp?'

'The tunnel had a door. And the room was tiled.'

'Why don't you open this door and show us?'

Jack shook his head. 'I'm not sure it'll open.'

If the door swung with ease, his theory of Jack using the tunnel to get to Erwin could be plausible. If it stuck…

Jack reached for the bolt, but Callan stopped him. 'Let me.'

He pulled on his gloves, leaned over to grip the iron lock and tugged. It didn't budge.

Callan tried again, and it slid enough to shake off encrusted mud. But it was far too heavy for him.

'Aaron made it heavy so none of us children

could go down there. You need two people to lift it up.'

'Thank you for showing us, Mr McCloughan.' Callan pointed to the suitcases in the corner. 'Going somewhere?'

'I'm headed to a conference. After all that's happened… Father packed off to my cousin's. Sarah and I decided to make a trip out of this conference.'

'What happens to the distillery, then?'

'Delegated a few tasks, as a good business owner should.' And like Pluto never had.

If Jack didn't have access to this door, he couldn't have made it to the crime scene and back in time. The man had motive and means, but a tight alibi, if the timing of the shots were to be believed.

Callan shook his head. The more he thought about it, the more Jack seemed to be innocent.

'Who is that?' asked Aileen.

He turned to her. Her face had paled to white. She gazed at one of the many picture frames on Jack's wall littered with smiling faces.

Beside him, Jack stiffened. 'No one.'

'Jack… That's my father, right there. Who is the woman next to him?'

'No one he'll remember now.' Jack ground his teeth. 'Nothing but his dirty little secret, wasn't she?'

'What do you mean?'

'It's none of your business.'

'Jack—'

'It's none of your damn business! He treated her like a chewing gum stuck to his boot by the end of it. Didn't care for the rock he'd put on her finger. Hadn't even introduced her to his mother. Then he dumped her and moved on. A bastard, all right. Your father's a bastard. No morals.'

'Who is that woman, Mr McCloughan?'

'A lieutenant general's overprotected daughter who deserved better than what she got. Had to marry that darned doctor! She's nothing to do with your case. If you're done, I'll see you out.'

'But—'

Callan wrapped his arms around Aileen and dragged her out the door. His mind had just clicked a few facts into place.

CHAPTER TWENTY

Dean knocked on the door, refusing to acknowledge the ball of anxiety, regret, guilt and much more burgeoning in his throat.

Ann was right. It was time to set things right, not repeat vicious patterns.

No one responded, so he tried again.

Jack hadn't been very cordial, had almost slammed the door in his face. It was hard to utter an apology. But this? He knew this would be much tougher.

More emotions involved. Stupid emotions. He hadn't had a rendezvous with them for a long time.

The click of heels sounded through the door. She was on the other side.

Breath stuttered in his lungs and his heart pounded.

The moment she appeared in the doorframe, his eyes drank her in, remembering her lush hair, twinkling eyes, slender stature, and the laugh. But now he found none of those.

'Eean.'

He swallowed, recognising her voice. But the woman in front of him didn't match. This was not the Melanie he loved decades ago. This was a husk. A doppelganger with hollow cheeks, a balding head, dead eyes and sad wrinkles. The sad wrinkles cut his heart.

She'd been his light in the dark tunnel, his cheerleader. As if the sun that glinted off her blond hair shone through her every second of the day.

'Melanie.'

'You're too late, Eean.'

He slammed his palm against the door, still staring at the thin woman. 'I want to talk. To apologise.'

She flipped her hair over her shoulder, revealing fallen strands. 'I don't think I can.'

'It's been decades, and——'

'They've been hell for me, Eean. Time has been my enemy and you should know that's your fault.'

'Please, let's sit and talk this through.'

'You're four decades too late.'

'Ann, my wife, says speaking through things helps.'

'Helps with what? Your guilt?'

'Please.' The plea sounded foreign on his

tongue, but he had used it with Jack. His profession had taught him men were easier in forgiving and forgetting. Not that Jack had done either of those.

A scorned woman?

'Please.'

Melanie's eyes narrowed, and her mouth pursed. Her skin looked dry, her lips chapped.

Eean rushed inside the moment she stepped to the side. She shut the door and led him to a living room of sorts.

His skin itched at the dark timber, as claustrophobic as an abandoned tavern. The sofa and armchair were in a dull puce shade. The dim lights invited in melancholy.

Their footsteps echoed like a death knell. The air felt suspended, as if George Erwin had sucked the life out of this house and his wife.

Eean swallowed, unable to crack even the slightest of smiles. More guilt piled into his gut.

Melanie dropped into the armchair, leaving him to take the sofa. 'Speak.'

He licked his lips, unable to form words. How did you apologise for a colossal, life-changing… mistake? But he couldn't consider his choices a mistake.

'I'm sorry, Melanie, for how life turned out.'

Her laugh smarted like a whip on raw flesh. 'I wouldn't call having a smart daughter and a strong marriage a sorry state for you.'

She wasn't making this easier. 'For you. I'm sorry.'

'That you left me? Left me so vulnerable I succumbed to a scam like George Erwin? You knew how oppressive he was. A numbskull with a silver spoon in his mouth that his father kept feeding him from. To shrivel in his shadow, and…' She gestured to herself, tears leaking down her face, staining her skin. 'This is what's become of me. Happy now?'

'Mel—'

'An unsympathetic husband and murdering son! The stress, Eean! All because you didn't want me.'

She was right, all of it. But… Eean intertwined his hands. He hadn't led her down the altar to George. All he had done was— Hell!

'I just wanted something beyond—'

'A life with me?' Her shriek reverberated through his skull and rang out in his ears. 'You prioritised Saville Row suits and sports cars over *me*?'

His life hadn't consisted of bespoke luxury for a long time. Ann and he had survived on canned food and bread for the first five years of their relationship. Not a bed of roses or a meander through a park. Melanie wouldn't understand that. She didn't like struggle.

She stabbed a finger at him. 'You gave me an ultimatum: my family or you. You never bothered to promise you'd return. Instead you moved to the city and found yourself a new woman.'

'Melanie, don't bring my wife into this. You and I called it off before I left.'

She held up her left hand and wiggled her ring finger. 'You had put a ring on this very finger. Remember, Eean? You said you wanted a lifetime with me. But you gave your vows to someone else, had a family with someone else!'

'Please, Melanie. Calm—'

'You wanted me to leave this and head to the city with you when you had no money. What was I to do? Make a home in a tiny matchbox and eat dry bread?'

'I wanted a better life, Melanie! And you knew—'

'Knew? I wanted to stay here, and you weren't willing to compromise.'

He wasn't willing to compromise, no. Eean knew that and was arrogant enough to think she'd change her mind about it. That his dream of making it big in the city and buying her all the things she wanted would make her move with him. That it wouldn't be such a struggle if they were together.

Aye, he'd been naïve. Too naïve to think what they had was enough. Meeting Ann had taught him otherwise.

His heart hurt for Melanie. She hadn't found what she'd wanted. 'I'm sorry for the way life's treated you.'

'You don't care! You strut in here, with your

fancy car and wife. You don't answer my calls!' Melanie bounced up and paced towards the back window. 'I called you. I begged you to come rescue me!'

'I—'

'You were a day too late!'

She whirled around, a revolver in her hand. And she knew how to use it.

His throat went dry. 'You killed him?'

Tears leaked down her face, blurring her makeup. 'You made me do it!' Her hand trembled.

She might end up killing them both.

'I called you every night after George went to bed. I called and begged for help. And you didn't have time! You never had time for me!'

They hadn't been close, hadn't so much as spoken since he left. Then she'd called him out of the blue.

'All you did was tell me to get help!'

'There was little I could do.'

'You made me kill him. I wanted out. So I had to kill him.' Melanie stalked towards him, head shaking, eyes wide. A terrible nightmare. 'He was blackmailing my best friend's husband, every one of my friends! No one would talk to me. And when I told him to stop? That bastard laughed in my face!

'My son murdered a boy, and he hid it. No one would talk to us when your daughter exposed us. The shame! The shame of it! And then he blackmails others. I had to put a stop to it, or I would have shrivelled into an old lonely hag. He didn't look at me once like you used to. Didn't mean it when he said he loved me. He only loved money.'

'Melanie.'

'Shut up!'

Eean breathed through the panic, tried to recollect survival tactics. But all that flashed in his mind were Aileen's questions. Aye, his daughter had been right. What he knew, his past, it had all mattered. And now he'd never get a chance to tell her how much he loved her.

'Get up! Get up! I don't want your blood staining my house.'

'Ple— please, Melanie.'

'I pleaded once. *Remember*, Eean? I pleaded for you to not leave. *Pleaded*. And you? You took off.' She stabbed the barrel into his chest and spat in his face. 'You deserve to die.'

'CALLAN! JACK SAID SHE MARRIED A DOCTOR! And—'

'You were right!'

Aileen froze, her eyes ready to pop out of her head.

'You were spot on about your father being in the centre of it all. It's Melanie Erwin; nee Matthews. She is Lieutenant General Matthews' daughter. That man…' Callan brandished his phone. 'That man has a license—'

'There's a Melanie Matthews who won second place in a rifle shooting competition in 1974.'

They were such fools to suspect everyone apart from the very person who had access to everything – even the printer in George Erwin's office.

A shrill ring trilled over the rustling of the leaves. Her mother. She was tempted to ignore it, let it go to voicemail, but…

'Hell—'

'Your father's missing. He told me he was fighting.'

'Fighting?'

'Making amends with the past.'

Aileen grasped Callan's arm. 'My father! He's with Melanie.' He had gone straight to Melanie Erwin – to a killer – to apologise for the past.

Like she had with Melanie's son.

'I've got to go!' She cut the call and glared at Jack, who'd stepped out of his house with a suitcase. 'Melanie Er—'

Boom. That wasn't the rumble of thunder.

'A gunshot!' Jack dropped the bags, braced. 'From the back! The peatlands!'

'Jack, call the police now.'

Aileen followed behind Callan, her feet moving of their own accord.

'Stay—'

'No way.' Raindrops smacked against her face

and déjà vu wrapped around her. They'd come a full circle.

They raced around rocks and stumbled over fallen branches, shivering in the breeze. But they continued. The wet peat sucked her boots. She tripped and pushed her limbs harder, jumping over a cluster of earth.

'What is it with you Mackinnons? Running into a burning fire like a damn firefighter?'

Darkness twisted around them and mist ran circles like a tornado.

'He couldn't have known.' The burn in her eyes turned into tears. 'Oh, where are they?'

He didn't respond to her.

Dread clawed. 'Callan?'

'Tread carefully.'

She continued and felt him beside her. He was drenched, but the look on his face was haunted.

'What's—'

He stumbled. Her hand shot out to grab him, and she realised he was trembling. 'Are you—'

'I'm okay. Stay behind me.'

They ran through the sheets of rain, water trickling into her trousers and her socks. Callan shielded her behind him, and she heard his low rumble despite the patter. She followed him into what felt like a timeless abyss. Thunder crackled overhead, and lightning ignited the silhouettes of trees.

Callan pivoted to the right, and she saw the wall

of trees. She'd been here, under a heavy dose of unconsciousness, hurt and bleeding.

Branches bowed and splattered water, such was the intensity of the storm. Just their luck. Aileen prayed to the gods above, those that played their fate like a puppet's strings, to keep them safe.

I want to tell my father I'm sorry.

Callan's hand clasped her arm, and he tugged her towards a tree. He placed his finger over his lips, commanding her silence. Something white reflected in his eyes.

She peered through the trees and saw the white torchlight illuminating a tent.

They were here.

Aileen wanted to leap into the clearing and demand Melanie let go of her father. But she wasn't stupid. She faced Callan, her back squashed against the tree stump with him at her front, his breath warming her forehead.

'The SOCO team built a tent over the tombs. Chances are she's taken him in there. Stay behind me at all times.'

A thought struck along with the lightning. 'Where's backup?'

'They're too far away to get here.' His blue eyes flashed into hers. 'Stay behind me, got it?'

And he moved. Like a puma, he slithered between the trees, his black clothes camouflaging with the dark.

Aileen put one foot in front of the other, tumbling over a fallen tree branch. If it weren't for the rain, they'd have been caught. Eejit. She refocused on the land: the tree barks, fallen branches, ditches, pines, moss.

Rain continued to crash against the earth, but when they hit the innermost tree, she saw it: a silhouette illuminated by a fluorescent white. It moved, just one person.

Aileen's heart leaped, seeing the figure, a woman's figure. Melanie. Where was her father?

The sheets of the tent fluttered, distorting the figure.

Aileen let go of the final tree. Her feet pounded on the floor before she realised she'd made a beeline for the tent's entrance. She'd promised to stay behind, but her father…

Where was he?

Her father…

Salt joined the scent of earth on her tongue. She loved him. And she hadn't told him. All she'd done was argue.

An iron shackle yanked her back, her waist pinned against Callan's. 'Stay back!' He threw her behind him, like she weighed nothing.

He lurched ahead, lunging into the tent.

Her boyfriend and father, the two men she loved most in this world, were inside that tent with a madwoman wielding a gun.

Her heart was in her throat.

Aileen followed Callan.

A loud shriek—

Boom. Dust splattered into the air.

She ducked, blinked and heard— 'Aileen!'

Her father.

Callan cursed, his voice inaudible over Melanie's cries.

Boom.

Rocks splintered everywhere, blinding her. Aileen threw herself towards her father's voice. His scent hit her, and her arm connected with flesh.

'Father! Dad!'

'What in the world are you doing here?'

She felt his face, head, arms. 'Are you hurt?'

'No.' And he embraced her, cocooning her into him.

Bright light flashed in her eyes, and she heard a thunder of boots. The cavalry had arrived.

Aileen turned to see what was happening and screamed. 'He's been shot! Help!'

Callan lay on the ground beside Melanie, blood oozing around him.

Oh, hell.

CHAPTER TWENTY-ONE

'Drive faster! I'm not a porcelain doll.'

Aileen snorted. 'Not porcelain, but a human who almost got shot.'

'The bullet barely grazed my arm.'

'You were unconscious.'

'Was not.'

Aileen rolled her eyes at her boyfriend. He'd frightened her when he lay unresponsive in the tent. Apparently, he couldn't hear her over the ringing in his ears from the gunshot.

She manoeuvred a bend in the road before intertwining their hands. The doctors had bandaged Callan's left arm, which had taken the worst of it: a grazed bullet wound and a sprained wrist. They'd advised him to refrain from picking up heavy objects or jostling the arm too much.

Aileen took a deep breath, thanking god for

keeping him safe. The oaf had gone against a gun-wielding madwoman. 'Thank you, Callan.'

'What did I do?'

Her eyes prickled. She could've lost him that night. Him or her father. 'Thank you for rushing in to save my father. He was rude to you, yet you risked your life for him.'

'It's the job, love.'

'You go above and beyond.'

Callan opened his mouth to say something, but shook his head.

Dachaigh loomed ahead. Its whitewashed walls gleamed under the sunlight, and its blue doors and windows matched the clear sky.

Aileen's parents had insisted on meeting Callan after his discharge from the hospital. She'd barely seen them the last two days as she'd been next to Callan's bed, ensuring he took his medicines. And now he'd stay at Dachaigh until the doctors gave him the 'all clear'.

Aileen cleared her throat. 'There's something I want to say. My parents don't own me anymore. And it's time I believe that.' She turned the car into the car park. Once she turned off the engine, she faced Callan. 'I want to start a catering business, and stay here with you, solve crimes, get into trouble, argue and make up. I love Dachaigh. If my parents cannot see what makes me happy, I won't change my life for them.'

Callan squeezed her hand and tugged her

closer. 'And I'm right here to support you.' He dropped a kiss on her forehead. 'Your mother's at the back door. I think we should head inside.'

Aileen looked over her shoulder at Ann Mackinnon. Her mother must have been to the hairdresser because her hair wasn't frizzy anymore. She didn't smile, and the dress she wore screamed 'chic'. Gold jewellery glittered at her ears and neck. 'She has her armour on.'

'I expected nothing less. She must want details about the case.'

Aileen faced Callan. 'Thank you for doing this. It's bound to be… difficult.'

Callan flashed her a grin and unlocked the car. 'It's now or never, darling.'

Aileen stepped out of the car and muttered to herself, 'You're a strong, independent woman.' She straightened her spine and took Callan's hand in hers.

Ann bobbed her head in welcome. 'Detective. Aileen. Come in.'

The aroma of home-cooked food hit her first, and then the sight of her glowing kitchen. Her mother had cooked and, since it was Ann, she'd cleaned up after herself.

'Eean's in the drawing room,' her mother said.

They didn't speak. Their footsteps echoed through the inn. All of her guests had left for various touristy spots earlier that day and weren't expected until late afternoon.

The TV crackled with the news.

'Give me the remote!' Siobhan roared.

'I'm sick of your crime shows, Mother.'

Aileen fought the urge to smack her forehead. Why couldn't her family stop arguing for once?

The moment they entered the drawing room, Siobhan grinned. 'Ah, this is better than TV.'

Eean stood from the sofa and held out his hand. 'Detective, I hope you're well?'

'I've been better. How are you?'

Eean sighed. 'Not good, if I'm honest.' For the first time, Aileen noticed the bags under his eyes. Her father appeared tired.

Ann stepped up to her husband and wound her arm around his. 'We wanted to know what…' She shook her head. 'I'm sorry. Where are my manners? Please, take a seat. I remember you take your coffee black with no sugar, Detective.'

How did her mother know Callan's coffee preferences?

Ann disappeared into the kitchen.

Siobhan clicked off the TV. 'I'm not one for being courteous when kept waiting. So, get on with it. What happened to Melanie?'

'Where's Nurse Nancy, Gran?' Aileen said. She wanted to wait for her mother to join them.

'Nancy's gone off to meet her cousin at the Mc-Cloughan's restaurant. I told her to get me some whisky. She refused.' Siobhan harrumphed. 'Ungrateful eejits, the lot of you.'

Ann walked in with a tray laden with a cafetiere and five coffee cups. 'You'll have to make do with coffee, I'm afraid, Siobhan.'

Aileen helped her mother pass the coffee cups. The clink of china filled the silence.

Finally, Eean placed his cup on the centre table. 'So, Detective—'

'Please, call me Callan.'

'Callan,' Eean nodded. 'I've been waiting to know why Melanie killed her husband. Was it… was it because of me?'

Ann squeezed Eean's thigh. The gesture said, 'I've got you.'

Eean sat back, rubbing his eyes. 'She was angry at her husband. At the life she had.'

Siobhan angled towards her son, and her eyes softened. 'It's one thing to be crushed after a heartbreak and another to wallow in it for four decades. If she still pined over you, why didn't she leave George Erwin? Why strike now?'

All eyes turned towards Callan.

'With Gerald's conviction and the societal scorn, life hasn't been fair to her lately.' Callan placed his cup on the tray. 'The stress had her losing weight, the doctors said. And her husband's "business" alienated her from society. She said in the interview that killing him was the only way out.'

Or leave him. But a twinge of sympathy wrapped its tendrils around Aileen's subconscious. Life hadn't been fair to the vivacious blond young woman.

Callan leaned forward. 'One night she heard her husband talking to Pluto McCloughan, saying he had plans to take pictures of the tombs and forward them to me. Melanie followed George with her weapon when he left for the peatlands. She'd been visiting a shooting range in the other town, and had borrowed Lt Gen Matthews' .44 Smith and Wesson Russian. We matched it as our murder weapon.'

Aileen's father sighed, holding on to Ann's hand. 'I wanted to go out into the world. I had too much ambition for this place but little money. She wanted to stay here, in a town she knew. To be close to her family and friends. And well provided for. We didn't talk about those things when we got engaged. We argued on the day we graduated.'

Ann squeezed his hand and nodded her encouragement.

'I broke up with her. It hit her hard. I was an arse about it. And I hadn't even introduced her to Mother. Somewhere in my heart, I knew she wouldn't like Melanie.'

'I still don't!'

Eean's face paled. 'Jack got into my face about it. Said I was an idiot for leaving what I had. We had words about it, said things I don't want to recall. I would erase them if I could. That month, I not only lost a fiancé, I also lost my best friend. And then I left.'

Aileen frowned. Her sympathy towards Melanie

had shattered after knowing the backstory. What kind of person measured someone's love based on their wealth?

Callan pulled out his notepad, struggling to get it out of his pocket using only his right hand. He flipped through the pages. 'Melanie said she called you every night last week, Mr Mackinnon. Did she?'

'Aye, she called using her husband's phone. And you thought I was speaking to George Erwin. I never spoke to that bastard after we graduated. I don't know where she got my number.'

'It's your official number, darling. Posted on our website.'

Eean sat back. 'Melanie called in the middle of the night asking for my help. Said she was in trouble, that I needed to come the next day and rescue her. You must know, we hadn't spoken since the day we broke up. I asked her to get help from someone she knew. I didn't know her anymore. Furthermore, her son almost killed my daughter. I wanted nothing to do with the Erwins.'

Aileen furrowed her eyebrows. 'But you came to Loch Fuar the morning after the murder.'

Her father sighed. 'Ann and I wanted to get you back to the city. We'd been talking about it for a while. And two nights earlier, Melanie had called again, sounding more hysterical. She was screaming, crying. I told her to go to a women's shelter. And, I must stress, she agreed. So, not once did I think, or even imagine, that she could have killed her husband.'

Eean rubbed his face. 'The Melanie I proposed to found joy in life. She drank in the seasons, nature, life, and love like a blind person seeing the world for the first time. To think that person could kill...'

'Rage, Father,' said Aileen. 'Rage makes humans do wild things.'

'It all distils to that, doesn't it?' Ann nodded. 'This murder was distilled from rage.'

They fell silent again, ruminating on the past couple of days.

Eventually, Siobhan stood up. 'I need some fresh air.'

The moment the door closed behind her, Ann beckoned to her husband. 'So... er... Believe it or not, we didn't call you here to ask about the case, Callan. We'd like to speak to both of you.'

With that one sentence, Aileen was sixteen years old again, sat in front of her parents after a parent teacher meeting, her latest report card in hand. She'd sweated buckets then, under her stuffy clothes. Even now, she felt sweat trickle down her back. But she sat up straight, reminding herself of her independence. 'Mother, I—'

'I'm sorry.' Eean interrupted and looked Aileen in the eye. 'I'm sorry for imposing my wishes on you all your life. For holding you back from your dreams.'

'Honey,' Ann cleared her throat. 'I'm sorry too, for berating you. I just… We just wanted – and still want – what's best for you. What'll make you happy. We wanted to let you know that. And Callan…'

'Thank you for running into that tent and saving my life,' Eean said. 'You have a commendable record with the police and I'm honoured to witness your persistence and determination first hand. But above all, you took a bullet for my daughter, saved her when Ricky Ridge or Melanie could've… I'll always be indebted to you for that.'

Aileen didn't know what to say.

By the look on Callan's face, her father's little speech had stunned him, too. 'I… I…' Callan took a deep breath. 'Aileen's as important to me, sir. I'll be there for her not because it's my job to keep people safe, but because I must. I… I love your daughter.'

A tear trickled down Aileen's cheek. She'd never expected this. She'd come prepared for an argument. But now, she stared at her parents, their eyes glistening with unshed tears.

It took both sides to want to make things right for a relationship to work. Her parents had taken the first step. She would be a fool, after wishing for a bond with them all these years, to not take a few steps towards them now.

She crossed to her parents and wrapped her arms around them, in what felt like the first time in forever. A warmth like no other invaded her world, soothed her aches. Parental love. 'Thank you for everything. For pushing me to do better, for seeing the potential in me. And I'm sorry too, for being so thick-headed and rude, for not understanding you. I love it here. I love you both, too.'

Ann caressed her back.

Eean straightened and looked over Aileen's shoulder at Callan. 'If you're ever in the city, please do come visit us. Both of you.'

Aileen grinned and said, 'We will.'

EPILOGUE

The call came on a Friday morning. Dr Brown's team had found Blaine Macgregor.

Callan, hand-in-hand with Aileen, had visited the morgue and identified Blaine. Pain had him dropping into a chair, uncaring of the tears trailing down his cheeks.

But he'd pulled through, and now he glanced at the portrait in front of him, of Blaine. His best friend could finally rest in peace.

They had had a closed coffin for him, adorned with white flowers to signify Blaine's pure heart and musical prowess. All of Loch Fuar had gathered at the church. Candace Willoughby, Blaine's piano teacher, had arranged for the organist to play a few pieces in memory of the prodigy that would have been.

It had warmed him, the overflowing of love for the boy who hadn't been accepted when he lived.

The wind ruffled his hair now, and the hum of conversation trickled in. Callan stared into the eyes he'd painted, so vivid in his mind, and the laughter Blaine had held in them. He had had a zest for life, like Melanie Erwin. Had dreams like Eean but parents unlike Aileen's who'd never come around to supporting him. And a best friend who didn't ask the right questions in time.

Callan shut his eyes, still unable to make peace with what he hadn't done.

Fingers squeezed his shoulder, and the scent of citrus intoxicated his mind. Home. 'You found him. Stood by him.'

Callan nodded, still unable to speak.

'He is smiling down at you. I can feel it. Look at the day outside. Sunshine, green leaves bobbing in the breeze, the Loch Fuar glinting under the blue sky and flowers still blooming. He's happy.'

Callan wrapped his right arm around her, gazed out at the loch. 'Not what I had in mind when I said we'd have a date here.'

'It's much better this way. This is a celebration of a beautiful life.'

'Aye, it is.' Daniel McIntyre clapped Callan on the back. 'He was one of a kind. Fiercely loyal. And you found him with the same determination he showed towards the people he loved. That counts, Callan. This is a win for the good. The Erwins tried their best to hide him away, but good won. Now he can rest in peace.'

'Aye, he can.'

A breeze brushed against Callan's face, like the tickle of peacock's feathers, carrying with it the fragrance of lilies. Aye, Blaine Macgregor was now at peace.

And Callan would have to be, too. With breath in his body, friends, and a girlfriend who loved him deeply, what did he have to complain about?

He smiled. 'Thank you. And farewell.'

THE END?
***

Aileen and Callan will be back with another mystery soon. Thank you for reading this story, and for the love you've showered on the residents of Loch Fuar.

There are six and a half novels in Aileen and Callan's world now. Each novel has been a journey for me and I can't wait to go on more adventures with our fav duo.

If you've read the previous books, you'll know I seldom include the point of view of a character that is not Aileen, Callan, the victim or the killer. However, this time I found Eean Mackinnon banging on my writing room door, wanting to share his story.

I knew Aileen's parents would be tough on her when I began plotting 'When Distilled From Rage'. Although I never could have predicted the love that governed their actions. But, as Aileen says, humans are as strange and contradictory as butter and bruises.

Whether you loved this story (or didn't) I'd be grateful if you could leave a review on the website you purchased this book from and/or on Goodreads and Bookbub—whichever platform you prefer. Your review helps me reach new readers. If you've never written a review before, don't worry. It doesn't need to be a long literary essay, just a sentence or two is perfect.

Your reviews and emails pull me through times when self-doubt injures my imagination. So thank you.

Until next time, if you haven't read the exclusive (and free) novella yet, you can get your copy at <u>Shanafrost.com/exclusivenovella</u>. This story includes Rory, Siobhan, Isla and many others. Turn the page to read a sneak preview.

But before I end this note, I have a list of people to thank, especially because this book had a tight turnaround time and without each of them, you wouldn't be reading this note right now.

Thank you to my lovely critique partners Janae Rogers and Kanika Bailey, who dedicated so much of their time to ensure this story was complete and emotionally resonant.

Special thanks to Charlotte Kane. Your analysis of this story, encouraging words, and love for Aileen and Callan inspire me.

Thank you to Rosie Walker for a thorough copyedit. This story reads so well all thanks to her! But any errors are my own.

And lastly, I must thank my parents for their support. Without them, all this would've been impossible to achieve.

I shall see you in the next book.

Lots of love,
Shana

PS: Don't forget to turn the page for a sneak peek at the exclusive novella!

WHEN WILT THOU DIE

Aileen sat in front of the ancient computer in the closet-like room no one used at the police station. She mumbled out the words she read and used her yellow notepad to make a note of all the ways Elizabeth Baines had spent the Council's money.

While Callan sat in the other room thinking over the crime scene, she hacked away at the numbers. The Council had handed over cash to Elizabeth from a common fund they'd initially collected to repair the Community Hall.

Had they even asked for a credit rating from Elizabeth, or was this donation simply on altruistic basis?

She hadn't a clue if it was dark outside because this room had no window. When the ancient computer froze, she let out a curse. Aileen pursed her lips. Callan's grumpiness was rubbing off on her.

When her eyes stung, Aileen leaned back. Elizabeth Baines was quite the spender: designer clothes, handbags, drugs, alcohol, and much more.

The list of people who hated her would truly be endless.

Aileen's phone chimed with a text from Nancy.

Come quick!

Panic welled inside her until her heart thudded in her throat.

Aileen dashed out the door. Was Siobhan ill? How could they get her to the hospital, being cut off from the rest of the world?

'Where ye off to?'

Without a backward glance at Callan, Aileen spoke in monosyllables. 'Siobhan… Something's happened… Urgent…'

Callan's heavy footsteps followed as he spoke hurriedly. 'Don't drive! Ye're shaking. Get in the car. I'll get us there quicker.'

Aileen clambered into his rugged car, trying to warm her frozen fingers. It took her three tries to click the seat belt in place. It alone told her how afraid she was.

Callan usually drove like the hounds of hell were following him. This time it was more like the entire police force was out to get them. He took sharp turns and honked to get any stray animals out of the way. Aileen didn't object.

Her mind was busy conjuring up all sorts of things that could've had gone wrong with her gran. Had she taken a tumble? Had she fractured her hand?

The whitewashed inn stood solitary against the overcast sky.

With a loud screech, Callan braked. Aileen threw open the door and bolted past the stone fence and into warmth.

'Gran! What's…?'

Her words died looking at the sight before her. Nancy sat on her gran's favourite sofa. Beside her, Siobhan's face appeared glummer than Aileen had ever seen.

But it was the flowers on the table which caught Aileen's attention. It wasn't a single bouquet of purple flowers, but three flower pots of what Aileen could describe as bell-shaped blooms.

Callan skidded to a halt next to her. 'What?'

Who had sent these flowers? And what was wrong with her gran?

Aileen panted, her lungs struggling to breathe. She glared at Nancy. 'What in the world? You said come quickly! I thought…'

Leaning on her walking stick, Siobhan stood. 'Don't shout at her. Can't ye see? The flowers!'

Callan strode towards the table. 'Ye asked Aileen to come quickly because ye got flowers?'

Siobhan huddled over, her usual strength and

energy missing. 'I wouldn't wish these flowers on anyone.'

She pointed at the purple blossoms. 'Those are Wolf's Bane plants, also known as Queen of Poisons. It signifies doom and they are poisonous.'

Aileen's legs suddenly became wobbly as if someone had sucked all the strength from them. She sank into the nearest chair. 'Someone tried poisoning you?'

To continue reading, download your free copy at Shanafrost.com/exclusivenovella

ABOUT THE AUTHOR

Shana Frost writes romantic mysteries as dramatic as the Scottish Highlands that inspire her. In every book, Shana shares the values she truly believes in: hope, justice, and love. Throughout her novels, you'll encounter a variety of characters—be their gender, ethnicity, disabilities, beliefs—all sharing their unique stories.

Always infused with a wee dram of the Scottish landscape and culture, Shana's stories take readers from Glasgow's gritty streets to the enigmatic Highlands. She promises that when reading her stories, you'll be at the edge of your seat, falling deeper in love with the characters.

To be enveloped in the world of Scottish romantic mysteries, visit Shana's home on the web at
Shanafrost.com

9 781738 499403